PYRAMID
BONES OF THE SUN GOD
HUNTERS

THE ADVENTURE BEGINS

PYRAMID HUNTERS #1
The Iron Tomb

PETER

PYR

BONES OF T

HUN

ALADDIN   NEW YORK   LONDON

VEGAS

AMID

HE SUN GOD

TERS

TORONTO   SYDNEY   NEW DELHI

ALADDIN

An imprint of Simon & Schuster Children's Publishing Division
1230 Avenue of the Americas, New York, NY 10020
First Aladdin hardcover edition August 2017
Text copyright © 2017 by Peter Vegas
Jacket illustration copyright © 2017 by Nigel Quarless
Interior illustrations on pages 24, 29, 44, 65, 133, 200, 202, 204, 206, 228,
239, 251, 301, 303, 317, 325, 348, and 384 copyright © 2017 by Mohammad Aram;
interior illustrations on pages 1, 37, 94, 193, 194, 213, 224, and 283 copyright © 2017 by
Simon & Schuster, Inc.; interior illustrations on pages 75, 101, 110, 152, 215, 274, 341, and 400
copyright © 2017 by Peter Vegas; swan logo on page 17 copyright © 2017 by iStock/milkal;
submarine on page 36 copyright © 2016 by Shutterstock/Gino Caron;
mayan calendar on page 51 copyright © 2017 by iStock/T-STUDIO;
mayan statue on page 92 copyright © 2017 by iStock/jezdicek;
sphinx on page 92 copyright © 2017 by ThinkStock/quintanilla;
dollar bill on page 207 copyright © 2017 by iStock/paulprescott72
For information about special discounts for bulk purchases, please contact
Simon & Schuster Special Sales at 1-866-506-1949 or business@simonandschuster.com.
The Simon & Schuster Speakers Bureau can bring authors to your live event.
For more information or to book an event contact the Simon & Schuster
Speakers Bureau at 1-866-248-3049 or visit our website at www.simonspeakers.com.
Designed by Karin Paprocki
The text of this book was set in Bembo Standard.
Manufactured in the United States of America 0617 FFG
2 4 6 8 10 9 7 5 3 1
This book has been cataloged with the Library of Congress.
ISBN 978-1-4814-4582-5 (hc)
ISBN 978-1-4814-4584-9 (eBook)

For KV and FV

PYRAMID

BONES OF THE SUN GOD

HUNTERS

1308 AD

DEATH WAS STALKING THE OLD KNIGHT.
The thought ripped him from his frozen, zombielike state. Behind him, the water churned; time was running out. He reached for the small pottery flask in his tunic, but clumsy fingers, numbed by the hours in the water, fumbled and it slipped from his grasp. He wouldn't have needed it if he had only followed his orders.

Summoning the last of his strength, he lifted himself out of the water and onto the stones etched with ancient carvings. The oil lamp spluttered and hissed, the flame wobbled like a tiny yellow sail in the darkness. It was only a few feet away, but it felt like miles to a body drained of strength. Behind him, the water frothed and boiled as death readied itself. His legs refused to function, as if the lower part of his body had already accepted defeat, but the knight would not give in. He cried out in anguish. Not at the prospect of a painful death, but the thought of failure.

At the very fringe of the weak yellow glow given off by the lamp, the knight could make out the wooden chest. Within it lay his salvation. He dragged himself across the stones, their dull chill a welcome relief after the freezing water. For two days he had worked in the pool; that was what his hourglass had told him. But in the darkness it had felt like one long night. It was a task that needed four, but was entrusted to just one. Stopping only for sustenance, he had toiled with ropes and wood and pulleys, but time and cold had wearied him to the point of exhaustion. His brain had dulled; mistakes had happened. After a short break he had reentered the water to resume his work, but without his protection. He'd only taken it off to recharge it. Now he would pay the price.

As he edged closer to the light, a monstrous black shape burst from the pool. The knight heard the meaty thump as it landed nearby. Claws scraped on stone, and the beast scuttled toward the light as if it had decided to race the knight to his prize. The man could only watch as it attacked the chest, swiping it with its tail. Sparks flew as the iron edges of the wooden box scraped across the stones, then darkness and a splash.

The lamp flame grew, fed by the new movement of air. It lit the beast, revealing shiny black eyes. The surface of the pool settled; silence descended on the chamber. The knight pushed himself up and reached for his dagger. The beast, sensing the man's last attempt at survival, lowered its head, locking both small black eyes on its target.

The familiar feel of the weapon in his right hand calmed the knight. He studied the fine lines and markings of the ornately carved blade for what he knew would be the last time and then reached for the waterproof pouch around his neck. From it he removed a well-worn piece of parchment. There was no need to look at it. He'd memorized his orders long ago and should have destroyed them as soon as he had. He'd almost left it too late. Ripping them in half, he screwed the first piece into a tight ball, cocked his arm, and let it fly toward the water.

That was when death came.

In the flickering glow of the oil lamp, the beast appeared to fly across the stones. Its glistening snout hit the ball of parchment, and the knight lost sight of it as rows of gleaming white teeth enveloped his legs. A loud *crack* echoed across the chamber as powerful jaws slammed together around his waist. With one last effort, he brought his dagger arm down onto his attacker's skull. Man and beast rolled as one onto the lamp.

And then there was only darkness.

SEPTEMBER 2015

THE BOY HAD LIVED BY THE RIVER ALL his life, but he had never been this far up at night. Desperation had brought him, fueled by rumors and stories.

A tortured screech echoed from the other side of the river. He froze in the ankle-deep water, twisting his head in the direction of the sound. The rhythmic beat of flapping wings reached his ears, then another screech as the creature of the night soared somewhere overhead. The boy released the breath he'd been holding. He had only stopped for a few seconds, but his bare feet had already sunk into the mud. He lifted his legs free one at a time, but the filthy slime clung to him as if it wanted to hold him there forever. Something small and scaly slithered between his toes.

He was close now. There was just enough light from the waning moon to make his way. The riverbank rose above his head on the left; a rocky wall dotted with large, rounded boulders. Above them were the jagged outlines of trees, and behind that the perfect blackness of a pyramid towered into the night sky, its outline silhouetted by the pinpricks of a million stars.

The boy removed a penlight from his pocket. The weak glow illuminated no more than a dinner-plate-size section of the riverbank. He didn't know what he was looking for, or even if he was in the right spot, so he studied the rocky surface inch by inch. Frogs serenaded him as he worked. The passage of time was marked by the moon's arc across the sky. His painstaking search took him no more than one hundred feet over a couple of hours. The moon was almost down to the trees when the frogs suddenly fell silent. Only now did the boy appreciate how loud they had been. Their deafening roar had accompanied him all night. Now the stillness filled him with a growing unease.

Then he heard the waves. Not waves, ripples. But in the silence they seemed to roar toward him. The boy stepped back against the riverbank and pointed his penlight into the blackness at his feet. The ripples rolled in. In the deathly silence, he heard each one break against his legs. He watched them, entranced by their perfect timing, but as he stared down he realized they were getting bigger, wider.

The boy aimed his penlight outward and saw the

beam swallowed by the blackness. He leaned forward, stretching his arm out. Two small, sparkling dots appeared. They grew, and the dots became eyes.

Too scared to scream and with nowhere to run, the boy watched the sparkling eyes float toward him. The water churned as he raised his penlight in a pointless act of defiance. In the glow, he made out the thick scales and then the perfect rows of white teeth as the crocodile's jaws opened.

Now the boy screamed. A cloud of white mist burst from the beast. With the pain came sudden understanding. The boy stared down at the silver dart sticking from his thigh. His eyes felt heavy, and as he fell to his knees, the crocodile spoke.

"Elio, you were told never to come here."

Elio wasn't surprised the creature knew his name. The last thing he heard as his world went black was the sound of the beast laughing at him.

One week later

1

SINGLED OUT

SAM BROKE OUT IN A SWEAT AS ALL EYES turned in his direction. Behind him, he heard Andrew Fletcher snickering. They hadn't been friends since Sam beat him to a spot on the four-man rowing team.

"I said come here, Force."

Mr. Stevenson's voice filled the classroom, and yet he hadn't seemed to speak very loud at all. Sam got to his feet, wondering if voice projection was a skill they taught at teachers college. He pushed in his chair, taking care not to scrape the legs on the floor. It was one of Mr. Stevenson's pet peeves. No point in making the situation worse than it already was.

Mr. Stevenson watched Sam approach, holding the

note distastefully between two fingers. He waved it in the direction of the nervous junior who had delivered the message. The boy understood the meaning and scuttled for the door.

As Sam got to the front row, Mr. Stevenson screwed up the piece of paper and tossed it into the wire basket in the corner of the room. It was a good shot, no rim. Sam hoped the mutterings of appreciation breaking out around the room might be enough to snap the teacher out of his foul mood. But they weren't.

"Settle down," Mr. Stevenson growled. "If you are not Mr. Force, then you should be attempting this!" He waved the black marker in his other hand at the algebra equation scrawled across the whiteboard.

"But you, Mr. Force, have been summoned to the headmaster's office."

Sam heard Andrew Fletcher mutter something from the back of the class.

"An urgent matter, no doubt. Can you think of anything important enough to warrant the interruption of your lesson in Advanced Algebra?"

Sam assumed he wasn't meant to reply, but he could think of hundreds of reasons to interrupt Advanced Algebra. For him, math ranked even higher than bathroom cleaning on his list of hated tasks at his boarding school.

"Well?" Mr. Stevenson pointed the marker at Sam accusingly.

"No, sir," Sam replied.

For a moment the man regarded him with the same look he'd given the headmaster's note, then he jabbed his marker at the door. "Off you go, then."

As Sam left the room, Mr. Stevenson spoke again, loud enough for everyone to hear.

"You'll have a lot to catch up on, Mr. Force. See Mr. Fletcher this evening. He can take you through the work you've missed."

Sam grinned as he heard Andrew Fletcher's muttered protests. He wouldn't make a very good study partner, but it served him right. As Sam walked down the deserted corridor, he reflected on his teacher's words. Mr. Stevenson was right. You weren't called for during class unless it was very important. So what was he walking into?

THE LONG OAK BENCH CREAKED AS SAM sat down. Looking around the office, with its floor-to-ceiling oak panels, old paintings, and grandfather clock, Sam realized that nearly everything in the place was creaky. That included Miss Ingle, the headmaster's secretary. According to one of the boarders, whose older brother had also attended St. Albans, Miss Ingle had been at the school since it was founded. Sam didn't think that was possible. It would mean she was . . . He couldn't work it out—maybe he could have if he'd paid more attention in algebra—but he knew it would make her very old.

St. Albans was a grand school, if you were into that sort of thing. Huge old oaks and big stone buildings covered with moss dotted a well-manicured lawn. Sam thought it belonged in England, fifty years ago, not modern-day Boston. Not that Sam had ever been to an English boarding school. He could hardly remember anything about England. His last trip to that country had been over five years ago, before his parents died. No, not died, he corrected himself—disappeared.

Five years ago, Sam's life changed forever when his parents were murdered. He'd been left to spend summer vacations in Cairo, with his uncle Jasper, and the rest of the year at St. Albans School for Boys.

But in July, everything changed again. In just a few days he had uncovered a conspiracy involving pyramids around the world and the famous Ark of the Covenant. He had learned his parents were involved, but more important for Sam, he'd been given hope that they were alive. His world had turned upside down, but almost as quickly as it had changed, he'd had to go back to being a schoolkid. It was impossible. Not with what he knew.

After his Egyptian adventure, he'd been desperate to keep going, to stay on the trail of his parents. But days had passed by with no progress. His uncle convinced him to return to Boston—a temporary situation, he had promised Sam, until he was able to get the appropriate resources in place. That had been six long weeks ago. Even Mary, who had been so keen to help him solve the mystery of his parents and the secret behind a world-wide network of pyramids, had lost interest. After Sam had returned to Boston, they had been in touch almost every day via e-mail, as they researched the information they had uncovered in Egypt. But in the last couple of weeks, things had changed. Her messages were less frequent, and the subject matter had become routine stuff about school and music. It was as if she had put their adventure behind her and moved on.

But Sam couldn't. Not while there was still hope his parents were alive.

Sam had a nagging feeling that his summons to the headmaster's office was to do with the events in Egypt. Since his return, he hadn't felt the same about anything, especially schoolwork. His grades were dropping almost as fast as his bangs. And both had become a source of tension.

St. Albans liked its boys' hair to look as well-groomed as its lawns, and both were cut often. Sam's hair had already grown beyond an acceptable length when he returned from Egypt. It had been one of the first things the head teacher had commented on: "Be sure you're front of the line when the barber visits this weekend, Force," he had commanded. After that, it had become a thing for Sam.

He found an excuse to miss the barber's school visit that weekend, and the next visit a few weeks later. In the outside world, Sam's hair would not have even received a second glance, but within the pristine walls of St. Albans he began to turn heads. It was a small thing, but to Sam it had become a symbol of defiance. A personal reminder that he didn't belong there anymore. Not when there were so many unanswered questions waiting for him in the outside world.

By the time the door to the headmaster's office opened, Sam had prepared himself for a showdown about his hair. So he was totally unprepared when the two men inside greeted him with a round of applause.

The headmaster was clapping politely, but the man beside him looked like he was about to cry with joy as he slapped his small hands together so fast they were a pink blur. He was a short man, but anyone looked short next to the towering Mr. Billington, St. Albans's headmaster.

"Come in, Sam, have a seat," Mr. Billington said. He immediately sat down, looking relieved to have an excuse to stop clapping.

Sam eyed the chair in front of him, but the short man darted forward, gripped his hand, and started shaking it with the same energy he'd put into his clapping.

"Mr. Force, St. Albans's best-kept secret, I think. How very, very exciting."

Very confusing, more like it, Sam thought as he watched his hand being pumped up and down. The man spoke with an accent, and something about him was familiar. Then Sam placed it. He was St. Albans's music teacher, Mr. *Ber*-something.

"Mr. Beroduchi has just received an e-mail informing us of your success, Sam," the headmaster said, holding up a printout. At the top, Sam saw an old-fashioned logo.

"Yes, yes," said the overexcited music teacher. He reached across the desk, grabbed the e-mail from the headmaster's hand, and waved it triumphantly in Sam's face. "My dear boy. Why did you keep your talent from me . . ." He glanced at the e-mail. "Well, no, this explains why. But, my boy, I can't tell you how excited I am to find a pupil with an interest in opera."

Sam had no idea what was going on. He studied the hyped-up music teacher, then the headmaster, searching for a sign that it was a stupid joke, but Mr. Beroduchi interpreted the look in a totally different way.

"Come now, Sam, the time for modesty is over. Now that you have fulfilled your dream."

"My dream?"

"Yes, Sam." The music teacher waved the e-mail in the air again. "Your acceptance into the Shonestein Opera Academy Scholarship Program."

The headmaster cleared his throat to get Sam's and the music teacher's attention. "Come now, Mr. Beroduchi." He motioned to the chairs in front of this desk. "Why don't we give Sam a chance to collect his thoughts. He must be overwhelmed by the news."

"Overwhelmed" wasn't the word. "Freaked-out" was more accurate. Sam sat, and the beaming music teacher pulled his chair close to Sam and continued his excited chatter.

"When I first read the e-mail, I was shocked, to say the least. I had given up hope of finding a student who has my passion for the art of opera. Don't worry, my boy." The teacher thumped Sam's shoulder with the same force he had put into his handshake. "The e-mail mentioned your reluctance to make your love of opera known."

"It did?"

"Yes," the teacher replied. "Your concern that you

might not be good enough. Your desire to prove to yourself that you can compete on the world stage by submitting an audition to Shonestein's Scholarship Program." The beaming teacher eased up on the shoulder patting as he turned to the headmaster. "We must share this good news with the school, Mr. Billington."

"Yes, we must do that," the headmaster agreed. Sam could see Mr. Billington wasn't as swept up in the moment as the music teacher. Fair enough. Opera? Wasn't that something fat old men did? There was a good reason Sam hadn't recognized Mr. Beroduchi straightaway. In his time at St. Albans, Sam had had nothing to do with the music department. He had zero interest in learning anything musical, and, until that moment, the music department had shown zero interest in him.

"Perhaps, Mr. Billington," the music teacher said, "we could entice Sam to give us a performance before his departure."

Sam's mouth dropped, and his mind scrambled, but before he could form the most basic excuse, the headmaster stepped in.

"Regrettably, that won't be possible. Mr. Force is required to leave this evening."

"Ah yes, of course," said Mr. Beroduchi.

"This evening? Where?" asked Sam.

"Why, Switzerland, of course," said Mr. Beroduchi. "To the Shonestein Academy. The details are all in an e-mail that was addressed to you." He took another piece of paper from the headmaster's desk, and thrust it into Sam's hand. It had the same fancy logo at the top. "This three-week course could set you on a path to operatic stardom, my boy."

Sam's head spun. Three weeks in Switzerland?

He tried to keep calm, but it was impossible.

Three weeks in Switzerland. At an opera academy he'd never heard of. When Sam couldn't carry a tune in a bucket.

Sam knew exactly what this e-mail was, and he needed time to study it.

He received a final supersized handshake from Mr. Beroduchi before being dismissed. A glance at the grandfather clock, as he hurried past the historically old secretary, told him he was about to be late for rowing training, but he couldn't bring himself to care.

Sam slowed and read the letter, then studied it line by line, letter by letter. By the time he reached the minivan that would take him to training, he'd found the hidden message. It was a trick his uncle had taught him, using the first letter of each line. But Jasper wasn't behind this. Sam knew the author of this e-mail because she had put the initial of her first name on the last line.

It wasn't a prank.

Sam was holding his get-out-of-jail-free card.

Dear Sam,

Today I am thrilled to confirm your scholarship with us. This is an honor you really should be quite proud of. As you may be aware, for an opera singer you're unusually young, but we were impressed by your audition tape, and our teachers see advantages in launching your operatic future as soon as possible. To that end, we would like you to join us in two days' time in Switzerland.

May I suggest you pack and prepare for your departure. It is booked for this evening. Your documents are at the airport information desk in your name.

May I wish you well and say how happy I am to line up this chance for you.

Yarm Ralmevu

2

FOILED

NOT EVERYONE WAS AS HAPPY ABOUT
Sam's operatic success as the music teacher. His rowing
coach, Mr. Holk, had already been upset about Sam
delaying the van. When he learned that Sam was
leaving the country that evening, his mood dropped
to the next level.

Sam sat through a lecture all the way to the river.
Did Sam know there was only a week until the inter-
school rowing championships? Was he aware that the
fours were a key event? Did he know how inconvenient
it would be to replace him this late in training? Sam
knew the answers to all these questions but kept his
mouth shut. He didn't want to anger the man further.

The student's nickname for Mr. Holk was "The Hulk."

But they always said it behind his back and well out of earshot.

The Hulk burned himself out as the minivan pulled up at the school's rowing facilities on the Charles River. Rowing was a popular sport in Boston, but Sam wondered if the school's obsession was influenced by the fact that a lot of English schools were into the sport. Uncle Jasper liked to point out that the sport originated in ancient Egypt, but Sam didn't think those Egyptians would recognize the lightweight fiberglass boats that competitive rowers used now.

St. Albans's rowing shed was a barn-sized building that held over thirty racing boats of various sizes and ages. As the boys formed their teams and went to collect their equipment, Mr. Holk called out to Sam.

"No point in you training with us, is there, Force?"

Sam's teammates looked confused, and for good reason. With the coach in his ear all the way to the river, Sam hadn't had a chance to tell them what was going on.

"For those of you who don't know," Mr. Holk announced loud enough for the group to hear, "Mr. Force has decided rowing no longer interests him. He is leaving the country tonight to spend some time at a singing school."

The looks among the group ranged from confusion

to amusement, but Sam only cared about the three guys in his crew. They looked hurt. Sam knew it looked like he was letting them down. He wanted to explain what had really happened, but Mr. Holk hadn't finished.

"Andrew Fletcher, you'll take Force's place in the fours. Okay, everyone, we are already behind schedule. Get to work."

The group dispersed quickly, and Mr. Holk headed for the small speedboat tied up to the jetty. "You might as well make yourself useful in the shed," he called out as he cast off. "The place could do with a fall cleanout."

Sam watched the fleet glide up the Charles River, tailed by Mr. Holk yelling instructions through a loudspeaker. As they disappeared around the first bend, Sam went into the shed to look for a broom.

The team returned two hours later. The day was getting late; the temperature had dropped, and the boys were in a hurry to get their boats up to the shed and cleaned so they could head back to school for warm showers. That was when the coach sprang his parting gift on Sam.

"Good news, boys," Mr. Holk announced as he walked up from the jetty. "Mr. Force has offered to clean up all the gear tonight. His way of saying goodbye and good luck with the national champs."

The news was greeted with a few cheers and a burst of exaggerated laughter from Andrew Fletcher. None of of extra warning, one of them managed to get an arm up, but both boys still received enough to sting them.

"Don't worry, it's biodegradable," Sam said as he sprinted for the door. He gave Andrew another burst, but his soapy ammo ran out. He tossed the empty bottle and it bounced off Andrew's head as Sam raced up the driveway.

Mr. Holk insisted his rowers were fit. The jog back to St. Albans was a regular part of the program, and Sam was always among the fastest, so he figured his chances of getting away were pretty good.

But as he reached the end of the driveway, Sam realized he had made a fatal error.

Andrew and his friends had arrived on bikes.

Sam's ex-teammates made eye contact with him as they got in the minivan. Mr. Holk was the last to board. "I imagine even opera singers need to stay fit, so I'm sure you'll be happy to jog back to St. Albans." He didn't wait for a reply. The doors shut, and the minivan drove off.

Sam wasn't surprised by the coach's reaction to his deserting the team. The rowing champs were a big deal. They had been important to Sam, too, but not as important as the chance to find his parents. Letting down his teammates was the thing that hurt the most. He wondered if he should leave them a note explaining the real reason he was leaving, but decided against it. He didn't want to do anything to blow his cover. He remembered the coded e-mail from Mary. He'd just have to hope she had it all worked out.

There were seven boats on the racks in the shed. Each one had to be squirted with the detergent bottle, scrubbed, and hosed down. It was a big job for one person, but Sam didn't mind. In a way, Mr. Holk had been right about it being a parting gift from Sam. He hoped the teams did well, especially his. Even if Andrew Fletcher had taken his place.

Sam worked fast; he had plenty of time before his flight that night, but he wanted to get back to school and say a few good-byes. He had finished the last boat and was about to lock up when he heard bikes skidding on the gravel outside. They clattered against the side of the shed; then the sliding door was pushed back. The rays of the setting sun silhouetted three boys. They stood in the entrance while their eyes adjusted to the darkened interior. Then one of them spoke.

"You still working, singer boy?"

They couldn't see Sam. He was behind one of the ceiling-high racks where he had just slid another boat into its cradle. He stood still, watching the boys. Fletcher's voice had a nasty edge to it, and Sam ran through the layout of the shed in his mind. The only other way out was a door at the back. To get to that, Sam would have to go around the end of the rack, and he'd be seen.

Then he remembered it was locked anyway.

Sam calmed himself with a slow breath and walked into the open.

"There you are, singer boy," said Andrew Fletcher.

"Have you guys come to help?" Sam smiled, trying to lighten the mood. It was the wrong move. He could tell Andrew thought he was being smart.

A sneer formed on the boy's face. "Sure," he said. The last boat was sitting on a washing rack. The boy kicked it and the lightweight fiberglass body flew off the rack and smashed onto the concrete floor.

"You fool! You've wrecked it," Sam yelled with genuine horror as he gaped at the ruined craft. It was

one of the newest boats, and the damage would impossible to repair in time for the championship glared at Andrew. "Why did you do that?"

"I didn't," he said, grinning stupidly at his two "We're not even here, Force. You must have He approached one of the boats Sam had alrea away. "Thing is, Force, now that I'm on the te to stay. And if you can't even be trusted to cle the Hulk won't want you back, will he?"

Fletcher's friends exchanged nervous glan we were only gonna break one," said one

Fletcher rounded on the boy. "On I'm going to make sure little singer for life!"

Sam knew he had only moment He bent down and reached for the fiberglass closest to him.

"Wouldn't bother tidying up, know there are boats missing."

But Sam wasn't tidying up. with the object he'd retrieve shell. He aimed the bottle Fletcher and squeezed.

The soapy liquid hit hi howled in pain. Before Sam swung the foamy je

Even as he veered off the road and onto the grass, he heard angry shouts and the whir of bicycle wheels. He didn't need to look back to know his pursuers were gaining on him, and Andrew was providing a commentary.

"I'm going to get you, Force! You hear me?"

Apart from his pounding heart, Sam could hear little else.

The sun had gone down, and the park got dark so fast the grass almost seemed to disappear under Sam's feet. He headed back down to the road and glanced behind, hoping to see a car. How was it that in a park in central Boston on a weeknight there wasn't one car to be seen?

There was no way he'd be able to get back to the dorms. A new plan formed in Sam's mind. If he made it back to the rowing shed, he could lock the door and wait for Andrew and his gang to lose interest. He jumped the guardrail onto the road and turned back toward the river.

Behind him, the bikes skidded to a stop. As he flew down the hill, he heard the rhythmic hum of tires on blacktop. The bike gang was back in hot pursuit and would be on him in no time.

The whole crazy marathon had only lasted a couple of minutes, and Sam was right back where he started. It was his turn to skid to a stop in the gravel and allow himself a backward glance. The three boys were powering down the drive, led by the red-faced and even redder-eyed

Andrew. He began mouthing words but was puffing so hard they weren't coming out. Sam didn't stop to lip-read. He stepped inside and heaved the sliding door shut. The last few inches slammed on a tire as Andrew Fletcher's bike collided with the steel door. The boy lost his balance in the crash, and as he fell, the tire slipped out of the gap. Sam seized the chance to slide the door shut and lock it.

The booming sounds of hands beating on the metal doors filled the shed as Sam ran to the office and grabbed the cordless phone off the desk. When he returned to the doors, Andrew was shouting above the din.

"Force. Can you hear me? You're dead!"

"I'm going to call the Hulk," Sam said.

The banging stopped, and Sam heard the gang conferring in hushed tones.

"You won't do it," Andrew said confidently.

Fletcher had called Sam's bluff, but he had no choice. He had a plane to catch. So he dialed.

"I made the call," Sam shouted as he hung up. "The Hulk is on his way."

"Sure you did," Fletcher shouted sarcastically as he and his gang continued to beat the metal doors.

Sam returned to the office and searched for a key to the back door, but then he spotted a shape through the frosted class. Fletcher had one of his mates covering the back.

Sam returned to the front to wait. He'd figured on

fifteen to twenty minutes, so the beam of light that washed through the gap under the sliding door five minutes later was a surprise. Fletcher and his mates were caught off guard too. Frantic shouts were followed by the sound of bikes skidding on gravel.

Sam eased the door open a fraction to check that the coast was clear. The plain brown car coming down the drive wasn't what he'd expected, but it had worked perfectly. As it pulled up outside, Sam prepared to deliver his story. The car stopped, the driver's window slid down, and Sam's plan died. He froze. It was as if his whole body shut down. He opened his mouth to say something, to scream for help, but nothing came out.

Sam hadn't seen the bearded man since the night in the desert, when his uncle lay trapped inside the buried ship. But he had thought of him every day. Now he was here in Boston.

Impossible.

Sam watched the man from the darkness. Part of him was screaming, *Run!* He might be able to break down the back door with one good kick. Damaging school property was the least of his worries now. But he didn't move. The man in the car worked for the people who had tried to get rid of him and his uncle.

But he was also the only link to Sam's parents. That kept Sam rooted to the spot.

The bearded man looked around and then appeared to make a decision. He opened the door and got out. Sam tensed, ready to run, but the man didn't move. He bent down and grabbed his shin as if he had injured it. When he pulled up the bottom of his right trouser leg, the light from inside the car caught the glint of steel. No, not steel—tinfoil.

The lower half of the man's right leg was wrapped in tinfoil.

"Who are you?" Sam yelled.

The man looked straight into the gap in the door, but Sam knew he couldn't be seen.

"It's okay, Sam. I don't mean you any harm. I—"

"Where are my parents?" Sam yelled. "In Egypt, before he died, the man who worked for you told me my parents were still alive. He said you told him that."

"He shouldn't have," the man growled.

"Why?" Sam yelled.

The man took a few steps forward. Sam tensed, ready to run for the back door, but the man stopped again and adjusted the tinfoil on his leg. Sam watched, more confused than scared. The man kept glancing up at the door as if he was afraid Sam was going to come for him.

"Are my parents alive?"

"I . . . I came to tell you . . ."

Another set of headlights swung into the driveway.

The bearded man turned and leapt back into his car.

"Wait," Sam cried. "Tell me what?"

As he turned the vehicle the man looked back to the shed. "If you're thinking of going to Belize, don't!" he called out. "Keep away from there. Belize is a dead end, Sam."

The car's wheels spun in the gravel as it sped up the drive. The bearded man had been spooked by Sam's trick, and he couldn't hang around either.

He slipped out, pushed the doors shut, and sprinted around the side of the building before the second car pulled up. Fletcher had been right. Sam hadn't called Mr. Holk, but he had needed someone to show up and scare the boys off. Someone who wouldn't ask questions.

Sam felt bad about ordering the delivery pizza. He had no money to pay, and no time to explain. All he cared about now was getting back to school to pack for a flight. The moment Sam realized Mary was behind the Swiss opera trip, he had known his true destination. And so did the bearded man.

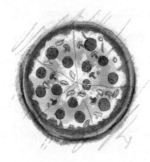

3

SLAYERS
OF MAYHEM

Dear Sam,

Oh dear, that sounds a bit grown-up, doesn't it? Dear Sam—mind you, this whole letter-writing thing is soooooo old-fashioned.

Now, to business. I hope you found the message I sent you in the letter from the opera school. Of course you did; you were the one who showed me the idea. But I bet you were surprised when your music teacher told you that you had won a scholarship for your opera singing! I remembered you saying how much you hate singing. Sorry, couldn't help myself. But, in my defense, it wasn't just for fun.

I needed a way to get you out of school for a few weeks—fast and without raising any suspicion. Shonestein Opera Academy is a real place, and they have a scholarship.

Once I found the opera school, I created a copy of their website and made sure that anyone using your school server to visit Shonestein would be rerouted to my site. That way, no one e-mailed the REAL teachers. Impressed? You should be.

Now, where was I? Oh, that's right. So your music teacher bought the story, but your headmaster, Mr. Billington, seemed a little suspicious. He contacted your uncle to confirm your interest in opera. Except he didn't. I took the precaution of monitoring any contact between St. Albans and Jasper, so I was able to intercept the e-mail and reply on his behalf.

Anyway, Sam, if you are reading this it means you found my hidden message, got to the airport, and received the package waiting there for you. Arranging a new passport and fake name was almost as difficult as the opera scholarship, but I'll save that story because my hand is getting quite sore. Honestly, Sam, I don't know how people used to write long letters. Typing on a keyboard is so much easier.

I hope you like your name. I think it's quite smart. We couldn't have you wandering into Belize as Sam Force, could we? There should be enough money, and I have booked you into the nicest hotel I could find in Orange Walk. I still can't get over that name. You must find out the story behind it for me.

So this is it, Sam. Your chance to pick up the trail of your parents and hopefully learn more about the pyramid network. Thanks to our efforts in Egypt (okay, I'll admit it was mostly your efforts, but I like to think I helped a little), we know my grandfather smuggled the Ark of the Covenant out of

Egypt on submarine 518 in 1942, and that it was sent to Belize to be installed in a pyramid. Now you get to uncover the next part of this mystery. I had no idea there are pyramids all over Belize. Did you know they refer to them as temples in that part of the world? I'm sure you do. I know you've done lots of research into Lamanai, the pyramid complex near the spot sub 518 was found. Me too. I've enclosed some of my notes for you, and a copy of that newspaper article that triggered your parents' trip. The more I read about Lamanai the more intrigued I get. The town of Orange Walk is the best place to start your investigation, don't you think? It's not too far from Lamanai, and it's where the policeman who found the sub came from.

I so wish I could be there, Sam. You've probably been wondering why I haven't been in contact much in the past few weeks. It's my father. The incident with the buried ship in the desert and your uncle almost dying scared him. I think he felt guilty because he was the one who hired your uncle to look into the mystery. The secrets behind the pyramid network destroyed my grandfather and have obsessed my father. I think he is worried I will end up the same. A few weeks ago he banned me from having any contact with you. I became concerned he was monitoring my e-mails. That's why they suddenly got so lame. All those boring stories about my schoolwork were to put him off the scent. Don't worry, I'm arranging a new number and e-mail address, and they'll be untraceable.

I got you a notebook that you'll be able to fill with lots of new sketches, and a fancy new smartphone. It's the latest model and has a super-long-life battery—two weeks, apparently. So keep it on, and I will be in touch as soon as I can.

Okay, I have to go now. I am organizing a trip to Switzerland myself. Not to opera school—ski camp. Why, you ask? Well, I love skiing, and it is one of the few places my father will agree to let me go without Bassem. You remember my very talkative minder, Bassem, don't you? He hates the cold and Father feels I'm safe up a mountain. It will be nice not to have the big guy watching my every move.

Okay, I seriously have to stop writing now. My fingers are cramping up big-time. I'll be in touch with more helpful instructions before you get to your hotel. The Orange Walk Excelsior is one of the oldest in town and the grandest. No expense spared for my friend. But I also thought there might be a chance it's where your parents stayed. Maybe they left some clues. Why don't you ask a few subtle questions?

But don't blow your cover. Remember, YOU ARE NOT SAM FORCE.

Good luck, not-Sam Force. I wish I were there to help. I'll be in touch soon.

xxx Mary Verulam

PS: Notice anything interesting in the name of the person who wrote the letter from the Shonestein Academy?

THE BELIZE NATIONAL

THURSDAY, JANUARY 14, 2010, ISSUE NO. 8279

STORM UNCOVERS SUB BURIED IN RIVERBANK

POLICEMAN FINDS WWII SUB BURIED IN RIVERBANK

A mystery, hidden in river mud for nearly seventy years, was uncovered recently. The discovery of the World War II submarine was announced by Felix Ramos, head of the Orange Walk Police Department, at a press conference yesterday. Officials say there are no records of the submarine in Belize in World War II, and they are mystified by the discovery. Superintendent Ramos said that a calendar found on board dates the sub's arrival to 1942. Experts were also surprised by the location of the sub, saying it was incredible that the vessel made it so far up the New River. Superintendent Ramos said the submarine had been hidden in a small side stream near the ruins of Lamanai. Had it not been for the recent typhoon that washed away large sections of the river-bank, it would have remained undiscovered.

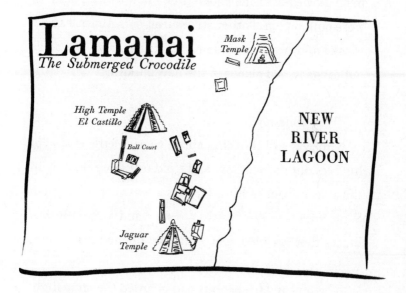

Lamanai

Located on the New River in Orange Walk District on 950 acres of archaeological reserve, Lamanai features more than a hundred minor structures and over a dozen major ones. Lamanai is known for being the longest continually occupied site in Mesoamerica.

The thriving crocodile population in the nearby New River Lagoon gave Lamanai its name. It means "submerged crocodile."

Only about 5 percent of the site has been investigated, and much remains buried or covered by jungle and bush. However, archaeologists do know that structures were built on top of other structures, sometimes leaving masks and other ornamental features from the older buildings in odd places in the new buildings.

"Hey, Chester."

Sam was still thinking about Mary's letter. He kept his eyes out the window and tried to ignore the boy in the seat in front of him. He was a few years older than Sam, with a mop of curly red hair and a mouthful of braces that sparkled every time he opened his mouth, which was a lot.

The boy and his parents had boarded the same flight as Sam in Houston, the last stop before Belize, and they were talkers, one of Sam's pet peeves on plane trips. Luckily for him, they had been seated a few rows in front, but he had still heard them tell the cabin crew and everyone around them that they were regular visitors to Belize. They loved the weather, the people, the scenery. In the two-hour flight, they covered every single thing that appealed to them about the country.

And lucky him, when they finally got to Belize, the family got on the same bus. He had kept his head down and stayed off their radar, till now.

"Chester, I'm talking to you."

Sam looked up and pretended he had only just heard his name. First Mary had made him a wannabe opera singer; then she had called him Chester. He decided that next time she created a false identity for him, he would have more input into it.

"I saw your name on your passport back at the airport." The red-haired boy beamed as if he deserved special recognition for his detective work. "We were ahead of you in the line."

Sam remembered. The boy's mother had greeted the customs officer like an old family friend, with a big hug and a sloppy kiss, but Sam got the impression the shocked man had never seen the woman before.

"Chester's a funny name," the boy said. Sam couldn't disagree. "Have they got lots of Chesters in England?"

Sam had no idea, but making him from England was another thing he would be asking Mary about.

Not that he minded. He was half English anyway, thanks to his father, but he had always had an American passport. Being English was just another thing to remember.

"Hello? I asked if there were a lot of Chesters in England."

"A few, I guess."

Sam's reply set the boy off. His screeching laugh filled the bus, attracting everyone's attention except his parents in the seat opposite, who, Sam decided, must have become immune to the excruciating noise.

"You got a real funny accent," the boy finally squeezed out.

Sam thought this was odd because he hadn't put on an accent. He'd thought about it, but decided it was too risky, and instead had just spoken politely. He figured he could tell people he'd lost his British accent after spending a year at a boarding school in . . . California. Somewhere as far from St. Albans as he could think of.

"Hey, Chester, you got Slayers of Mayhem in England?" the boy asked.

"What's that?"

"Greatest band in the world." The boy knelt on his seat facing Sam and pointed to his T-shirt. Splattered across the top in red were the words

SLAYERS OF MAYHEM. Under this ominous banner were four shirtless men with long hair, tight purple pants, and dog collars. Sprawled across their feet was a tiger. Sam figured the purple pants were fireproof, because the tiger had flames coming out of its mouth.

"Oh," Sam said thoughtfully. "Those Slayers of Mayhem."

"You heard of them?"

Sam shook his head. "No. Sorry."

The boy pulled a pair of earbuds out of his pocket. "You wanna listen?"

Sam almost gagged as he spotted a lump of earwax on one of them. "No thanks. I'm into opera," he said politely.

The boy's brow wrinkled with concentration. "I've never heard of them. They from England?"

Thankfully for Sam, the conversation came to an end as the boy's parents began informing their son of their plans for that evening.

Sam sat back and gazed out the window, relieved to have the boy's focus redirected. But as he listened to the family's animated chatter, part of him felt jealous and sad. He imagined the conversations he would have had with his mom and dad on vacations, and at home. The kind of simple family moments that had been stolen from him when his parents disappeared.

The emotions got stronger, hanging over him like a dark cloud. Sam twisted in his seat to snap himself out of the mood. He focused on the view, scared of where his thoughts were taking him and angry he had let himself go down this path. For five years he had lived with the idea his parents were gone. Then in Egypt, he'd been given hope. He'd been told they were alive.

At first Sam had been overjoyed. Back in Boston, he had begun researching Belize and Lamanai. There was plenty to read; the Internet was great for that. But over the weeks, he had gotten bogged down and frustrated. Nothing he found offered any obvious links to his parents. Then Mary seemed to lose interest. As time passed, new questions arose for Sam and doubts began to grow. Five years with no word. How could that be possible? And why had the bearded man turned up in Boston to warn him away? Sam had come anyway. But after five long years, he was scared about what he would find.

Sam got out his notebook and started to draw. There was no point in thinking about what could have been, or what might be. There was only now. He was here, and this was his best chance to find his parents.

The bus rolled down a two-lane highway, lined on each side by dense green forest. Every few miles, the green walls would drop away to reveal a small, dusty town or homes surrounded by fields of churned brown earth. The landscape was different from anything Sam had seen before. With his yearly trips to Cairo, Sam had begun to think of himself as a well-seasoned traveler, a man of the world, but sitting there he knew he had been fooling himself. Until now, his world was only Cairo and Boston.

When the red-haired boy finished his family conversation, he didn't turn back to Sam. Instead, he inserted his earbuds and rocked his head rhythmically to what was surely the torturous sounds of the Slayers of Mayhem. Sam was relieved, but it meant he was left alone with his thoughts and doubts. He checked his phone for the hundredth time since he had gotten off the plane. Why hadn't Mary gotten in touch? She would have known what time his flight got in.

The forest got thicker and crept closer to the road, blocking out the sun and plunging the bus into semi-darkness. Sam stared at his blank phone screen in the gloom, willing it to light up. Then he returned to his notebook.

The phone was still blank when the bus arrived in Orange Walk. The parents of the red-haired boy wandered off, making a loud fuss about finding a taxi to take them to their motel. Sam got a map from a battered information stand and located the Orange Walk

Excelsior. It was only three blocks away, and he decided the walk would do him good.

The town was smaller than Belize City, where his plane had landed, but he was relieved to see it wasn't a village like the ones the bus had driven through. It would be easier to blend in. Assuming that a young, white schoolkid traveling alone *could* blend into a town in Central America.

Orange Walk was full of old, colonial-style buildings, mostly two or three stories high and painted in a variety of bright colors. The place had a tropical island feel, with dusty streets and trees dotted between buildings. It wasn't hard to spot the Orange Walk Excelsior. The brown, seven-story box towered over the buildings around it.

Sam checked in, using his exchange-student cover story. An elderly lady with a tanned face and big white teeth that shone as if they had just been painted gave Sam a key to a room on the third floor and wished him a pleasant stay. Her English was so thickly accented, it was difficult for Sam to understand.

The room, like the hotel and the town, was tired, but it was clean. In the corner, the double bed had a bedspread with a crazy pattern of orange and yellow swirls that seemed to move when Sam stared at it. A battered wooden coffee table in the middle of the room was lined up between a faded brown couch and an old-school television the size of a refrigerator.

The pattern on the bedspread was so busy that Sam didn't spot the envelope lying on it until he put his bag on the bed. *Mr. Billington* was scrawled on it in black pen. His undercover surname was Mary's final joke. Sam wondered how St. Albans's headmaster would feel about being used for a fake identity.

In the envelope was a note from the hotel manager informing him a secure fax from Yarm Ralmevu was waiting for him to access at reception. Mary had gotten in touch.

4

BATHROOM STOP

SECURE FAX To: Chester Billington
From: Yarm Ralmevu

Well done, Chester Billington.

If you are reading this, that means you
rang the number and answered the security
question—What is the anagram of Yarm
Ralmevu? Mary Verulam, of course. But I
know you spotted that little clue when you
read my letter from the Shonestein Academy.

When I saw your hotel had a secure fax
number, it was perfect. How cute that they
still use fax machines in that part of the
world. I'm still sorting out a new e-mail and
phone number.

Now, to business. I have been trying to track down Superintendent Ramos, the policeman who found sub 518. It seems he left the Orange Walk Police Department soon after his discovery. I've had even less success tracking down the submarine.

So I've decided that the best place for you to start is the Orange Walk Police Department. I rang them pretending to be your teacher and explained you're a big fan of World War II submarines and are keen to talk to anyone who might be able to help you track down sub 518. They are expecting you this afternoon at two p.m., Chester, so that should keep you busy. You might even be able to find out what happened to Superintendent Ramos.

I have also been monitoring your school e-mail account in case anything important pops up. We can't have you accessing it, can we? Imagine if someone traced you to Belize. But I'm sure you already thought of that. ;)

The night you left, I intercepted an e-mail from your uncle. I printed it and added it to this fax. I've rerouted his e-mails so that from now on they will come to the new mail account I set up on your phone—this is where you give me a round of applause. ;)

Good luck at the police station. Remember your cover story. Talk soon.

xxx Yarm Ralmevu

From: Jasper Force j.force@eef.com

Date: Friday, Sep 18, 2015

To: Sam Force s.force@stalbans.com

My Sam,

How are you, dear boy? I must apologize for my lack of correspondence. Since you saved my life in the desert, an act for which I will be eternally grateful, I have had quite the time with the legal system here in Cairo. The case to clear my name of the money-laundering charges with my employer, the EEF, is moving at glacial speed, and I fear it may take many more months. In the meantime, I have been forbidden to leave. Guilty till proven innocent, it would seem. Sadly, dear boy, this is an unwanted distraction at a time when my thoughts, like yours, I am sure, are more concerned with your parents.

Our adventures inside the iron tomb of the *Panehesy* uncovered more than the possibility that your parents are alive, Sam. The knowledge that the Ark of the Covenant was designed to fit inside the sarcophagus of the Great Pyramid in Giza, and that there were once many Arks in pyramids around the world, is information some have killed for. Those same forces are behind the false charges I face here in Cairo. This should be a warning to you, Sam, that you must be careful.

Your parents and this conspiracy are irrevocably linked, but please be patient, my boy. I promise you that as soon as I extricate myself from my legal problems I will devote my full energies to solving the mystery of your parents' disappearance.

You asked me if I could recall the details of the last piece of correspondence I received from them. The answer is yes. Your mother penned the letter, she spoke of pirates and buried treasure; she used the phrase "X marks the spot," I remember. All of this made perfect sense to me as I was under the impression they were in the Caribbean, the heart of pirate country, so to speak. How these details fit in with what we know now, I am unsure. But as I said, Sam, as soon as I am able I will begin to unravel this mystery.

I can imagine how difficult it must be for you, stuck at your school in Boston. I am sure, like mine, your thoughts often drift to Belize.

It is an intriguing country, Sam. From the research I have done, I can see why your parents believed that by following the lost Ark there they would learn more about the link between the pyramids around the world. Belize is full of them. They are mostly credited to the Maya, a civilization that flourished for hundreds of years in central South America from 1800 BC. The Maya are famous for their obsession with time and their long count, which ended in 2012. What you may not be aware of was that the pyramid building and the long count were in fact inherited from an even older civilization that predated the Maya, called the Olmec. All intriguing stuff, I think you'll agree. Rest assured I will be doing more research into the Maya and Olmec, because I am sure it will help us understand what happened to your parents.

I will not let this rest, Sam. On that, you can be sure. But for now I ask you to bear with me and let me know if there is anything I can do for you.

xxx Jasper

PS: Here is a picture of the Mayan calendar. Is it just me or does this design appear to show a circle of pyramids? One might say a network.

Chester Billington, Chester Billington, Chester Billington. Sam sat in the waiting room repeating the name in his head. On the walk to the police station, Sam had reflected on his latest correspondence from Mary and his uncle. For weeks he had been thinking about getting to Belize. But not alone. He'd always figured Jasper would accompany him. And Mary. She'd never actually said it, but Sam assumed her promise to help meant she would be coming with him. Sam knew he had to get over it. He was on his own; he had to start thinking for himself. That's why he was so angry with what happened when he entered the police station.

He'd walked up to the woman behind the plastic window at the front desk and introduced himself as Sam Force. It didn't even sink in what a grave mistake he'd just made.

The woman, who spoke English, had looked at her computer screen and then questioned Sam. Yes, he'd assured her, he was there to see someone about the old submarine.

There was a flicker of understanding in the woman's eyes, and she checked the screen again. That was when it hit him. "Sorry. Not Sam. My name is Chester. Chester Billington. I'm, um, reading a book, and the author's name is Sam Force."

The excuse was so flimsy he was sure she'd seen through it.

If the woman seemed surprised by the schoolboy who had got his own name wrong, she didn't show it.

Sam watched her pick up a phone. As she dialed, she nodded for him to take a seat.

And now he couldn't decide if he should bolt and find some place to hide. But he'd come so far . . . and this was his only lead.

Besides, the lady hadn't really reacted to the name Sam Force. Chances were she had never heard of him.

A few minutes later, a man in a faded black suit walked in the front door. The woman behind the counter saw him and nodded in Sam's direction. When the man turned, Sam's mouth dropped. He was dark-skinned, like most of the locals, and in his late twenties or so, with long hair pulled back behind his head. But what shocked Sam was the angry scar on the right-hand side of his face. Sam had seen scars before, but nothing this big or ugly. Instead of a lumpy line of scar tissue, a jagged red trench ran from above his eye down to his jaw.

The man watched Sam gaping at him with something like amusement. "You are Chester, yes?" he said with a thick accent.

Sam nodded, moving his eyes away from the man's face.

"Come this way, please." The man waved Sam toward an open door and a set of stairs. Sam went up, with the man close behind. On the second floor, the man slipped past and opened the door, ushering Sam down a narrow corridor, past a bathroom, and into a small interview room. It was painted pale green and contained an old wooden table and two chairs the same color as the walls. The man pointed toward the nearest chair. As Sam sat, he heard the door shut, and then the man settled into the seat on the other side of the table.

Sam swallowed. It looked like an interrogation room.

"Tell me, Chester, why are you interested in the submarine?"

The harsh white light of the single bulb above the table made the man's scar look even more gruesome, something Sam wouldn't have thought possible downstairs. He couldn't take his eyes off it, but then he noticed the look on the man's face had changed. His smile had gone; his eyes narrowed as he waited for Sam to answer.

"I'm . . ." Sam took a breath. *I'm Chester, and I'm English*, he reminded himself. That is, if the lady downstairs hadn't already spilled his real name. "I'm here on a student exchange," he said slowly and politely, hoping it sounded English enough. "And I heard about the submarine found near here a few years ago."

"From who?" the man demanded.

Sam swallowed, caught himself staring at the scar, and averted his eyes again. "I read about it in a paper."

"Which paper?"

"The *Belize Times*."

The man laughed. It was more of a snort than a laugh. He leaned across the table. "You get the *Belize Times* in . . . Where are you from?"

"England," Sam answered quickly.

"Really?"

Sam was shaking, and his hands were getting sweaty. He rubbed his palms together under the table. "I read about it on the Internet, on the *Belize Times* site."

The man nodded as he considered Sam's answer. "Would you like to see it?" he asked, looking down at his watch.

"The submarine?"

"Yes," said the man. "I can take you there. But we have to go now." He got up and walked to the window. "My car is parked outside. Look," he said.

Sam walked to the window, trying to steady his heart. He didn't trust this man, but his apprehension warred with excitement. He *needed* to see that submarine, and here was his chance.

He glanced down to see what the man was pointing at so proudly. It was a bright yellow convertible Mustang.

"Shall we go?" the man asked, moving toward the door.

Sam watched him, but this time it wasn't the scar he

was focused on. It was the man's eyes. The way they kept darting to his watch.

"Okay," Sam said.

The man smiled as he opened the door. Sam slipped past him and into the corridor, heading for the stairs, but when he got to the bathroom he darted inside and shut the door.

"I'll just be a sec," he called out as he quietly slipped the bolt into place.

The bathroom wasn't much bigger than the interview room. It had the same kind of window and, more important, the same fire escape balcony outside. Sam turned on the taps to cover his sounds, then he grabbed the window and lifted. It didn't move. Apparently, fire safety wasn't a big concern for the Orange Walk Police; the window had been nailed shut.

The door rattled. "We must hurry," the Scar-Faced Man called out.

There it was again. Why the rush? It felt to Sam like the man was keen to get out of the building. And what about the car? Hardly standard police issue.

There was another knock, faster, more insistent, but the man spoke in a hushed tone this time. "We must go now!"

Sam didn't reply. He moved back to the door and placed his ear against it. He could hear breathing and shuffling feet, and then the shuffling became footsteps that faded away down the corridor. Sam turned off the taps and returned to the door, listening for any signs of life in the corridor, but it was silent.

Sam raced to the window just in time to see the Scar-Faced Man getting into his bright yellow car. As the man sat back in his seat, he twisted his head and looked straight up at the bathroom window. Sam stepped back into the shadows, but he was sure the man had seen him.

A loud knock made Sam jump. He turned and stared at the door.

"Hello," said a voice from the other side. "Mr. Billington, are you in there? I'm Officer Castillo; you have an appointment with me at two thirty."

Sam took another look out the window. The yellow car was gone. He unlocked the door and opened it. In the corridor was a round-faced man of medium height wearing an Orange Walk Police Department uniform.

"I'm Jerry Castillo," he said, grinning and holding out his hand. "Someone downstairs told me a foreign boy had come up here. You are early, yes? I was told you had changed your appointment to three."

Sam gathered his thoughts as he shook the man's hand. The woman at reception had definitely been expecting Sam at two, the time Mary had booked for him, and she had called the Scar-Faced Man. Sam had known there as something wrong about him, but how did he know if he could trust this new guy, even if he was a cop?

"So, how can I help you, Chester?"

"I was interested in the World War Two sub that was found here a few years ago," Sam said.

"May I ask why?" Jerry said, still smiling.

"I'm here as an exchange student, and I read about the sub, so I thought it would be cool to check it out," Sam replied casually. "I heard it was found by a policeman, so I figured this was a good place to ask about it."

"That's right," said Jerry. "Superintendent Ramos."

"Is he still around?" asked Sam.

"Kind of," said Jerry. "These days Felix Ramos is a very rich and powerful man. He owns the Xibalba Crocodile Park, and he says he is a follower of Kinich Ahau."

Sam stared at the policeman, trying to work out if he was serious or not.

"Do you know who Kinich Ahau is?" asked Jerry. Sam shook his head.

"He's the Sun God." The smile faded from Jerry's face. "But also"—the man lowered his voice—"the god of the underworld." Jerry stared into Sam's eyes, then broke out in another big grin and slapped him on the back. "It's all for show," he said cheerfully. "But the tourists seem to like it." Jerry made a show of looking around, then lowered his voice. "Personally, I think the guy is a bit loco."

"What about the submarine?" asked Sam.

"That's locked away in the scrap yard by the river. Superintendent Ramos had it towed there after he found it. You can't get in there, I'm afraid. It is private property." Jerry placed his hand on Sam's shoulder and guided him toward the stairs, signaling the end of their meeting. "You should forget about the submarine. It's been rusting away for years. The thing is a death trap. There are a lot of other fun things to do in Orange Walk. Have you checked out the pyramids at Lamanai? They're pretty spectacular."

There was a new woman at the front desk when they got to the ground floor. Sam thanked Jerry for his time and assured him he would visit Lamanai. Before he stepped out of the building he checked for the yellow car, then he walked quickly back toward the hotel, checking behind him at regular intervals.

When the soft tones of a male opera singer reached Sam's ears, he stopped to locate the source. It took a few moments to work out that it was coming from his pocket. His new phone was ringing.

"How's it going, Sam For—uh, I mean, Chester?" said Mary, on the other end of the line. "How do you like the ringtone I programmed into your phone?"

"Very funny," said Sam. He was trying to sound angry, but it was good to hear her voice.

He explained what had happened at the police station and what he had found out about Felix Ramos.

"You've done well, Sam, but you're going to have to be careful. That man with the scar could be a problem."

"I'll be okay," Sam said, sounding a lot calmer than he felt. "I came here to find out what happened to my parents. I'm not going to let some creep in a yellow sports car scare me off."

"Good on you, Force," said Mary. "So, what next?"

"I need you to do something for me," said Sam.

"Name it."

"The cop said the submarine is in a scrap yard near the river. He said *the* scrap yard, so I reckon that means there is only one in town. Do you think you could locate it for me?"

"Sure," replied Mary. "What are you going to do now?"

"I'm going to follow Jerry's advice and see the sights of Orange Walk. Starting with a trip to the Xibalba Crocodile Park."

5

DINNER AND A SHOW

DESPITE HIS ENCOUNTER WITH THE Scar-Faced Man, Sam felt more confident than he had since his adventure to Belize had begun. He had a plan. Tracking down Superintendent Ramos was a good step forward.

He asked directions to Xibalba and marked it on his map. The walk took half an hour, and Sam stuck to the backstreets, keeping an eye out for a yellow car and the man with the hideous scar. Who was he? An opportunist who saw the chance to make some money off a boy who wanted to see an old submarine? That made sense. The woman at reception could have been a friend of his.

Or she could've recognized the name Sam Force and tipped somebody off.

As Sam wandered through Orange Walk, a text arrived from Mary with the address of what she assured him was the only scrap yard in town. He felt his confidence growing.

The dusty streets gave way to fields of crops and lumpy green stands of palms trees. For a while, Sam enjoyed the walk. The first pangs of apprehension hit him when he saw Xibalba. Even from a distance, it was impressive. A twenty-foot stone wall surrounded the complex. The name had been carved into the stone in giant letters. In front of the wall was parking for hundreds of cars. It was less than a quarter full, but as Sam approached the entrance a sleek white tour bus rolled in and stopped by the two big wooden doors.

A stream of chattering people poured out of the bus and bustled through the entrance. As Sam merged with the crowd of excited tourists, he saw they were all Asian and wearing identical white baseball caps with a logo that matched the one on the side of the bus.

A small man with a red baseball hat led the way, talking excitedly into a loudspeaker in an Asian language. Sam was caught in the press of people as they flowed through the doors. He kept his head down, and that's how he spotted one of the white caps lying on the ground. He grabbed it and slipped it on his head.

The heat of the afternoon sun faded away as they entered the gloom of a long tunnel. It was lit along each side by a series of small glass boxes. As the crowd slowed and bunched around the first box, Sam peered over the shoulders of the people in front and saw a huge stuffed crocodile head. Its rows of razor-sharp white teeth were gleaming under a spotlight, and the black marbles in the eye sockets gave it a ghostly stare. The group moved on, stopping to peer into each box. They all contained crocodile heads of various sizes.

Sam couldn't see the end of the tunnel, but the reason for that became clear when the tour group rounded a sharp right turn and entered a dimly lit gift shop. Rows of shelves were packed with an array of souvenirs. There were caps, T-shirts, golf balls and key rings, and they all had the same design on them—a fierce-looking croco-dile head. People began fussing over the merchandise, but the man in the red hat activated his loudspeaker and directed them toward the light.

They stepped into a small, open-air arena, with a large circular pool in the center. Rows of seats ran around the pool; each row was higher than the one in front. There were ten rows in all, and Sam's group was led up the stairs to the very top. Each seat had a Xibalba brochure on it, and Sam picked his up before sitting down. From his bird's-eye view of the pool below, he saw huge symbols carved into the stones around the pool, and recognized them as the Mayan calendar that his uncle had sent him. And then Sam noticed something. Four tall white poles positioned evenly around the pool and angled in to meet at a center point high over the water. The effect, for Sam at least, was the frame of an invisible pyramid.

The man with the red hat switched on his loudspeaker and said something to the group. Sam guessed it was a request to switch off cell phones, because the people on either side of him fussed over their devices, but then the man was peering down the aisle, checking his instructions were being obeyed.

Sam ducked his head and raised the Xibalba brochure in front of his face. He made a show of studying the crocodile design and prayed he hadn't been busted.

Suddenly the seats began vibrating as the sound of trumpets blared out of speakers mounted on the wall behind the seats. Sam lowered the brochure and saw that the man had sat down. The music faded just as the

sun dipped below the rim of the amphitheater. The temperature dropped, and a cool breeze blew across the crowd as the sound of drums echoed around the pool. But it wasn't coming from the speakers. Sam followed the direction of turning heads in the crowd. A small door had opened in the wall near the entrance to the gift shop, and out of it marched a line of figures. They looked like monks, wearing bulky black robes with the hoods pulled down over their heads. There were four of them, and each one was beating a small drum in time to their steps.

The crowd clapped enthusiastically as the procession marched slowly around the edge of the pool until each of them was standing by a pole. The drumming stopped, the applause died and for a few moments the only sound was the clicking of cameras. Then a loud voice boomed out of the speakers.

"Welcome to Xibalba. Home of Kinich Ahau, Sun God!"

Down at the pool, the black monks began to beat their drums again, faster this time. White smoke billowed out of the doorway, and Sam saw a flicker of movement, then a huge man in a white robe stepped out. His hood was also pulled over his head, and around his neck hung a wooden disc with a cross carved into it. He thrust his hands in the air like a boxer entering the ring, and the crowd rewarded him with a fresh wave of applause.

The frantic drumming continued as the voice began again.

"At night, Kinich Ahau, Sun God, becomes god of the underworld, and he summons his guardians."

The figures by the poles peeled off the tops of their drums and pulled out hunks of meat, which they tossed into the water. The blood in the meat spread like stains across the surface of the pool. The crowd made loud, appreciative noises, and cameras clicked. Then, long dark shapes appeared in the pool. The surface of the water began to churn, and the crowd gasped as four crocodiles rose to seize the meat. The picture taking became a frenzy; white bursts of light flashed around the amphitheater.

"The guardians of the underworld demand sacrifices," boomed the voice. "This is the key to rebirth."

The lights dimmed and spotlights lit up each of the four robed figures as they stepped down onto a ledge running around the inside of the pool. The water lapped around their waists. Sam narrowed his eyes. Why would someone get in the water with crocodiles when they'd just been tossed an appetizer and were surely eager for the main course?

At first the crowd kept taking photos. The man

beside Sam clapped wildly. When the first monk went under, Sam thought they had slipped. One moment they were standing there, hands outstretched; the next, they were gone and the spotlight switched off.

Somewhere in the crowd a woman screamed, and that was when it clicked.

The crocodiles were attacking the people.

Two more went down, the first rammed from the side, the second pushed from behind. Arms flailed, water churned, and then there was only one person left lit up in the water. It was a young woman; her hood had fallen back, and Sam could see she was terrified. When she screamed, Sam realized it was the first noise that had come from any of the victims. The piercing tone echoed around the crowd and triggered new screams from the spectators. Down at the pool, the woman scrambled back toward the edge, but before she could climb out, her legs were pulled out from under her and she disappeared beneath the surface.

Many of the audience were hysterical by now. Women were crying. A mother and child got up and ran for the gift shop.

But Sam was frozen to the spot, confused and horrified. Had he really just seen four people die?

The man in the white robe had remained still, with his head bowed the whole time, but now, as a spotlight hit him, he thrust his hands back into the air, and the speakers crackled to life again.

"Only he who is ordained by Kinich Ahau can control the guardians of the underworld."

A fresh wave of screams erupted as the man stepped down into the water. At the same moment lights in the bottom of the pool switched on, illuminating the crocodiles, who were still holding their human sacrifices. The surface was choppy as the black, scaly bodies, twisted and turned with their victims in their mouths. Suddenly, the man thrust his arms out and took another step forward. He dropped and the water rose to his neck. "Watch now as the power bestowed by Kinich Ahau controls the forces of life and death," the voice said ominously. The crowd went crazy as the man waded toward the beasts. And then the four objects on the bottom of the pool became eight as the beasts appeared to spit out their victims. The crocodiles, unburdened by their prey, swam to the far side of the pool and disappeared into the tunnel.

The crowd went silent as one by one, the black-robed sacrifices moved to the edge of the pool. The screaming and yelling began again, but it had changed. The crowd clapped wildly as the four figures stepped up onto the ledge and out of the pool. Clearly exhausted, they stumbled to their original places by the poles, their robes dripping water onto the stones. The white-robed leader climbed out last and then signaled to his followers. They picked up their drums and walked toward the tunnel.

"Sacrifice is the key to rebirth," the announcer declared. "You have just witnessed the power of Kinich Ahau, god of the underworld." The clapping got louder. "Now is your chance to meet the followers of Kinich Ahau and pay your respects." Then the announcer added, "Please make gratuities in US dollars only."

The crowd rose quickly; everyone was eager to meet the freaks that had cheated death. Sam kept his head down, wary of the man in the red hat, but he soon heard him screeching through his loudspeaker about US dollars. Sam had been so distracted by the performance he'd forgotten the reason he had come to Xibalba, but now he was focused on his mission again and he knew he needed to get down by the pool as fast as he could. He hadn't seen the face of the man in the white robe, and he didn't even know what Superintendent Ramos looked like, but he was sure they were the same person.

Movement along Sam's row slowed to a few shuffling inches at a time, so he took a shortcut by stepping over a seat and down into the next row. He repeated the move four more times until he was in an empty row, then cut along to the stairs and joined the line heading for the bottom.

Sam could see the four crocodile attack survivors lined up along the inside of the tunnel in their soaking robes. Their hoods were draped back over their heads, but they hung like wet towels. And they were holding their empty drum containers out in front of them like strangely dressed beggars. A traffic jam of tourists had formed at the entrance to the tunnel and people tossed dollar bills into the drums as they squeezed in for photos with the death-defying monks.

The white-robed leader wasn't with his disciples, and Sam pushed around the edge of the crowd, looking for the door the group had come out of. The frame had been painted to blend in with the stone, but as Sam grabbed the door handle he realized the whole wall was plaster, made to look like stone. He turned the handle and pulled the door open to look down another long corridor. At the far end, Sam caught a glimpse of the man in white, but the door was suddenly slammed shut in his face. Standing next to him was the woman who had tried to escape from the pool. Sam saw her looking at him from under her hood. She pointed to the door and shook her head, then stepped back into line beside her colleagues.

"I just want to see Mr. Ramos," Sam said, loud enough to be heard over the excited chatter of the tourists. The woman ignored him, and Sam was about to say something else when the hood of the monk at the far end of the line shook. Drops of water splashed onto an elderly lady who had backed up to the monk for a picture. The hood moved as the head inside turned toward Sam. He saw an eye under the wet cloth, then the second, and beside it an ugly red line.

Sam stared back at the Scar-Faced Man. The man sneered and stepped forward, but the woman was in his way. She turned, thinking he was giving her a hug. The man pushed her to one side, and in those few seconds, Sam acted. He dropped to his feet and crawled like a speeding toddler, hidden from the Scar-Faced Man. But he didn't head away; he aimed for the tunnel.

Sam had no idea if there was a back way out, but he did know where the entrance was. His only advantage was the mass of people. He crawled forward, over feet and between legs. The curses and yelps of surprise were lost in the chaos of over a hundred people struggling to take photos and buy souvenirs.

The tunnel was about ten feet wide; the four robed people were lined up against one side. Sam's course took him as close to the other wall as he could get. The tunnel widened as he got into the gift shop, and he rose to a crouch and ran across the shopping space, around the corner and into the narrower section that led to the entrance. As the space around Sam darkened, he risked a glance back.

At first all Sam saw were tourists loaded down with purchases, and then he spotted the Scar-Faced Man pushing through the crowd. Eager fans reached out to touch him and ask for photos, undeterred by his angry face. He ignored them and spun around, looking for a glimpse of his quarry. Finally, he looked up the tunnel and began moving toward the entrance. Sam ran on, swerving left and right to avoid the glow of the boxes containing the crocodile heads.

A crack of light running along the bottom of the two big wooden doors signaled the end of the tunnel. Sam tried the handle—locked. He looked back the way he had come and saw the outlines of bodies moving toward him. A camera flash went off, and for a fraction of a second the front group was illuminated. In the middle of them, moving fast, was the Scar-Faced Man.

Sam dropped to his knees and shuffled into the corner. There was no way he had been spotted, he told himself, but that would change once the man got to the doors. Sam pushed them again. They were heavy and bolted firmly. He hit them in frustration and was shocked to be rewarded with a *click*. He pushed again, and one of the doors swung outward. Sam's confusion faded as he stumbled into a surprised man wearing blue overalls and a Xibalba cap. The light streaming in made Sam an easy target. Shouts erupted from the other end of the tunnel. He slipped past the man in the doorway and ran into the parking lot.

Sam had seconds to get away, but where? The football field–sized lot was less than half full. The big white bus was still parked in the middle, and beyond it was the gate. Sam's only hope was to use the bus for cover as he ran for the only exit. Once he was out, he knew he could hide in the fields. Sam sprinted for the bus, but with every step he braced for the yell of the Scar-Faced Man.

THE SCAR-FACED MAN BARKED ORDERS at the men gathering around him while the tourists, oblivious to the drama, chatted happily to each other as they boarded their bus. The engine started, and the vehicle moved toward the exit, but an urgent cry brought it to a jarring stop. The hydraulics hissed as the door opened, and boots thumped up the stairs. The engine idled, and the passengers continued to talk. There were more heavy footsteps, and then the

XIBALBA CROCODILE PARK
GUARDIANS OF THE UNDERWORLD

Xibalba (Place of Fear) is the name of the Maya underworld and is ruled by the Maya death gods and their helpers. It is believed that the entrance to Xibalba is a cave in Belize. The Maya believed that when you died you entered the underworld through a cave.

Kinich Ahau (He of the Sun / Face of the Sun)—In the daytime, he is the Sun God on his daily trip through the thirteen levels of the sky. After sunset, he is god of the underworld, lord of night, as he descends to the underworld (Xibalba). Kinich Ahau is a personification of the number four.

Crocodiles—The relationship of the crocodile with the underworld, home of the dead, may be suggested for different reasons. Crocodiles live in caves, and caves are viewed as entrance points to the underworld. Crocodiles also spend much of their time underwater, and water is a feature of the underworld and one of the component parts of Xibalba.

door hissed shut. As the bus moved off, the Scar-Faced Man yelled to his men to search the rest of the parking lot.

The bus rolled back into Orange Walk, heading downtown. At the first set of lights, no one on board heard the *click* of the baggage compartment door as it opened and was then shut again. As the bus drove off, Sam stood up and crossed the road onto a small side street.

6

LOST AND FOUND

THE CONFRONTATION WITH THE SCAR-
Faced Man had thrown Sam. His getaway had been
down to luck. And a basic knowledge of bus loading.

The idea hit him as he ran past it. A flash back to
a rowing trip and helping to load the team bus. Sam
remembered the huge baggage compartment. Thankfully,
this one hadn't been locked. That, Sam soon discovered,
was because it was empty. He slid in with a sense of dread,
positive it would be the first place they would search.

It was the second. But the fact that it was empty had
saved Sam.

If there had been any bags, it would have triggered a
closer inspection. Whoever checked the compartment
only looked long enough to see that apart from the spare

tire, it was empty. If they had known anything about the baggage compartments in modern buses or had to pack them on team trips, they would have known that the spare tire was usually tucked away in a locker. A space just big enough for a thirteen-year-old boy.

Running through the backstreets of Orange Walk, Sam went over his options. He knew he shouldn't return to his hotel, but he had no choice. He called Mary, but there was no answer. On her way to Switzerland, he figured. He had to return to the hotel because he'd left his passport and extra money in his room. It was a rookie mistake, and he promised himself he would keep his passport and cash with his notebook in his backpack from now on.

When he reached the hotel, Sam waited across the road in the doorway of an apartment building. He watched the main entrance for the Scar-Faced Man and his helpers. After thirty minutes, there had been no sign of anyone. Did that mean he was safe? The Scar-Faced Man had his name, and he worked for Felix Ramos; surely he could find where he was staying.

He gave it another ten minutes and then, using his best young-exchange-student-out-for-a-walk look, he sauntered in past reception and headed for the elevators. Sam wasn't sure if he was sauntering, but he'd read the word in a book and thought it meant "walking casually."

There were no guests in the hotel lobby, and on

Sam's floor the only evidence of other people was a big room service cart. Judging by the number of plates, Sam could tell the people in the room next to him had enjoyed a real feast, and he felt a pang of hunger.

The room was how he'd left it. The first thing Sam did was go to the window and check the street; it was still empty. He pulled the curtains and turned on the light. Ignoring the temptation to call Mary, he dug a local directory out of the bottom drawer and turned to *Accommodations*. He needed to check in somewhere else under a different name. He found an ad for a cheap-looking motel a few blocks away and was about to ring the number when his phone beeped. He dug it out of his backpack, relieved that Mary had finally made contact. But then he saw the screen.

From: Jasper Force j.force@eef.com
Date: Saturday, Sep 19, 2015
To: Sam Force s.force@gmail.com

Sam,

I KNOW YOU ARE IN BELIZE.

I have been contacted by someone. He, or she, won't tell me who they are, but they go by the name TF—does that mean anything? TF told me you had left St. Albans and gone in search of your parents. Sam, I can't tell you how much this concerns me. We both know there are powerful people involved in this hunt for the Ark. I know you want to find out what happened to your parents, as do I, my boy. But please consider putting off your search until I can extract myself from Cairo and help you. You could leave Belize now and return to school. I could contact St. Albans with a cover story. Is that something you would consider?

Alas, I fear, knowing you as I do, that the answer is no. If you have shown the initiative to get yourself to Belize, then I imagine my pleading will not alter your determination. Therefore, I will pass on the information that TF asked me to convey to you.

I was asked to tell you that your parents used the name Sobek while they were in Belize. Sobek, by the way, was the Egyptian crocodile god. I don't know if this will be of any use and if I am contacted again I will pass on any information I receive. TF has also insisted you do not mention any of this to Mary. They do not want her involved.

So there you have it. Please do consider my suggestion to leave. Your parents would not think any less of you, and it would help this old man sleep much easier. If you cannot bring yourself to heed my wishes, then please stay safe, my boy. I hope some of my lessons will stand you in good stead. If you need anything, anything at all, contact me immediately.

xxx Jasper

Sam had no idea who TF was. The fact so many people seemed to know he was in Belize was a worry. First the bearded man and now the mysterious TF. At least he wanted to help. That should have been welcome news, but Jasper's words weighed heavily on Sam. He was embarrassed by his uncle's faith in his abilities. After being so eager to get to Belize, now he felt an overwhelming urge to run away.

Sam had been there less than a day, and things were already getting out of control. Should he move to another hotel? Or head for the airport? His mind wrestled with the question as he fidgeted with the directory. He opened the battered book again and looked up *Airport Transfers*. He found the listing and picked up the phone next to the bed to call for an outside line, but just as he dialed he turned back to the page with the ad for the cheap motel.

"Hello, reception," said the woman from downstairs.

"Hi. This is Chester Billington from room three oh seven. I need to make a local call."

There was a pause on the other end of the line.

"Mr. Billington, I was just about to ring you. I have a man here asking for you. I told him I couldn't give out your room number." The woman stopped talking, and Sam pressed his ear to the phone, straining to hear what was going on. She was talking to someone, then shouting. The words were faint, and Sam only made the last few out, but they were enough—*You can't go up.*

Sam dropped the phone, grabbed his backpack, and sprinted to the wardrobe. He threw back the doors and jabbed at the numbers on the small safe. An age passed between the four beeps of the buttons and the *click* of the door unlocking. He scooped up his passport and cash and ran from the room.

A solitary *ping* echoed along the corridor. The elevators were at one end around a corner. The other exit, the fire escape, was roughly the same distance in the opposite direction. Sam knew he'd never make it.

THE SCAR-FACED MAN WAS ALONE. HE'D changed from his soggy black robe into jeans and a black jacket. He walked quickly to Sam's room and knocked on the door softly, then harder. He checked up and down the corridor, then dropped to his knees and inserted two pieces of wire into the lock. There was a dull *click*, and he rose and slipped into the room.

A few seconds later, he was back in the corridor with his phone to his ear. As he spoke angrily in Spanish, the *ping* of the elevator announced another arrival on the third floor. A young man in a crisp white jacket rounded the corner and walked toward the Scar-Faced Man. He nodded respectfully when their eyes met and then moved behind the room service cart and pushed it back toward the elevator. The waiter didn't notice the extra weight, and Sam was wheeled away, crouching under the table on wheels. Through a gap in the tablecloth, he watched the Scar-Faced Man continue his conversation in the doorway of Sam's old room.

WHEN THE ELEVATOR STOPPED, SAM FELT the trolley being rolled out onto a concrete floor. He could hear the clanging of pots and instructions being shouted in Spanish. His plan—and it didn't deserve the title—was to leap out, apologize, and run. But he didn't need to. Someone yelled, "Pedro," which must have been the name of the waiter, because the cart came to an abrupt stop, and he rushed off toward the sound of the pots and yelling people.

Sam pulled back the tablecloth. He was in another long corridor, but not nearly as fancy as the one he'd come from. Guests were never meant to see this part of the hotel. Plain white walls and a concrete floor. Sam rolled out and headed away from the kitchen, toward a glowing EXIT sign at the far end of the corridor. He'd almost made it when another door opened in front of him. Sam just had time to open the door of the room he was passing and dive in.

It was pitch-black inside. Sam took one step forward

and kicked a bucket, sending it skidding across the floor. The noise was horrendous. He froze, listening for a sign that he had been busted. The squeaking wheels of another room service cart drifted past, and the corridor outside fell silent. Sam put his hands out, feeling for the door and then the wall beside it. He found the light switch, and a single bulb flickered to life above him.

He was in a small, windowless room. There was a desk beside the door. The rest of the space was filled with rows of floor-to-ceiling shelves stacked with all kinds of stuff. Sam put on his backpack and turned to leave the room. As he reached for the door handle, a large book on the desk caught his eye. Written on the cover were the words *Lost Property.* Inside were pages of neatly written dates and names. The first entry was October 2007. Sam flicked through it; the same neat handwriting filled every line. Whoever was in charge of lost property at the Orange Walk Excelsior took their job seriously, and they had been busy. 2008 took up three whole pages. 2009 was five. In early 2010, someone had even left a microwave oven in their room. Who took an appliance to a hotel? Sam wondered. A few lines below that entry, Sam spotted the name he'd been looking for. It seemed Mary had picked the right hotel. Next to the name Sobek, it said *Coat 414.*

There were no noises coming from the corridor, but there was no way to know how long it would stay like that. Sam knew the Scar-Faced Man could be searching the place for him. He had to get moving, but a potential clue was too important to pass up. He checked the book one more time and looked at the rows of shelves. Numbers on small cards were taped to the end of each unit. Sam moved toward the back of the room until he saw a card with *400–520* on it. Halfway along the bottom shelf of that row he spotted the microwave. Each shelf had numbers along it, and it didn't take Sam long to find 414. Folded neatly above it was an old brown trench coat. Sam knew it well; it was his father's. He picked it up and headed for the door.

That's when the alarm went off.

7

FIRE ESCAPE

OVER THE CLANGING BELL, SAM HEARD footsteps thundering down the corridor. They stopped outside, and he leapt into the corner as the door swung open. Three men spoke urgently in Spanish as a drawer in the desk was pulled open. There were more shuffling footsteps, and the door was slammed shut. They hadn't even noticed the light was on. The voices and footsteps faded away.

Then Sam smelled the smoke.

Stepping out from the corner, Sam saw the open drawer and one remaining fire warden vest in the bottom. The alarm was still ringing, but the corridor sounded empty. Sam stuck his head out to make sure the coast was clear. Down near the elevators, he saw wisps of black smoke in the air, so he ran the other way, toward the exit. He pushed down on the metal bar and burst out into a loading bay. It was empty, except for a delivery truck, but then the man who had been hiding behind it stepped out into the light. A flicker of recognition crossed his face, and he ran toward Sam.

Stepping back inside, Sam slammed the door and flicked the bolt at the top. Looking back along the corridor to the elevators, he could see a lot more black smoke now. Then the man outside began pounding on the door and shouting in Spanish.

Sam ran for the elevators. The smoke got thicker as the wall on the left-hand side disappeared to reveal a large kitchen. Steel benches and industrial ovens filled the space. On the far side, a frying pan was sitting on a gas hob with something small and black in it. Matching smoke was wafting into the air forming a thick layer on the ceiling. Sam could tell immediately that it wasn't the cause of the fire alarm. One of the panicking fire wardens must have been responsible. But it would soon bring people down, so he hurried on.

He reached the elevators and hit the button before remembering they stopped working during a fire. Cursing himself for wasting time, Sam entered the stairwell beside them. He went up one flight and found himself looking through a strip of glass in the door that opened out into the hotel reception area. There was more smoke, thicker and blacker, coming from the entrance to the bar on the far side of the space. Men in bulky black suits with yellow tanks on their backs and full face masks were walking backward and forward, ferrying equipment and escorting scared guests in pajamas and dressing gowns.

Sam wanted to get out of the stairwell and out of the hotel, but he resisted the urge to run. He calmed his breathing and kept staring through the window. On the hotel driveway, the flashing lights from two fire engines spread a red glow across the lawn and onto the crowd of spectators lining the footpath. Sam scanned the faces from one end to the other.

He missed him on the first pass. The Scar-Faced Man had put on a baseball cap and was standing behind the front row of the crowd with his head down, talking into his phone. But Sam saw his small dark eyes watching everyone who left through the hotel's glass doors. As he watched him, Sam knew the man's visit to the hotel during the fire was no coincidence.

Suddenly his view went black, then a face behind a mask peered through the glass strip. The door was ripped open, and the fireman grabbed Sam's arm.

"Are you all right?" he asked in accented English.

Sam could only nod as the man took his arm and

steered him toward the entrance. The big glass doors loomed ahead, and Sam knew he'd be spotted the moment he stepped out. Luckily, the reception area was crowded. Beside the front desk, a woman in a waiter's uniform was lying on a stretcher, breathing into an oxygen mask. It gave Sam an idea. He buckled over, slipped out of the fireman's grip, and burst into a violent coughing fit.

"Smoke, smoke," he gasped between coughs.

The fireman lifted his mask and called out in Spanish to a medic near the stretcher. The man came running with another oxygen bottle and mask. "Breathe in this," the man said, slipping the mask over Sam's face.

The fireman said something to the medic in Spanish and left.

"Wait here, please," the medic said to Sam. He returned to his patient on the stretcher and Sam used the time to pull on his father's trench coat. He didn't even bother taking off his backpack. The effect made him look like a hunchback, but Sam was happy with anything that disguised his appearance.

The medic didn't seem to notice the change in his patient when he returned, pushing the stretcher. He motioned for Sam to follow, which was fine with him. Head down and collar up, with a hand holding his mask in place, Sam stumbled out behind some other injured guests. The medic led them to an ambulance that shielded him from the crowd on the footpath. Sam waited nervously, expecting to see the Scar-Faced Man coming around the side of the vehicle, but after a few minutes he began to think he had made it without being spotted.

The medic was busy tending to half a dozen patients. Sam waited until he climbed inside the ambulance, and then he put down the mask and oxygen bottle and stepped back into the garden that ran down the side of the building. Knowing there was a man behind the hotel, Sam only went halfway before he climbed a fence and found himself in a narrow alleyway.

He didn't know how long it would take for the Scar-Faced Man to realize Sam had given him the slip again, but he wanted to put as much distance between them as he could. He started running, sticking to the backstreets and hiding whenever a car passed by. Ten minutes later, he reached the river and slowed to walk. He followed it away from town until he came to an old wharf jutting out into the water. Making sure no one was around, he ducked down and crawled under the decaying wooden structure. There was just enough room to sit, and he leaned back against one of the posts and closed his eyes. Despite his situation, he couldn't help smiling. He'd gotten away, again, and he'd done it on his own. He knew he should be scared, but he felt calm. Tired but calm.

Sam checked the contents of his backpack. Passport, cash, phone, notebook, and, thanks to Jasper's mysterious contact TF, his father's coat. Sam held it to his nose and sniffed, hoping for a scent, a memory of his father and his past. All he got was musty cotton, but that didn't matter, because he finally had the first physical proof his parents had been there.

The coat reminded him of long walks with his father; he'd always worn it. Another memory came to Sam: candy. It was his father's weakness and one his mother tried to prevent. On their walks, his father always had a supply of the banned goodies hidden in the deep pockets of his coat.

Sam's mouth watered at the thought. He searched the pockets. There was no candy, but he did find a piece of paper folded into a thin strip and tucked at the very bottom.

Some of his mother's research notes—he recognized the handwriting and her doodling at the bottom.

The Olmecs

Olmec artists carved large man-jaguar warriors that are similar to the Egyptian sphinxes on display showing lions with the heads of gods or kings.

The Olmecs disappeared
from history sometime before
1000 BC. Despite the best efforts of
archaeologists, not a single, solitary
sign of anything that could be
described as the "developmental phase"
of Olmec society had been unearthed
anywhere in Mexico (or, for that
matter, anywhere in the New World).
These people, whose characteristic
form of artistic expression was
the carving of huge negroid heads,
appeared to have come from nowhere.

The Long Count

The long count is a sacred calendar handed down to the Maya from the much more ancient Olmecs. The Maya, as with almost all other ancient world cultures, believed that the earth, as part of its natural cycle of being, lives through a series of successive "world ages," each separated by sudden physical planetary upheaval.

The long count calendar was established in ancient times to forecast or mark out the very transition points between these world ages.

The fourth sun ended with "torrential rains and floods." The fifth sun was said to have begun in darkness in 3114 BC and was known as "The Sun of Movement." This 5125-year cycle was divided into thirteen baktun cycles of 144,000 days and is *predicted to end on December 21, 2012. It is said the end of the fifth sun will come with the violent movement of the earth.*

▽∨⟨▷◁ ⍦▽ ◁▽▷ ◁▷◁

There had been a lot of talk about the end of the world in 2012. Sam hadn't paid much attention to it. His parents had been gone for two years then, and he was adjusting to his new orphaned life. Had his parents taken the threat seriously? Were the Olmecs the connection between Egypt and pyramids in Central America? His parents must have felt they were onto something if they made the effort to hide their research.

Sam leaned back against the pillar; the rhythmic sound of the lapping water was hypnotic. He was exhausted, his eyes were heavy, and the urge to close them was powerful. He knew that wasn't a good idea and dug into his backpack for the map of Orange Walk. Flicking it open, he traced his escape route from the hotel to his current position. The scrap yard didn't look too far away. He remembered Jerry the policeman's warning about it being private property. But how secure would a scrap yard be? A late-night visit would be the best chance of getting a look at the sub and the best way to take his mind off how tired and hungry he was.

Sam crawled out from under the wharf, put on the coat and backpack, and headed off to see the submarine that had brought his parents to Belize.

8

MIDNIGHT SNACK

SAM SMELLED THE SCRAP YARD BEFORE he saw it. He followed the river away from town for an hour. Old buildings gave way to fields that ran right to the water's edge. The journey felt much farther than it had looked on the map, and Sam wondered if Mary had gotten the location right.

He slogged along the riverbank, ankle-deep in sticky mud. It would have been faster using the light on his phone, but he didn't want to risk being spotted.

Hundreds of croaking frogs accompanied Sam on his journey, and occasionally, from the darkness overhead, a bird would add its loud screech to the din. But there were no man-made sounds, and that was just how Sam wanted it.

When he caught the first whiff, he thought he was approaching a farm. It was the smell of something dead. In the darkness, he made out a wall blocking his way. When he reached it, he saw it was a wire fence with hundreds of rusting cars stacked tightly behind it, creating a wall of iron. The fence stretched across the field, disappearing into the night. It also ran the other way, into the river. Coils of rusted barbed wire topped the barrier, and Sam realized he would have to get wet.

He waded into the river but had only gone a few feet when he saw the end of the fence, anchored in the water with a thick metal pole. Obviously, the builders had decided water-based break-ins weren't likely. Given the state of the yard, Sam wondered if the fence's main job was to hold the junk in, rather than keep people out.

The water was only up to his waist when Sam rounded the end of the fence. He waded back to shore between the shell of an old fishing boat and a half-submerged car chassis. The stink was much worse. It smelled like it was coming from the mud, but it was too dark to see.

As well as the smell and the mud, Sam had to contend with the small engine parts and other metal objects littering the ground. After almost tripping, he decided to risk using the flashlight on his phone. The first thing he saw in the light was a big dead something. Judging by the feathers scattered around, the thing had been a bird. But not for at least a week.

With the mystery of the smell solved, Sam moved on. He raised his phone, aiming the beam of light in front of him, and got his first look at submarine 518. It was bigger than it had appeared in the newspaper article. A gigantic black tube sloping down the riverbank into the water, but only the tail fin and propeller were submerged. The conning tower stuck out on top, and on the side he could just make out the numbers 518 in chipped, faded paint.

The sub was even more impressive up close. The huge curved body rose above Sam, blocking out the night sky. He placed his hand on the hull. The pitted steel plating felt cold and slimy.

This was the sub that had brought the Ark to Belize in 1942. Five years ago, Sam's parents had come here looking for answers, and now it had drawn Sam here, searching for answers of his own.

The body of the sub narrowed at the tail. Sam figured this was the best place to climb on board. As he followed the hull of the sub down into the water, his hands ran across on old rope ladder. Someone had already solved the problem.

In a place full of metal and junk, it was odd that someone had built a ladder out of old wood and rope. The contraption creaked and groaned as Sam climbed.

Each time his feet hit the side of the sub, the dull, echoey thud reminded him he was climbing something big and hollow.

Finally, his hands found the rusting iron rail the ropes were attached to. Clouds drifted overhead, blocking what little moonlight there had been, and as Sam stood on top of 518, he was forced to use the flashlight on his phone again. He waved it around him low and fast. The scrap yard felt deserted, but from the top of the sub he knew he'd stand out like a human lighthouse to anyone nearby.

The walkway ran toward the conning tower that rose off the deck like a small metal skyscraper. Steel steps, welded to the side, ran all the way to the top. But just as Sam prepared himself for another perilous climb, he spotted the open hatch a few feet from where he was standing. If he hadn't used the flashlight, he would have stepped into it.

Crouching next to the black hole, he shone the beam from his phone down into the sub. A ladder of rusting iron dropped down to a steel-plated floor. The pungent smell of rust, oil, and decay wafted up, and Sam regretted his decision to visit at night. But in the same instant, he knew he'd had no choice. He turned off his flashlight and climbed into the dead machine.

The blackness of an already dark night got even darker as he descended into the sub. Every scrape of his boots was amplified by the steel walls. Even the sound of his breathing bounced around, making it feel like someone was right next to him on the ladder.

The moment Sam's feet touched the steel floor, he reached for his phone. The blackness swirled around him as he fumbled for the button that activated the flashlight. He swung the phone left and right, knowing he was alone but comforted by the act of proving it. The beam lit up curved walls of rusting steel and gauges and switches covered in a layer of black sludge. Aiming forward, he recognized the periscope hanging from the roof, exactly like the ones he had seen in submarine movies.

To the rear, Sam saw a polished black floor that sloped up toward the roof of the sub the farther back it went. The space didn't make sense, and Sam moved closer. His feet reached the edge of the polished floor, and ripples ruined the effect. It was water. The river had claimed the back half of the submarine.

Moving around the ladder, Sam headed up toward the periscope. This was the heart of the ship. Tables stuck out from the wall, covered in a slimy gunk that had once been charts. An old clock was bolted to the hull, its glass cracked, the hands snapped off.

Sam waved his phone light around, hoping to see a sign his parents had been there, but everything was caked in seventy-three years' worth of dirt and decay.

Then, in the shadows, Sam saw something he recognized. It was a drawing of a crocodile, the same design as the one used at Xibalba.

As he looked closer, Sam noticed differences. This one had been filled with tiny designs, but someone had tried to remove them, leaving the center of the design a blurry white mess. Sam could still make out some of the details, and his instincts told him this was a clue. He got out his notebook and began to sketch, then remembered his fancy new smartphone had a camera.

Sam swiped at the screen until he found the app and made sure the flash was on. He took a series of

close-ups, and then a final shot of the whole design. As he stepped back to give himself room, he hit the periscope. The phone flew out of his hand, and Sam cried out as the glowing device hit the floor and slid past the ladder. The crash and scraping of the phone sounded like an avalanche on the metal-plated floor, then a *plop* signaled that it had hit the water.

Luckily, his fancy phone was waterproof, and it had landed with the light aiming up. Sliding one foot at a time, with his hands out in front, like a blind man, Sam moved toward his lifeline. For the last couple of feet, he dropped to his hands and knees and crawled.

Sam winced as he made contact with the ice-cold water. He edged forward, ignoring the discomfort, and finally got close enough to reach out and grab the phone. Just as he did, the screen died. Sam backed out of the water, got to his feet, and dried the phone on his T-shirt before turning it back on.

As his breathing settled, Sam could hear the water sloshing on the steel floor. He accessed the phone's settings and looked for the screen timer; he wouldn't get caught out again. The sound of the disturbed water grew, and, curious, Sam pushed the flashlight button. The beam shot out across the black space, but in the light Sam watched wide-eyed in horror as the surface became a churning white mess. Then, from out of the foam, rows of jagged white teeth and an impossibly pink fleshy mouth appeared.

Sam screamed as he stumbled back. His boot caught on a metal plate, and he fell sideways. The crocodile launched itself out of the water, slamming its jaws together in the exact spot its prey had been a second before. With a meaty *thump*, the crocodile hit the floor. Sam felt the impact through his body. His fall had saved him. He scrambled to his feet as the hunter twisted its head and locked its eyes on him.

Sam kept the phone's flashlight aimed at the crocodile; he put his other arm out behind him, feeling for the ladder. As he moved backward, the crocodile followed him step for step. In the glow of the flashlight, its two big, glassy eyes were locked onto Sam. He wanted to turn and run to the ladder, which was somewhere near in the darkness, but he couldn't take the light off the crocodile, so he continued with his awkward retreat.

And then he fell again.

It was a lump of slime. Sam stepped onto it, and his foot shot out from under him. As he crashed backward, he clutched his phone, blocking the light. There was a soft *thud* in the darkness as Sam landed on his backpack, then the scramble of claws on steel. The crocodile was coming.

With no time to get to his feet, all Sam could do was roll. The wall of the hull was only a few feet away;

he rolled once and then again, driven by the urge to avoid death. Halfway through his second roll, he didn't hit the hull as he'd expected; he dropped.

Sam hadn't spotted the narrow trench that ran between the floor and the hull, but it was just wide enough for a boy and just deep enough too.

Sam felt like he had dropped into a metal coffin. He'd landed on his side, facing the hull, with death lurking above. The crocodile's claws scraped across the metal plates as the beast tried to get to its prey. Sam listened to its long, raspy breaths just inches away. As he lay there in the darkness, the idea of being attacked from behind triggered a fresh flood of panic. Sam twisted to face the threat, even though he couldn't see it. But suddenly he was rolling again.

He hadn't fallen into a trench. It was a gap that led to a narrow space under the floor. Sam stopped and lay there listening to the crocodile as it slithered backward and forward on the steel plates just above him. He inspected his hiding space with a quick burst of his flashlight and spotted an identical gap on the other side. Sam rolled in super slow motion to the opposite side of the sub. He kept his phone off and moved by feel, listening for the sounds of the crocodile to work out where it was.

Sam eased into the gap next to the floor and readied his phone. He sat up, aimed it in the direction of the ladder, and flicked it on and off. In the brief flash of light, he spotted it, just a few feet from where he was lying. He lay down again, listening for signs that the crocodile had spotted his new position.

The sub stayed quiet.

Sam inched his way up the sub, keeping track of the distance in his head. When he figured he had gone five feet, he sat up and used his light again. He was now directly opposite the ladder.

Sam lay back down, breathing slowly and listening for the crocodile, but the man hunter had gone deathly quiet. He imagined the crocodile hatching its own plan, stalking him as he lay there. His heart beat faster, and his mind screamed at him to get out of there.

Sam sat up, climbed out of the gap beside the floor, and lunged toward the ladder, hoping he had the angle right. His hands hit cold steel; his feet found the bottom rung. As he climbed, he heard the scrambling of claws on steel plate, but the noise was drowned out by the sound of his feet thumping the rungs of the ladder.

Sam burst out into the cool night air and flung himself away from the hatch, powered by the fear of the beast below. He lay on the slimy deck, breathing so loudly he didn't hear the approaching footsteps. Then a new wave of panic ripped through Sam as a hand gripped his shoulder and a voice said, "You are under arrest."

9

FRAMED

HE WAS COLD, WET, AND TIRED. EVERY
part of his body ached, and then his nose began to itch.

It got worse, and he flicked his head from side to
side, trying to shake off the sensation. It didn't work.
One quick scratch would have solved the problem, but
his hands were cuffed behind his back.

Sam leaned forward, straining to reach the back of
the front seat. It was a couple of inches too far. Then
the police car braked, and Sam pitched forward, slamming into the worn vinyl. The itch disappeared as a
jolt of eye-watering pain shot through Sam's nose. He
groaned, prompting the policeman in the passenger
seat to turn and say something in Spanish.

Sam eased himself back and rested his head on the

window, watching orange streetlights pop in and out of view, to take his mind off his throbbing nose. It was a bad end to a rough night, but he knew it could have been worse.

When rough hands grabbed him on the deck of the sub, the wave of panic that hit him had been fueled by the thought that the Scar-Faced Man had tracked him down. When he heard the words *you're under arrest*, he almost felt relieved.

The two policemen led him to the front of the sub and down a shiny new ladder. Safely on the ground, they were almost apologetic when one of them produced a pair of handcuffs. Sam didn't understand their Spanish explanation but guessed they were telling him it was procedure. Their car was parked at the front gates. They helped Sam into the backseat and headed for town.

Orange Walk was deserted. The digital clock on the dashboard said 11:20 p.m., but it felt much later. After escaping the Scar-Faced Man and facing death inside sub 518, Sam felt strangely calm about returning to the police station. If he kept to the story—a naughty exchange student, exploring a junkyard at night—he was sure he could get away with just a telling off.

They pulled up outside the building Sam had visited only that afternoon. Now it seemed like a lifetime ago. The policeman from the passenger seat led Sam into the darkened reception area. As he removed the handcuffs, Sam heard footsteps on the stairs.

"Hello, Chester Billington," Jerry said, crossing the floor. He nodded a dismissal to the other policeman and stuck out his hand to Sam. "You have had a busy night, yes?"

Just stick to the story, Sam told himself. *I'm just a naughty exchange student on a midnight adventure.* He offered an embarrassed smile. "Yeah. I'm really sorry about all this."

"Are you hungry?" asked Jerry. "I can offer you some soup." He pointed to the stairs. "Let's go upstairs to my office?"

The offer of food got Sam's attention. He nodded eagerly and followed the man.

Jerry led Sam to a small office a few doors down from the room where he had gone with the Scar-Faced Man. The policeman sat down behind a desk covered in paper and motioned Sam to the one opposite. He fussed over some documents, moving a couple of stacks of paper from one side to the other. He looked up at Sam and shook his head slowly, the smile still on his face.

"You know, Chester, when I told you the submarine wasn't safe, I had no idea there was a crocodile living inside it. You must have been terrified."

"A bit," Sam replied.

Jerry's eyes widened. "A crocodile is not to be messed with, my friend. You would have seen that at Xibalba. It is just lucky my men happened to be passing by."

Sam nodded, but Jerry's comment seemed odd. The police car just happened to be passing? The junkyard was a long way from town. And how did the policeman know he had been to Xibalba—a lucky guess?

"Ah, here it is." Jerry produced a pink sheet of paper. "I need you to fill this in, Chester. And while you do, I'll get that soup."

Jerry left, and Sam studied the piece of paper. The title was in Spanish, but the English translation was next to it in brackets: *Incident Report*.

Jerry called out from down the hall. "I just need you to write your name, address, and phone number. That's all."

Sam wondered how many lies he could get away with, but then he realized Jerry hadn't given him a pen. He scanned the desk but only saw paper. Behind it, under the window, was a bookshelf jammed with folders full of more documents. Sam scanned the shelves, looking for a pen, but his eyes locked on to a small wooden picture frame, and a chill ran through him. He sat bolt upright, ears straining. The sounds of a running tap and clanging pot drifted up the corridor.

Mounted behind the glass in the frame was a roughly drawn stickman family—two big ones, and a smaller one in the middle. A large yellow circle, representing the sun, loomed over them and beside them was a blue oval shape. That was a lake.

Sam knew this because he had drawn the picture.

He had been three and half; the drawing was a birthday present for his mother. She had framed it and kept it by her bed from then on, even when she traveled. She referred to it as her little family. Sam's heart raced. He could still hear Jerry in the kitchen. He got up and retrieved the frame, then glanced out the door. The corridor was empty, so he walked quickly to the stairs.

The whole thing had been a setup. *Of course the police weren't passing by*, Sam thought as he took the stairs three at a time. He entered the darkened reception area, hoping the doors were still open. His luck held.

Sam sprinted across the tiled floor. As he leapt down the steps to the footpath, he checked the road, relieved that the police car had gone. That feeling lasted only a couple of seconds. The man had positioned himself behind the streetlight. As Sam ran past, he stepped out and grabbed him. Sam recognized the uniform, then the face. It was the policeman from the passenger seat. Two giant hands gripped him in a meaty vise, and Sam understood that the wide-open doors had also been a setup, and he'd fallen for it.

As he was guided back up the stairs, Sam heard the front doors being bolted. Sitting on Jerry's desk was a bowl of tomato soup and plate with two pieces of toast. The smell was delicious, but Sam forced himself to turn away from the mouthwatering display. He looked at Jerry. "Those policemen weren't just driving past the junkyard, were they?"

"No," the man said. "I thought you might try to visit the submarine, and I was concerned for your safety."

"You knew who I was?"

Jerry nodded. "I suspected you were Sam Force, but I wasn't sure."

"So you left the picture out for me to see."

Jerry nodded again then pointed to the soup. "Please eat."

Sam looked up at the policeman. "Did you know my parents?"

Jerry shook his head. "No. The discovery of the submarine and your parents' visit took place before I came to Orange Walk."

Sam couldn't hold back any longer. He grabbed a piece of toast and took a bite, then began spooning the soup into his mouth.

"Who's the man with the big scar on his face?" he asked between mouthfuls.

Jerry glanced toward the door then sat down and stared at Sam, the smile gone from his face. "How do you know about him?"

Sam explained how the Scar-Faced Man had arrived to interview him before Jerry and how he had gotten cold feet and locked himself in the bathroom.

Jerry listened intently, writing notes on a small pad.

"The man with the scar is called Azeem Rochez," Jerry said when Sam had finished. "He was a police officer here in Orange Walk. He left the force soon after Superintendent Ramos. He was the first to join his cult."

"Cult!" said Sam. "I thought Xibalba was a crocodile park?"

Jerry smiled, but it was thin and forced. "The park and show are for the tourists. There is a darker side to Xibalba. People used to come from all over Belize, and the world, to witness the power Felix Ramos has over his crocodiles. He says it is a gift from Kinich Ahau."

Jerry leaned across the desk and lowered his voice. "I told you he was crazy. I meant it. Sam, if he knows you are in Belize, you are in more danger than I thought."

"But why?" Sam demanded. "Has he got something to do with my parents going missing? Please, I need to know."

Jerry stared at his desk as if he hoped to spot a piece of paper that could help. "I can only tell you what I know," he said. "Felix Ramos was a long-serving police officer here in Orange Walk. When he found the submarine, he received a lot of attention from the press and television. And then your parents arrived."

Jerry paused. Sam could see him deciding how much to say. He wanted to yell at him to hurry up but fought the urge.

"Soon after your parents' visit," Jerry continued, "Superintendent Ramos was attacked by a huge crocodile. He killed it, but his injuries were very serious. After his recovery, he claimed to have power over all crocodiles. He also became very wealthy. There was talk that he found a lot of gold. He used his new wealth to build Xibalba."

Sam felt his anger flare. "You said *after* my parents' visit, like they came here and went home. They didn't. I haven't seen them for five years!"

Jerry sat back, running his hands through his short black hair. "I'm sorry, Sam, I didn't mean to make light of your parents' disappearance. But I have looked into the matter. Your parents left the country, and I don't believe Felix Ramos had anything to do with it, but . . ."

"But what?" Sam demanded.

"The submarine, the gold, and the power of Kinich Ahau. I think these are linked, although I cannot prove it. I suspect your parents believed that too. If Felix has discovered you are their son, he may see you as a threat to his power."

"Not if he hasn't done anything wrong."

"I didn't say he hadn't done anything wrong," Jerry said. "I told you I don't believe he had anything to do with your parents' disappearance. But people have gone missing at Xibalba." Jerry picked up a stack of papers that were perched on the far side of his desk and dropped them between him and Sam.

"These are missing persons reports. People who came to witness the power of Felix Ramos and then disappeared." Jerry tapped the pile with a finger. "But only after signing their possessions over to him. I have been researching this case since I came to Orange Walk. That's how I know about your parents."

Sam stared at the document and said nothing. Jerry broke the silence. "So you see, Sam, there is nothing here for you. There are no answers. But if you push a man like Felix Ramos, I won't be able to protect you. You have to leave Orange Walk."

Jerry looked up, and Sam realized someone else had entered the room. He turned to see the policeman who had brought him into the station.

"Officer Martinez and his partner will drive you to the airport in Belize City," Jerry said. "I have booked you a ticket back to Boston. I presume you want to travel under your fake identity?"

Sam looked at Jerry. The smile returned to the policeman's face for a moment.

Sam could feel his choices slipping away. "Hang on a minute."

"Sam," Jerry said firmly. "I have told you everything I know. Your parents were here, but they left. There are no more answers here."

"Left for where?"

"I don't know. Now, please. For your own safety, you must leave." Jerry rose to his feet and nodded to the other policeman, who placed a hand on Sam's shoulder.

The three of them went downstairs to the reception area. While Officer Martinez opened the front doors, Jerry said good-bye to Sam, then handed him over to the men who would make sure he left the country.

10

GREEN LIGHTS

THE STREETLIGHTS LIT UP THE INTERIOR of the police car with flashes of orange light as it cruised along the highway leading out of town.

A hundred questions crowded Sam's mind. The ones he knew he should have asked when he was with Jerry. Why was the policeman so sure his parents had left? Why was he so sure Felix Ramos was not involved? There were too many questions, and now he would never have a chance to get answers. Sam had been dismissed. Like a visit to the headmaster's office, his time was up, the adults had other things to do. With every streetlight they passed, Sam's frustration and anger grew.

The car rolled through the deserted street as its

passenger seethed in the backseat. The two policemen sat silently, staring ahead. Sam's anger cooled as he began to focus on thoughts of escape. It couldn't end like this. He would never have this chance again. He studied the door handle and lock beside him. When the car slowed, could he jump out? He thought back to the final moments at the police station.

The passenger-seat cop had put him in the backseat and closed the door, but Jerry had opened it again, just as they were about to drive off. He had handed Sam a business card. *Send me your real details when you get home, and I promise to contact you if I ever find out anything to do with your parents*, he'd said. Sam had ignored him, and Jerry had shut the door and they had driven off. But sitting there now, playing the scene over in his head, Sam realized that meant the door was unlocked.

Sam sat up and ran his hand across the bottom of the window. A slow, unconscious stretch, or that's how he hoped it would look. In the dark, his fingers felt for the lock. It was up. The door would open.

The car slowed as they reached a set of lights that led onto a bridge. Sam remembered it from the bus trip. It had signaled their arrival into Orange Walk. At the other end, the car would make a sharp turn then speed up along the highway that led to Belize City.

This was his last chance to get away.

Sam sat up, pretending he wanted a better view of the river as they crossed the bridge. He put out his other hand, feeling for the backpack on the seat beside him. The bridge was high, but what he remembered most about it were the boys he saw jumping off it. Sam just had to hope that neither policeman would want to follow him over the rail. That worry took his mind off the fact he was going to jump from a moving car and off a bridge in the dark.

Sam was so tense that when the car braked, he almost went headfirst into the back of the seat again. The jolt and burst of Spanish that followed from the men in the front seat brought Sam's attention to the road ahead.

Parked in the middle of the two lanes was an old car. Its hood was up, and three men were leaning over the engine. None of them had noticed the police car, and Sam's escorts cursed and fidgeted in their seats. Finally the passenger-seat cop wound down his window and shouted. Hands were waved in apology as the men closed the hood and gathered in front of the car to push it out of the way.

Sam knew this was his chance. Open the door, three quick steps and over the rail. But what came next? Where would he go? What could he hope to achieve? He didn't know. All he was doing was acting on the urge to stay free. He couldn't let them send him away now. Not with so many unanswered questions.

The policemen watched the men on the bridge impatiently. The passenger-seat cop leaned out of his window again. Sam gripped the door handle. He would go when the man yelled, hoping the noise would cover his exit. Suddenly, there was a blur of movement at the broken-down car. Two of the men spun toward the police car. They had guns. There were two flashes of light and everything went black.

The headlights had been shot out; the guns had been fitted with silencers. The only noise was the tinkling of glass, then running footsteps. Figures appeared on each side of the car. A man pulled Sam's door open and wrenched him out. As Sam was dragged to the old car, the struggling policemen fell silent.

The man threw Sam into the backseat and pushed him to the far side as another man wearing the same helmet and mask jammed in beside him. The engine started with a roar, tires screeched, and the car took off. Through the open window Sam saw they were heading out of town. In the darkness, he found the opening of his backpack, put his hand inside, and found the picture frame. The car slowed for the turn onto the riverbank highway. Sam slipped the frame out the window, and as the car swung around the bend, he tossed it into a clump of bushes.

The man in the passenger seat turned to look at Sam, and he thought he'd been caught. At that moment, the car sped past a streetlight. The orange glow lit up the interior, but all Sam saw was the long, ugly scar running down the man's face.

11

SUN GOD

THE SCAR-FACED MAN DIDN'T SAY A WORD.
No one in the car spoke during the ten-minute drive
to Xibalba.

The car stopped at the entrance to the tunnel. Sam
felt the man beside him move, and as he turned, a
bag was shoved over his head. Panicking, he began to
struggle, but the door opened and someone pulled.

Firm hands on each shoulder steered Sam into the
tunnel, but they hadn't gone very far when the group
stopped. Sam heard the *click* of a door opening and
sensed the walls closing in as they moved down a long
corridor. The pace increased until they came to stairs.
Sam stumbled twice, but each time he was hauled back
to his feet.

There was another corridor at the top of the stairs, then another door. This time one of the men knocked politely. The group waited in silence and then, from inside a booming voice called, "Enter."

The door opened, and the hands pushed Sam forward until he bumped into a chair. He slid into it, and the room descended into silence. Minutes passed, and Sam's ears began to compensate for his lack of vision. He sensed the three men behind him, breathing and shuffling their feet. He heard the ticking of an old clock in the corner of the room. It reminded him of the secretary's office at St. Albans. And then, below the ticking and shuffling, he heard another sound: the scratching of a pen on paper.

Finally, the scratching sound stopped. A moment later someone pulled the bag off Sam's head. The rough cloth scraped his nose, and Sam's eyes watered. As he wiped the tears away, he saw the large, moon-shaped face of a very well-fed middle-aged man staring at him. Sam dropped his hand, embarrassed by his reaction.

The man was totally bald, with only the faintest trace of eyebrows. The effect was a large brown blob sitting on top of a white collared shirt. He sat on the other side of a desk, covered in paper, staring at Sam with dark, unblinking eyes. Sam tried to hold his stare but couldn't and looked away.

The man took this as a sign of victory. He slammed

his hands onto the desk and pushed his bulky frame up. As he rose, he looked past Sam and gave the briefest nod. There were hurried footsteps and the sound of the door opening and closing.

They were alone.

"Sam Force?" The man lowered his head, fixing his dark eyes on his guest. "That is your name, yes?"

Sam nodded.

"And do you know who I am?"

"Felix Ramos."

"That is correct," the man said, smiling as he placed his hands behind his back and moved out from behind the desk.

Sam relaxed as Felix lifted his piercing gaze from him, and he took his first proper look around the room. The office was fancy. The huge wooden desk had thick legs with the images of plants and animals carved on them. It sat on thick red carpet. The walls were painted the same color but covered with large oil paintings of old people and landscapes. But it was the object behind the desk that caught Sam's eye.

Mounted on the wall was a thick gold frame. But instead of a painting, the space inside was black fabric. Mounted in the center was an antique silver dagger. A spotlight in the roof aimed at the weapon lit up every detail. It had a large, rounded hilt with a cross on it like the one carved into the necklace Felix had worn in the show at Xibalba. The wide grip was bound with silver wire, and the blade was engraved with the image of a crocodile.

Sam recognized the design. He had seen it on the Xibalba brochure and in the sub. His interest must have shown because behind him the man spoke.

"Have you seen that before?"

Sam shook his head.

"Those are the tools I used to create Xibalba."

Beneath the dagger, a faded scrap of paper was pinned to the black fabric. It didn't look like much of a tool, and Sam couldn't make out the handwriting on it, but at the bottom he saw a sketch of a pyramid.

A dull hum filled the room as the entire frame sank back, and then a panel, the same color as the walls, slid down over it and clicked into place. It was as if the framed dagger had never been there. The man moved back behind his desk and put down a small remote control unit. Sam understood that the dagger and piece of parchment had been on display for his benefit. The man sat down again; his eyes bored into Sam.

"Did your parents send you?"

"What? No! I came here to find them."

Felix laughed, deep and throaty; his huge frame shook like a mountain of jelly covered in material.

"It's true," Sam pleaded, angry with how lame his statement sounded. "What do you know about my parents?"

Felix kept laughing. He got back to his feet and walked to a small door. He stabbed at the keypad next to it with a pudgy finger until there was a clicking sound; then he motioned for Sam to follow him as he pushed the door open. Sam stood nervously, glancing back at the main doors he had been brought in through.

"There is no escape," Felix said, reading Sam's mind. "My men are waiting outside. But if you do as I say, you will be okay."

Sam followed him through the door into a narrow hall lit by small lights set into the roof. At the end of it, stairs descended to another corridor that led to another door. Felix grinned as he pushed it open and waved his arm like a doorman in a fancy hotel. Only his dark eyes betrayed the friendly act.

Most of the room was taken up by a large indoor pool. It was circular, like the one in the amphitheater, only slightly smaller. The room had no windows—the only light was coming from the water, and it filled the space with an eerie blue glow. It would have been quite beautiful if it hadn't been for the circumstances.

As Sam's eyes adjusted to the low, blue light, he saw the far wall was glass. Behind it, steel cages were stacked from floor to ceiling. As he stared at them, they faded from view, the glass transformed from see-through to the same off-white color as the other walls.

Felix grinned at Sam's confusion and produced another remote control from his pocket. "I designed every part of Xibalba myself," he said, waving in the direction of the glass wall. "And no one will take it from me. Not you, not your parents."

"I don't care about Xibalba," Sam said. "I told you. I came here to find my parents. That's all!"

Felix considered Sam's statement for a moment, then pointed to the pool. "Leave your bag there," he said, pointing to Sam's feet. "I want to show you something."

He walked to the edge of the pool and stared into the water.

"You see it?" he said, pointing to the center of the pool.

Sam stood next to the giant man and looked, but all he could see was the white-tiled bottom of the pool. "See wha—"

Sam wasn't expecting the shove. Felix hit him hard in the center of his back. His arms flapped pathetically and got caught in his trench coat as he tumbled into the water. He'd had no time to take a breath, and as his head broke the surface, he gasped for air. He looked up at Felix, angry and confused, but the man smiled and pointed to the far side of the pool.

Directly opposite, Sam spotted a hole in the wall. As he stared at it, a long black object slid out and settled on the bottom of the pool. Sam felt sick. A shiver ran through his body as he turned and looked up at Felix, unable to hide the horror on his face.

"Don't move," the man said. "Answer my questions, and you have nothing to fear."

Sam was beyond fear. He couldn't stop his body shaking. He inched his body back around to see the dark outline of the crocodile lying motionless on the white tiles.

"Why are you here, Sam Force?" Felix said behind him.

"My parents. I told you," Sam pleaded. "I came to find them!"

"Liar," shouted Felix. "They have sent you for the treasure. You know where the other two locations are."

Sam was out of his mind with panic. He had no idea what the man was talking about.

"The other two locations. Where are they?" Felix demanded.

"I don't know!" Sam screamed. "I don't—"

"On!" Felix shouted.

On command, the beast slid forward. Sam couldn't help it, he screamed, a loud, shrill cry of terror.

"Tell me," said Felix.

The crocodile surfaced. Water glistened on the

green scales; its dead eyes, large and unblinking, were fixed on Sam.

"The other two locations," Felix said again.

"I don't know," Sam sobbed. "I don't know what you're talking about."

The crocodile opened its mouth.

"Enough!" Felix yelled. The crocodile froze in the water, but its jaws continued to open. Sam stood rigid in the water, staring at the beast.

And then he heard the laugh. Not from behind him. It was coming from the crocodile.

As he stared into the jaws of the crocodile, human eyes appeared at the back of its mouth. Sam's brain couldn't understand what his eyes were showing him. He was looking at the face of a man wearing a dive mask. The man's cheeks moved up and down around the edge of the mask as he laughed.

Legs appeared under the crocodile. Sam watched as a man dropped out from underneath the animal and swam to the edge of the pool. He was wearing a skin-tight black wet suit and propelled himself out of the water in one smooth move. As he pulled off his mask, the Scar-Faced Man was still laughing.

"Get him out," Felix ordered.

The Scar-Faced Man walked back to the edge of the pool, leaned down, and stuck out his arm. Sam took hold of it and let the man pull him out. He collapsed in a wet heap. Water drained out of his trench coat, spreading in a pool on the stone around him. He lay there, not trusting himself to stand up and unable to take his eyes off the lifeless beast in the pool.

"That thing . . . Is that the secret to your show? How the sacrifices survive?" Sam asked.

Felix laughed as he stared at Sam, then pointed a meaty fist at the pool. "That is just a toy. I assure you, the power given to me by Kinich Ahau is very real. As you will find out if you do not tell me the truth!"

"I told you," Sam said. "I just came here to find my parents."

"Liar. Your parents sent you here for gold. My gold!"

"No they didn't!" Sam protested. Despite what he'd just been through, Felix's comment had angered him. "My parents came here because of the sub. They were interested in a link between the pyramids of Lamanai and Egypt."

"Ah yes," Felix scoffed. "The pyramids, and the end of the world in 2012. That was a lie. A cover story. I found the sub and I claimed the real secret of Lamanai." He began hitting his chest as he spoke. The meaty thumps punctuated the words. "I . . . found . . . it. Not them! And now that they know the truth, they have sent their boy to do their dirty work."

In the blue light coming from the pool, Felix's angry red face looked even more grotesque. He glared down at Sam, who suddenly forgot about his run-in with whatever it was in the pool. Now Felix was the threat. He stood over Sam, breathing heavily as beads of sweat broke out across his face and head, and his chest heaved as if he'd just run a race.

Sam looked up, too tired and too scared to move. Felix's dark, unblinking eyes bore into him, and then, as quickly as it had come, the storm passed. His breathing calmed, and he lowered his arms and unclenched his fists. A weak smile formed as he turned and headed back to the door.

"Azeem, find our guest somewhere to sleep for the night," he called out as he left.

The Scar-Faced Man had slunk out of the way while his boss had worked himself up to a frenzy. Now the man darted in, pulled Sam to his feet, and pushed him toward the glass wall. As they passed Sam's backpack, Azeem grabbed it with his spare hand. They went to the right-hand end of the wall. Azeem leaned on the glass, a door-sized panel swung open, and he pushed Sam into the room full of steel cages.

Stacked two high along both walls, each cage was twice the size of a dog kennel. The room smelled of rotting meat and damp living things. In the dim light coming from the pool room, Sam saw dark eyes watching him from the cages. Some of the crocodiles were so big their tails had been bent around to fit into the cages. Halfway along the room, an old wooden table had been slotted in between the cages.

"Take your coat off and put it here," Azeem said, pointing to the table where he had tossed Sam's backpack.

"What's happening?" Sam asked as he put the coat down.

Azeem shoved Sam on past another stack of cages before stopping.

"Top or bottom?" he said, grinning.

Sam looked at the two empty cages, one on top of the other. "You can't be serious?"

"Where did you think you were going to sleep?" the man hissed. "Choose now or I will."

Sam looked at the small, dirty cages and decided the one on the bottom would be more comfortable.

He crawled in, and as he struggled to turn in the cramped confines of the cage, he heard, and felt, the door slam behind him. Sam looked back just in time to see Azeem placing a padlock on the latch.

"Have a good night's sleep." Azeem tapped the cage cheerfully and laughed to himself as he headed back to the door.

Sam sat back against the side of the cage, listening

to the echoing footsteps fade. The bars dug into him. He shifted, but it made no difference. He was cold and tired and beyond despair. It had taken all his strength not to break down in front of the two men out by the pool, but now he sobbed quietly. All around him he could hear signs of life, but they weren't human. There were low growls, the scrape of claws and scales on concrete, and breathing. Sam felt more alone than he had ever been in his life.

And then someone whispered his name.

12

SEWING CLASS

SAM DIDN'T UNDERSTAND WHAT HAD happened. Had he just imagined a boy calling out to him?

Then he heard it again.

"Sam. Can you hear me?"

"Who is that?" he asked, expecting to hear nothing and be forced to admit he was losing his mind. But the voice replied.

"My name is Elio."

Sam felt relieved. Not because he had company, but because he wasn't going crazy. "Where are you?"

"I am in a cage next to the desk. I saw you come past me."

"Why?" Sam asked. "Why are you here?"

"I used to work for Mr. Ramos, but I was caught . . ." The boy's voice trailed off.

"Caught? Doing what?"

"Mr. Ramos thought I was stealing from him. But I wasn't," the boy insisted. "Not really."

Sam was confused, and he still couldn't get over the fact there was someone else in the room, and in a cage.

"I was on the riverbank at Lamanai," Elio continued. "I was looking for the entrance to the chamber."

"What chamber?"

"The chamber where Mr. Ramos found the power of Kinich Ahau, and a lot of gold. I don't need much. My mother is sick. One coin would be enough."

Sam thought back to Ramos's bizarre questions about treasure and the two other locations.

"Do you know where this chamber is?"

"No."

"But Felix caught you looking for it?"

"Not Mr. Ramos. Azeem," the boy said. Sam could hear the bitterness in his tone. "He was in his machine."

"What machine?"

"The one you saw in the pool."

"That fake crocodile. What's it for?"

"Mr. Ramos had the machine designed to catch crocodiles for Xibalba. It is a miniature submarine. One man lies inside and controls it. Always Azeem.

He used to go into the caves and catch the babies. It has a dart gun in the mouth."

Sam sat in his cage shaking his head. A miniature sub disguised to look like a crocodile. Ramos had to be rich if he could waste money on contraptions like that. Sam wouldn't have believed it if he hadn't just seen it with is own eyes. "It looked so real," he said, more to himself than to Elio, but the boy heard him.

"Yes, Sam. I, too, have been where you were. On the river, when it came for me; I thought I was dead."

"So Azeem was hunting crocs and found you."

"No," the boy said. "Xibalba has enough crocodiles. Mr. Ramos sends Azeem to watch over his secret in Lamanai. I didn't think he would be out that night. I was desperate. My mother is sick. I only need one piece of gold. I thought if I could find the chamber . . ."

The boy fell silent, and Sam thought about what he had just learned. It felt like a tiny piece of a huge jigsaw puzzle had slipped into place. He had no idea what the final picture looked like, but he was almost grateful that Azeem had stuffed him into the cage.

The feeling of success was fleeting. It faded as the cold bars digging into his back reminded Sam of the danger he was in.

"Elio, how long have you been here?"

"I was caught a week ago."

"You've been in that cage for a week?!"

"No," the boy said. "At first I was locked in a storeroom upstairs, but a few days ago there was a fire. Not a bad one, but the fire department came. Azeem was worried they would find me when they evacuated the park, so he moved me here. We are underground. This room is not on the plans."

"How do you know?" Sam asked.

"I have worked here since Mr. Ramos opened Xibalba. I knew of this place, but was never allowed here. This is where Mr. Ramos trained his followers."

Sam didn't reply straightaway. His mind began to tick over. "Could you find us a way out of here?" he asked.

Now it was the boy's turn to go quiet.

"Elio?" Sam said.

"I think perhaps yes," he replied. "But first I would need to get out of this cage."

Sam nodded slowly. The boy was right. One problem at a time. The first was getting out of the cage. He examined the padlock on the door—twenty seconds. He knew he could have it open in twenty seconds, maybe less.

Picking locks was a skill his uncle had taught him in Cairo. On a rainy afternoon at his apartment, Uncle Jasper had produced a padlock almost identical to the one Sam now faced. Jasper had said lock picking was a handy skill to have, and he had been right.

Chocolate and other banned food confiscated from the boys in Sam's dormitory at St. Albans was locked in a cupboard. On more than one occasion, Sam's roommates had persuaded him to put the skills his uncle had taught him to use. For a decent cut of the proceeds.

"Sam, what's wrong?" Elio asked, the concern obvious in his tone.

"Nothing," Sam said. "I'm just thinking, Elio. You're next to the table. Can you reach my bag?" As he spoke, he looked down the room. He could just make out the table and the outline of his bag, but it was too dark to see the boy in the cage beside it.

"Yes, I think I can," came the reply.

"I want you to get my pocketknife out of my bag. It will be at the bottom."

The pocketknife was the key to Sam's plan. It had been a present from Uncle Jasper—*To mark your graduation as an official lock picker*, he had said cheerfully at the time. Jasper then pointed out the attachment on the knife he had personally modified to turn it into a lock-picking tool.

Sam held his breath and listened for signs of Elio's progress. He heard a grunt and imagined the boy leaning through the bars, straining to reach the bag. If it was too far away, the whole plan would fail before it began. There was a scraping sound. A bag buckle on wood? The sound faded, and Sam couldn't hold his breath any longer. He let out a lungful of old air and gulped another.

"Elio. Have you got it?" he called out.

There was no answer.

He tried again. "Elio?"

Finally the boy replied, "Yes, Sam. I have the knife. Now what?"

Sam leaned back against the bars again; they were warmer now, thanks to the heat from his body. They didn't seem as uncomfortable. Or was it because his mind had no time to be bothered with minor discomforts?

"Sam?" Elio said again. It was his turn to be impatient.

"Hang on," Sam snapped, then, feeling bad about his tone, he added, "I just need a second to think."

The knife was the key, but he had to get it. Could Elio skid it along the floor to him? It was a long way, and if he got it wrong, or Sam missed it, the knife would race off into the dark. Sam studied the space around him. Through the bars of the cage above, he saw something solid.

He stuck his fingers through and prodded the dark shape. It was soft and fleshy. His prodding dislodged the object, and it fell into his lap. Sam flung the rotting meat away in disgust. It hit the bars on the far side of his cage, but he forgot it instantly as a low growl rolled out of the dark.

Sam had been so focused on Elio and the table, he hadn't realized there was an occupant locked up on the other side of him. Like the cage between him and the table, he'd thought it was also empty, but now he heard claws scraping on concrete, and as he watched, a crocodile slithered out of the dark corner.

Compared to the other specimens Sam had seen that day, real and fake, this one was a baby, no more than five feet long. Sam's neighbor pressed its snout against the bars between them and locked its small black eyes on the meat sitting a few inches away.

As the surprise wore off, curiosity took over. Sam retrieved the hunk of steak, ripped a small piece off, and tossed it through the bars into the crocodile's cage. It swung away with surprising speed, and Sam heard jaws snap as it grabbed the rotting snack. Then it was back, in the same spot, its eyes locked greedily on the rest of the meat. Sam couldn't help laughing. The crocodile had performed like a hungry dog, and as quickly as that thought came, it was replaced by the germ of an idea.

"Elio," he called out.

The boy replied instantly, "Yes, Sam."

"Is there any meat in your cage?"

There was a pause, then he said, "Sam, don't eat the meat. It is rotten. It will make you sick."

Sam smiled. "No, Elio, it's not for me. It's for a crocodile. I have an idea to get us out."

"I see," Elio replied. "Let me check." Almost immediately, he spoke again. "Yes. There is a large piece in the cage next to me. I can get it, but how will I pass it to you?"

"You don't need to," Sam replied as he took off his pants. "Just give me a few minutes to get ready."

One of the things St. Albans boarding school prided itself on was preparing their boys for life and career. Life preparation covered everything from gardening and cooking to sewing. To make a sewing class more acceptable for boys, it was called Soft Materials Technology, or Soft Tech for short. But the fancy name didn't disguise the fact it was lessons on how to use a sewing machine and needle and thread. Skills that Sam and his friends agreed they would never use again.

Despite his misgivings, Sam enjoyed Soft Tech. In his first year, he had made a bean bag and a pencil case. His least favorite project had been the one on mending, but now, as he took off his pants, he'd changed his mind.

The boys were required to bring an item of clothing to repair. Sam had picked his canvas cargo pants, the pair he wore on archaeological digs with his uncle. During his escape from the ship buried in the desert, they had developed a big rip in the seat. Sam's mending solution was a large canvas square, hand-stitched over the rip. The job had earned him a C from the teacher, who had noted the loose stitching and the use of thick, waterproof thread. Sam had disputed the low mark. He felt the teacher had failed to understand that he was going for the Hobo look. But sitting there in the cage, Sam was surprised by how easily the thread came out—surprised but also grateful. Thanks to his poor work in Soft Tech, he soon had a couple of feet of the thick thread wound around his hand.

The crocodile had ignored Sam and his pants, keeping its eyes locked on the meat as if it was hoping it would fly across the floor and into its mouth. Sam picked up the rotten steak, ripped off another piece, and tossed it behind the baby croc. The moment it turned, Sam shoved his fingers out through the front of his cage and grabbed the latch of the crocodile's cage. Luckily, only the humans warranted locks on their cages. Sam lifted the latch and flicked the door open just as his hungry neighbor returned to his spot against the side of the cage.

The crocodile was more interested in the prospect of another snack than taking advantage of the open door, and Sam had been counting on this. He made a loop in one end of the thread, then ripped off another piece of meat, but he tossed this chunk outside the front of his cage. The crocodile spotted the morsel, turned, and moved cautiously out through the open door. As the creature slunk along the front of Sam's cage, he hung the looped thread out between the bars. At the moment the crocodile snapped up the piece of meat, Sam dropped the loop onto its tail and gently tightened it.

Sam released the lungful of air he'd been holding, but there was no time to lose. He needed to keep the hungry crocodile outside. He ripped the last of his meat in half and hid one piece behind him. He put the other out between the bars above the crocodile and tossed it down the room toward Elio's cage.

The beast shot off like a little green dragster.

"What's happening, Sam?" a nervous Elio called out.

"There's a crocodile coming to you," Sam said, almost laughing at the crazy statement. "Listen, Elio. You need to throw some of your meat onto the floor in front of your cage, so the crocodile comes all the way to you. Do you understand?"

"Not really," he replied.

Sam heard the boy moving about, then there was silence. He was about to call out to him when a squeal came from his cage.

"Sam! It's here."

"That's good," Sam said. "Can you see its tail? I tied some string to it."

"Yes," Elio replied. "I can see it."

"All right. Now, I want you to put some more meat out on the floor. But listen," Sam said. "This is important. Don't put the meat in front of your cage. Throw it to the left. Not too far. Just enough for the crocodile to bring its tail to you. Do you understand?"

"Not really," he said again.

"The crocodile will go past your cage to get the meat. When it does, you need to grab the string and tie the pocketknife on."

In the silence that followed, Sam replayed the crazy instructions he'd just given out. Of course it was never going to work. What had he been thinking? He felt the familiar pangs of panic surfacing as his mind raced away.

"Okay," came the boy's voice out of the darkness.

"You'll give it a go?" Sam asked.

"I've done it."

"What?" Sam didn't try to hide his amazement.

"I did exactly what you said. I tied the knife on and put it on the floor outside the bars. The crocodile is right in front of my cage, watching me."

"Nice work," Sam called out as he retrieved the last of his meat. He dangled it between the bars and swung it backward and forward. The stench of the rotting meat filled his nostrils. "Is the crocodile coming?" he asked.

"No."

Sam pinched a small piece off and flicked it down toward Elio's cage. He peered into the darkness, willing the beast back to him. Suddenly, Elio squealed.

"He's coming," the boy hissed.

Sam heard the scratching of claws on concrete, and something else—a scraping sound.

The beast came at full speed; Sam only just had time to drop the meat and pull his hands inside before a blur of white teeth snapped together in the place where his fingers had been just seconds ago. But the crocodile didn't stop. Spotting the open door of its cage, it made a beeline for home. The tail slid past, towing a thin white line behind it. The thread seemed to go on forever, but suddenly the small block of red plastic popped into view.

As the knife skidded and bumped across the floor in front of Sam's cage, he thrust an open hand through the bars and grabbed the moving thread. He felt it slipping under his skin and then the knife was pulled into his hand. His fingers locked around it tightly, and he pulled it back to him. The thread was supposed to snap, but the thick, waterproof cotton was tougher than Sam realized. As he pulled the knife to him, the line went tight, and suddenly an angry, snapping crocodile came racing back to the cage, intent on attacking the threat that had struck from behind.

Sam shied away from the bars as the crocodile's snout

smashed into them. He put the knife to his mouth and worked furiously at the thread with his teeth. The line went tight again as the crocodile whipped its tail away from the cage. The thread ripped across Sam's face, went taut, and finally snapped with a loud *ping*. The angry croc scuttled off into its cage, and Sam slid to the back of his, one hand on the stinging cut across his face, the other clutching his precious knife.

"Sam, are you okay?" Elio asked.

It took Sam a few moments to calm down enough to answer. "I got it," he finally said.

Sam retrieved the last piece of meat from the back of his cage and tossed it between the bars. The crocodile slithered out of the darkness and back into its home. It snapped up the last bit of meat and turned to lock its black eyes on Sam again.

It took over a minute to pick the lock. Sam put the extra time down to his lack of practice and shaking hands. It took even longer to open the door of his cage. Conscious of being watched by his food-obsessed neighbor, Sam edged the door open a few millimeters at a time. When he had it fully open, he got into a crouch and edged out onto the floor. He waited near the opening, collecting his thoughts and running through what he was about to do. When he was ready, he sprang to his feet, took three steps forward, grabbed the door to the crocodile's cage, and slammed it shut. As he slid the latch into place, the crocodile still hadn't moved. Sam wasn't sure if it had been surprised by his speed or was too full to care.

The stench of meat, the fact he had been caught and locked up in a cage, none of that mattered as Sam strode down to Elio. The boy peered up with a smile so big his white teeth took up most of his face.

"Hi, Sam," he said, as if they were meeting up in the school yard.

"Hi," Sam said with equal cheer.

He knelt down and grabbed the lock, and his smile faded.

"What's wrong?" Elio asked. "You still have your knife, yes?"

Sam nodded then looked at the boy. "I'm sorry, Elio. I'm so sorry."

"I don't understand," the boy said.

Sam held the heavy silver lock in his hand. In the center, five small wheels were lined up side by side with numbers around them. "This is a combination lock," Sam explained. "The lock on my cage was an old brass key lock. I can't pick this, Elio. I don't know how to. I'm sorry."

13

SUIT UP

"YOUR BAG IS SINGING."

Sam, pacing backward and forward outside Elio's cage, didn't hear him.

"Your bag," the boy said again. He pointed to the table, and Sam heard the muffled opera coming from inside his backpack.

"It doesn't matter," he said. He knew it had to be Mary. She could wait.

"Sam, listen to me," Elio said. "I heard Mr. Ramos talk about your parents. He thinks you are after his gold. You need to get out of here. Don't worry about me."

"No. I can't leave you," Sam insisted. He knelt down

by Elio's cage again and inspected the hefty combination lock. "If I can find a crowbar, or something solid, I might be able to break it."

He got up and raced to the end of the room, looking for anything that would help him break Elio out. All he saw were more cages. Most were empty, but some had crocodiles similar in size to the one he'd been locked next to.

"Sam," Elio called out. "On the wall is a suit. Bring it here."

Sam wondered why the boy was worried about dressing up, and then he saw the dark lump of clothing hanging on a hook. It was rubber, cold and wet.

"You mean this wet suit?" Sam replied.

"Yes. Please."

Sam lifted the suit off the wall, surprised by its weight.

"Hurry," Elio urged. "Morning can only be a few hours away."

Sam dumped the wet suit on the floor, surprised by Elio's cheerful look. "How will this help get you out?"

The boy's face became serious. "Listen, Sam. If you get away, you can send help for me, yes?"

Sam nodded slowly.

"Good." Elio beamed. "It is agreed, then. Do you have pen and paper?"

Sam took his notebook and pen out of his backpack and gave them to Elio. Then he checked his phone. It had been Mary calling. He wondered what time it was in Switzerland. He could see from the clock on his cell phone that it was three a.m. in Orange Walk. It had been a long night, and it wasn't over yet.

"What are you doing, Elio?" Sam asked.

The boy kept drawing as he replied. "I know every part of Xibalba. I have worked here since it opened. I am drawing you a map. And a place to go if you need somewhere safe. Put on the wet suit."

Sam looked at the pile of rubber on the floor, and Elio spoke again as if he had read his mind. "It will go over your clothes."

"Oh, good," Sam replied with a touch of sarcasm. He had worn a wet suit a couple of times on school rafting trips, but this one was different. The rubber felt twice as thick, and on the chest was a strange plastic box.

It took a few minutes to get into the suit. It felt cold and clammy and far too big. As Sam stumbled around trying to adjust to the extra weight, he saw Elio watching him.

XIBALBA

1. Main pool
2. Secret pool
3. Cage room
4. Gift shop
5. Tunnel
6. Main doors
7. Mr Ramos office
8. Boat jetty
9. Car park
10. Main entrance
11. Tunnel to river
12. River
13. Tunnel to main pool
14. Seating
15. Staff area

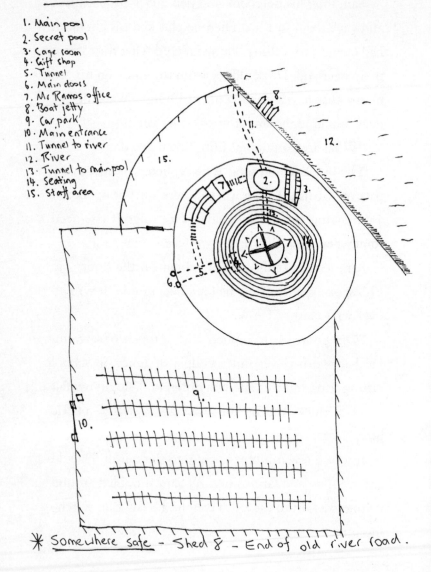

✲ <u>Somewhere safe</u> – Shed 8 – End of old river road.

★ ★ ★

"THIS IS THE BEST I CAN DO, SAM," THE boy said as he pushed the notebook out through the bars.

"We are under the small pool," Elio said. "This and Mr. Ramos's office and the staff quarters are all under the seats of the main arena."

Sam studied the rough map. "What's this?" he asked, pointing to the two sets of dotted lines leading away from their pool.

"Those are tunnels. This is how the crocodiles swim into the main pool and the river."

"Swim?"

"Yes," Elio said. "The tunnels are filled with water. You need to swim out to the main pool."

Sam pointed at the other dotted lines. "Why not this one out to the river?"

Elio shook his head. "No. That tunnel has a door to the river that closes on a timer. Every night at midnight, Mr. Ramos sends his crocodiles out, and the door stays shut till six a.m."

"So they come back in like pets," Sam said.

"Yes, that's right. Mr. Ramos has trained them."

"And not just to come and go," Sam said. "I saw the show."

Elio let out a small laugh. "All is not as it seems here, Sam."

"What do you mean?"

"I have learned much since I have been locked down here. That suit you have on is one of the secrets to the show," Elio said. "It is how the Sun God's sacrifices avoid death."

"This rubber thing protects them from the crocodiles' teeth?" Sam asked, prodding the suit.

"It is called pressure-expanding Kevlar," Elio said, as if he was reading it from a manual. "The more pressure put on it, the stronger it becomes, so it can withstand even the bite of the crocodile."

Sam ran his fingers across the rubbery fabric. "But even if they weren't bitten," he said, "I saw them dragged under the water. Why didn't they drown?"

"There is also a built-in breathing device."

"So that's what this is," Sam said, prodding the plastic box on his chest. "How does it work?"

"A button on the left arm," Elio replied. "Try it."

Sam found the button and pushed it. There was a *click* as a small mouthpiece popped up out of the plastic box. He leaned forward and wrapped his lips around it. As Sam sucked in, he felt the tangy taste of oxygen. He pushed the button again, and the mouthpiece retracted back into its compartment. "Nifty," he said. "But where does the air come from? There are no tanks."

"It is stored in the rubber," Elio said. "I don't

know how. I heard Azeem talking about it with Mr. Ramos out by the pool. It is the latest technology from America. Very expensive. Mr. Ramos spared no expense with his park."

"This is pretty cool," Sam said, admiring his suit with newfound respect. "So the sacrifices are grabbed by the crocs and dragged under the water and they breathe on the mouthpiece until Mr. Ramos makes the crocodiles leave?"

Elio nodded.

"But why do the crocodiles let go of them?"

"I do not know," Elio said. "Mr. Ramos says he has the power to command the crocodiles, given to him by the Sun God."

"Do you believe him?"

Elio shrugged. "The crocodiles never touch him. And on his command, they release the sacrifices."

Sam looked at his suit. "Your idea for my escape doesn't involve me being grabbed by a crocodile, does it?"

"No," Elio said. "I told you. Except for the untrained crocodiles in these cages, all the rest are sent out to the river at night to hunt for their food. You will be quite safe."

Sam didn't share Elio's confidence in his statement, but he stayed quiet. "So, what is your plan?" he asked.

"You can swim up the tunnel to the main pool."

"Swim?"

"Yes. That's why you need the suit. It is too far to hold your breath. You will need the air in the suit."

Sam nodded. In the dark, he couldn't see Elio's face, and he had no idea how confident the boy was, but he didn't sound as if he was sure about the idea. "Then what?" Sam asked.

"You can pick the lock to the door into the gift shop and escape down the tunnel."

"Won't the main door be locked too?" Sam asked.

"Yes," Elio replied. "But neither are combination locks, so you can open them, yes?"

Sam wasn't so sure. A door lock was tougher than a padlock. Not impossible, just time-consuming. Then he thought of something else. "What about alarms?"

"Not in the pools. Only once you get into the gift shop," Elio said helpfully. "But you can be out before Azeem comes, yes?"

"What do you mean, before Azeem comes?" Sam asked. "Do he and Ramos live here?"

"Not Mr. Ramos. He goes home to his mansion," Elio replied. "But Azeem sleeps in a room near Mr. Ramos's office."

"Oh, great," Sam said. Even if he could pick the first lock, he would have to run down to the main doors and attempt that one. There was plenty of time for Azeem to grab him. His slim chance of escape was becoming a zero chance, but then his mind went back to alarms.

"Elio, why did the fire brigade come the other day?"

"A fire in the gift shop," the boy replied.

Sam thought about the fire Azeem had set at the hotel. His inspiration for the stunt must have come from the Xibalba fire. "Are there any fire alarms by the pool?"

"No," the boy said. "They are all inside."

The silence in the cage room was interrupted by the muffled opera singing coming from Sam's phone again. This time he reached into his bag and grabbed the device. He clicked accept, but before he could speak, Mary's high-pitched voice screeched out of the earpiece.

"Sam Force, are you there? Now, before you get mad, I know it is three a.m., but I couldn't sleep. I had to call and see how you are doing."

Sam rubbed his ear and moved the phone away from his head, but he could still hear Mary perfectly.

"Are you there, Sam? If I've got your voice mail again, I don't know what I'll do."

"I'm here. Okay." Sam laughed. "Has anyone ever told you that you talk really, really fast? No. Don't answer that," he added quickly. "Look, Mary, I can't talk right now. I'm in a bit of trouble."

"And let me guess, you don't have time to explain."

"No, I can explain," Sam said. "Felix Ramos caught me and locked me in a cage in his crocodile park."

The line went silent for the first time since Sam had answered the call. Then Mary said, "Are you telling the truth?"

"Kind of," Sam replied. "I got out of the cage, but I'm still stuck in the crocodile park."

"Sam, are you okay?" The humor had left Mary's voice. "I mean, you're obviously not okay. What can I do?"

"I don't know. What can you do?" Sam knew he should sound more worried. He wasn't trying to impress Mary by acting cool about the situation. Perhaps, he thought, he was just too exhausted to get any more afraid.

"Do you have a plan?" Mary asked.

"I did," Sam replied. "I was thinking about setting off a fire alarm—you know, for distraction."

"Would that work?"

"Maybe," Sam said. "If I could get to a fire alarm without setting off the burglar alarm."

"Maybe I can help with that?"

"Are you talking about hacking into Xibalba's computer system?" Sam said.

"No," Mary said. "I tried that when you told me about Felix Ramos. But it has better security than the US government websites."

"Figures," Sam said. "This guy likes his tech."

"But I don't need to get into his computer."

"What do you mean?"

"I bet the Orange Walk Fire Department doesn't have an encrypted computer system," Mary said confidently. "I bet little old me could walk right in there, digitally speaking, and trigger Xibalba's fire alarm from that end."

Sam smiled, and Elio saw the change. "Sam, what is it?" he asked.

"I'll tell you in a minute," Sam said to the boy.

"Is there someone with you?" Mary asked in Sam's other ear.

"Yeah," Sam replied. "But that's a long story. How much time will it take you to set off the fire alarm?"

The line went quiet for a few seconds. "Give me thirty minutes," Mary answered.

"What?!" Sam protested. "I can't hang around here. It'll be morning soon."

"Okay, okay. Twenty minutes. Give me twenty minutes to get in position."

"In position? What do you mean? What time is it in Switzerland?"

"Just be ready," Mary answered firmly. "I have to go. I have things to do."

The line went dead, and Sam put the phone down.

"Who was that?" Elio asked.

"A friend," Sam said. "Tell me about the tunnel into the main pool?"

14

HELP FROM ABOVE

THE CROCODILE WAS STILL IN THE POOL.
Sam still couldn't believe how real it looked.

"Have you found the control box?" Elio's voice
sounded dull behind the glass wall. Sam had another
pang of guilt about leaving the boy trapped in his cage,
but he had insisted and time was running out.

"I found it," Sam hissed, not brave enough to shout.
According to Elio's map, Azeem was well out of earshot, but he didn't want to risk it.

The fuse box on the wall opened to reveal two
rows of red buttons. Following Elio's instructions, Sam
pushed B1 and B2. He felt the vibrations under his feet
that Elio had told him would mean the door to the
tunnel that led to the main pool was opening.

"I'm going now," Sam said in the direction of the cage room. He heard Elio's muffled "Good luck" as he lowered himself into the water.

In his suit, he didn't notice the change in temperature. The Kevlar-impregnated rubber insulated him from the cold. Sam checked the zip at his neck was pulled up tight, and he placed a hand on his waist, where he could feel his notebook and phone. They were essential, but he had been forced to leave his backpack and his father's trench coat behind. Elio's last words to him in the cage room had been a promise to look after his father's lucky coat.

Sam pushed the button on his left sleeve. The breathing unit popped out, and he wrapped his mouth around it and took a breath. The air tasted stale and rubbery, but it was breathable. As he slipped below the surface, Sam took another, deeper breath. His lungs filled, and he kicked off the side, heading for the tunnel below.

Sam hovered outside and peered into the gloom. At first all he could see was black, but then he made out a tiny blue rectangle of light. The exit into the big pool looked a long way off. He felt his doubts growing, but before the feelings could take hold, he started kicking. His body straightened, and he entered the tunnel with his legs pumping up and down the way the swimming coach at St. Albans had taught him.

It was pitch-black inside the tunnel, like swim-ming in ink. The only guide Sam had was the small block of blue light in the distance. It didn't change in size, and as he swam on, he got the feeling he wasn't making any progress. He imagined a current coming down the tunnel holding him in place, trapping him in the darkness. His breaths got shorter and faster. How long would the air last? Surely the suit couldn't hold much. This new thought triggered fresh fears. With every breath, he expected the unit to fail. He kicked harder, fueled by the image of an agonizing death in the watery tomb.

Gradually, the block of light ahead got larger. Sam's legs were aching, and his lips stung from holding the mouthpiece in place, but the pain was forgotten as he popped out into the main pool. Sam surfaced, spat out the breather, and sucked in a lungful of the fresh night air.

Lights in the bottom of the pool cast a soft blue glow out of the water into the front rows of seating. As Sam hung there, treading water, he suddenly felt like a massive target. A black blob in the middle of a glow-ing blue circle. The image spurred his legs back into action, and he kicked to the edge of the pool.

Water dripped off his wet suit as he clambered out. The noise echoed around him and sounded disastrously loud. Sam ran for the shadows of the second row of seats but looked back in horror at the wide, wet trail he'd made from the pool to his hiding place. He hoped Elio was right about there being no guards inside the complex at night.

Loosening the zip of his wet suit, Sam fished out his phone. The message on the screen from Mary read, CALL IF YOU CAN, and Sam's heart sank as he hit the green button.

"Sam, is that you?" Mary whispered.

"Why are you whispering?" Sam whispered back. "I'm the one who's hiding."

"Sorry, a nervous habit," she replied, but she kept her voice low. "Are you ready?"

"Yes," Sam said. "What's wrong? Can't you get into the fire department's system?"

"That's all set," Mary said. "I'm ready to go. But I think I can be of more help."

"How?" Sam asked.

"I can guide you out," she said. "Once you get to the main door, I'll have eyes on you, so I can help you across that car park."

"Really?" Sam was impressed and confused. "How are you going to do that? Have you hacked into a satellite or something?"

"Something like that. I don't have time to explain.

Call me the moment you get out the door, and keep the phone to your ear. You might not be able to talk, but I'll be able to tell you where to go to avoid the people in the car park. . . . Sam, are you still there?"

Sam was; he just didn't know what to say. He knew Mary was good with computers, but this was way beyond anything he could imagine.

"So what next?" he asked.

"My computer just told the Orange Walk Fire Department computer that every fire sensor in Xibalba is going off, so they're responding to a massive fire. Get ready."

After Mary hung up, Sam moved closer to the double doors that lead to the gift shop and tunnel. Last time he had been here, he was on his knees, crawling through a crowd of tourists. Not for the first time, he reflected on what a bizarre day it had been.

The amphitheater was deathly still. The terraced seating blocked out any wind, and the only noise came from Sam's movements. He stood by the doors like an overeager shopper lining up to be first for a sale. Away from the light of the pool and decked out in his black rubber, he felt almost invisible, but as he stood there, paranoia got the better of him. He imagined security cameras watching him and decided to move back to the cover of the nearest seats.

Sam lay down between two rows and ran through what was about to go down. The place had stayed silent. That meant the fire alarms had only been triggered at the fire department, which was a good thing. There would be little or no warning for Azeem when they arrived. What would he do? Elio had said the small pool and cage room were secret. Azeem wouldn't be worried about the firemen finding his prisoners. His first instinct would be to run straight to the main entrance to find out why they had turned up. Then what? Sam pictured the Scar-Faced Man and the firemen rushing down to the gift shop to fight the fire. They would spend a few minutes checking before deciding it had been a false alarm. That was when Azeem would get suspicious. He would run back to Ramos's office and down to the small pool and find Sam gone.

Sam suddenly felt sick. Lying there running through the events that were about to go down, he spotted a huge flaw in his plan. The firemen were expecting a fire in the gift shop. Sam was in the amphitheater. If they didn't come out through the door, he couldn't get away. He patted his body madly, like he was on fire. He finally felt his pocketknife. He had tucked it in along with his notebook and phone. He pulled it out of his wet suit and opened the lock-picking attachment. He was going to have to try his luck on the door anyway.

Sam heard the sirens as he got to work. He couldn't believe he had been so stupid. Picking a door lock was hard enough, but he had just made the job even tougher. The first bit of good news was that the lock didn't look too complicated. Sam tried to block out the noises drifting into the amphitheater. Over the sirens, he could hear screeching tires, and then men shouting. From the other side of the door, he heard a thumping sound that had to be the main doors being thrown open.

He moved the picking device around; the urge to speed up the slow, circular movements was overwhelming, but he knew it would be a mistake. The first rule of lock picking was patience. He stopped, took another cautious breath, and resumed his work, ignoring the sudden noise of shouting men in the tunnel.

Finally, Sam was rewarded with a tiny *click*. He let out a hushed *yes* in celebration. He grabbed the door handle, then froze as he remembered the burglar alarm. Would it be off? As he weighed up the risk, the noises on the other side of the door grew louder, and he knew he had to make a move.

He pushed down on the handle, opening the door just enough to slip through, and then shut it immediately.

The only light in the gift shop came from a small aquarium behind the counter. Sam moved away from it, searching for the long row of shirt racks he remembered. He found it just as a group of men, weighed down by bulky equipment, burst into the space.

Sam kept moving, using the cover of the clothing racks. He knew it would only take a few moments for the men to work out that there was no fire and, worse, find the light switch. He ran at a crouch, out of the gift shop and up the tunnel, relieved to see the light boxes with the croc heads weren't on; the tunnel was pitch-black.

Sam was in another black tunnel heading for a rectangle of light. Instead of blue, this was filled with flashing red. Sam could see more figures rushing around outside. Judging by the noise levels, Mary had done a great job summoning the fire department. He ran on, wary of the side door he had been taken through to meet Ramos. He didn't want to run into Azeem, not when he was so close to escaping.

He reached the door and peered out, surprised to see only three fire trucks in the parking lot. From inside it had sounded like the entire Belize fire brigade.

A car with a flashing red light sped in through the front gate. The men standing by the fire trucks walked over to greet the new arrival and Sam used the opportunity to dart out into the darkness and move along the wall toward the staff car park.

Immediately, his phone began vibrating in his hand. He'd been ready to call Mary, but she had beaten him to it. He put the phone to his ear, and she started speaking.

"Stop. Get down," she ordered.

Sam's first thought was that Mary's ridiculously complicated scheme was going to fail. He had been doing fine without her. There was nothing coming his way. He stopped anyway, thinking of the simplest way to tell her he didn't need her help. As he got down on one knee, a car roared into life, and moments later it sped out through the gates of the staff parking lot, heading for the main entrance.

"That was close," Mary said.

Sam could only manage a whispered "Thanks."

"There's no one else near you," Mary said, and Sam took comfort from her calm tone. "When I tell you, I want you to run straight ahead. And don't stop till you get to the fence."

Sam's doubts came racing back. The fence looked a mile away, across wide-open ground. He'd be spotted for sure. He desperately wanted to question Mary but held his tongue.

"Don't go until I say," Mary said.

Sam forced himself to relax. He took a deep breath, but Mary shouted, "Now!"

Sam got up and ran. The sound of his feet thumping on the concrete sounded so loud Sam expected to hear the men by the trucks call out with every step.

"Keep going. You haven't been spotted."

Mary seemed to be reading his mind, and Sam wondered how she was seeing him. Was he a tiny, grainy, night-vision-green image on a screen? Could she really know he was safe? The doubt and fear gave him more energy, and he increased his pace, or at least he imagined he had increased his pace.

The pitch-black sprint came to a sudden and undignified end. Sam had run the whole way holding the phone near his ear, but he'd struggled to keep it in place. A few feet from the fence, he heard a few garbled words, and as he wondered what she'd said his foot hit empty space and he crashed down a small bank.

"You okay?" Mary asked.

Sam lay sprawled on his back in a ditch that ran along the base of the fence, but the rubber suit had cushioned the impact.

"That's the ditch I warned you about."

Sam didn't care. He was listening for the sounds of running feet.

Mary, sensing his thoughts again, said, "No one heard you."

"Now what?" Sam whispered.

"Now it gets a little difficult."

Sam didn't know if he felt like laughing or crying.

"Move along the ditch," Mary said. "The car that came past you stopped at the gate. The man in it was sent to back up the guard on the gate. You're going to have to get past two sets of eyes."

Sam was already in a crouch, moving toward the gate. He listened to Mary and tried to imagine what Azeem was doing. He'd know Sam had escaped by now, but he wouldn't know where to. Sending a man to the front gate had to be a precaution; otherwise he would have been there himself.

"The man in the car. Can you see if he has a scar on his face?" Sam asked.

"He doesn't," Mary answered.

Her tone was definite, and Sam realized the surveillance technology she had tapped into was state-of-the-art.

The ditch was empty, and Sam made good time along it. On the other side of the car park, he could see the firemen packing their gear away. They would be gone soon. Sam had to beat them out.

The front gate was just ahead. The light in the guard booth cast a glow over the two men standing by the barrier arm. One of them was in blue overalls; the other looked like he'd just gotten out of bed, which he probably had.

Sam crept forward until he was near the ring of light coming from the guard booth. He stopped and waited. He knew Mary was watching, so he didn't bother speaking, but he was dying to ask about her plan for getting the men away from the exit.

The sounds of the firemen drifted across the car park. The two guards were talking quietly. There was a crackling sound, and the man in blue overalls pulled a walkie-talkie off his belt and said something in Spanish. It had to be Azeem asking if they had seen anything. Sam looked up into the night sky, hoping Mary could still see him.

"I'm going to distract them, Sam. You need to be ready to go through the gate."

Sam got to his feet and edged forward. A fire truck started up, but Sam kept his eyes on the two men and waited for Mary's distraction. When it finally happened, it wasn't as dramatic as he'd expected. Both men turned and stared down the fence line on the other side of the gate. They spoke in hushed tones then ran off.

Sam didn't wait for Mary's signal. He sprinted along the ditch to the guard booth, jumped up onto the concrete, and ducked under the barrier.

He'd done it.

Just as that thought entered his mind, disaster struck. As he got back to his feet on the other side of the barrier, his phone slipped from his hand and skidded across the concrete and into the ditch on the other side of the road. Sam stopped and spun around, following the noise of the phone.

He looked down the fence line for the two guards. In the darkness, all he could see was a thin beam of red light bouncing around. Then a truck roared to life, and the first fire engine swung slowly toward the exit. Its headlights caught the two guards at the fence line, standing by an empty car. They turned to head back to their post just as the fire engine's lights lit up the guard booth and a boy in black rubber.

Sam ignored the shouts of the men as he went for his phone. The fire engine's headlights had shown him where it was. He slid down into the ditch and grabbed it, then scrambled back up and under the barrier. As he got to his feet, Mary yelled into the earpiece.

"Run straight across the field."

"Why?"

"Just do it," Mary said.

With the phone still stuck to his ear, Sam ran across the road. If there had been a fence or ditch, it would have been all over, but the ground was flat, the dirt was smooth and firm. As he sprinted on through the darkness, Sam could hear a man shouting behind him.

"Now what?" he puffed into the phone.

"Keep going. On the other side of the field is a hill. There are trees on it. Look for a red light. Run straight for it and you will avoid hitting anything."

There was no time to ask what was going on, so Sam just ran. He glanced back once to see the lights of the fire truck heading down the road. As it faded away, he made out the sound of a man thumping across the field behind him.

He was getting closer.

"You're nearly at the hill," Mary said.

Sam made out the incline ahead. His feet started hitting small bushes and weeds.

"Can you see the red light?" Mary asked.

"Yes," Sam said. The flashing pinprick looked as if it were in the sky. The hill got steeper, and Sam began to slow down. He could hear the heavy breathing of the man behind him.

"Run faster, Sam!" Mary urged.

Sam tried, but his strength was fading. The thick rubber suit wasn't helping. The joints were stiff, and its weight made it feel like he was carrying someone on his back.

"When I say stop, I want you to drop to the ground, okay?" Mary said.

Sam couldn't imagine what Mary had planned, but he couldn't keep his pace up, and he was grateful for the excuse to stop. He ran on, waiting for Mary's signal, first expectantly, then desperately.

Finally, she gave the command.

Sam dropped to the ground with his pursuer only a few steps behind. He could hear his feet crashing through the undergrowth. Sam lay there, defenseless. He rolled onto his back and saw the silhouette of the man looming over him. Suddenly, the red beam hit the man's face. For a second, Sam made out his features—curly hair, thick, bushy eyebrows, and a wide, flat nose—then the man threw his hands to his eyes and howled in pain.

"Sam!" Mary's voice called from the phone. "Get up, keep going."

Sam rose unsteadily. Staring up the hill, he spotted the red pinprick of light again and stumbled on up the steep rise. Behind him, he could hear the man howling.

Then the light went out.

"Sam," Mary said.

"What?" Sam said into the phone.

"Sam," she said again. But her voice wasn't coming from the phone. Somehow she was speaking to him from the ground in front of him. When the hand grabbed his arm, he yelped pathetically.

"Sam," Mary said again. "It's me."

"What?" Sam couldn't see a thing in the darkness, and he couldn't believe his ears. "How . . . how can you be here?" he said, reaching out and grabbing his friend. Before he could say anything else, another cry of anguish drifted up the slope.

"We should get going," Mary said.

"What did you do to him?" Sam asked, still gasping for breath.

"A high-powered laser pointer," Mary said, holding out a small metal cylinder. Sam's eyes were adjusting to the dark, and he could just make it out.

"I didn't think anyone would follow you up the hill," continued Mary. "I had to aim it at his eyes. You're not supposed to do that. It says so in the instruction book."

"I'm kinda glad you did," Sam said. "I wondered what had gotten the guards' attention in the parking lot?"

"Yeah. I aimed it at the wing mirror of the car so they couldn't tell where it was coming from. Pretty neat, eh?"

"Pretty neat. I still can't believe you're here. How did you do it?"

"I'll explain when we're safe. The blindness won't last long," Mary said. "We need to get going."

Halfway down the hill, Sam could just make out

the guard, who was now sitting on the ground, still clutching his eyes.

He looked out toward Xibalba. The fire trucks had gone, but there were more men in the car park.

"This way," Mary called out.

Sam turned to see his friend heading up the hill and, with a hundred questions forming, he followed after her.

15

DEAD END

THE ADRENALINE PRODUCED BY HIS escape drained away as Sam followed Mary over the hill and down the other side. It was the hardest walk of his life. In the darkness, he had trouble picking his way between the trees and rocks. Twice he tripped. Each time he treasured the few seconds on the ground before Mary pulled him back to his feet. After the second fall, she stayed behind him, guiding him to the bottom of the hill with short, stern commands until they came to a large tree. Behind it was a motorcycle.

"We're nearly home, Sam," Mary said as she removed the branches covering the bike. "I know you're exhausted. You just need to hold it together for a little longer. Take off that wet suit and we'll get out of here."

Sam dumped the suit behind the tree and then Mary started the bike. The noise of the engine sounded like the world had exploded around Sam, but even that couldn't break him out of the trancelike state he had slipped into. In the glow of the headlight, Mary mounted the bike and motioned to Sam to get on. She steered them carefully along a small track and up onto a road.

The journey into Orange Walk was a blur for Sam. He held on to Mary as they sped toward town, the wind whipping his face. Mary left the bike in an alley, and then they walked. Or Mary walked and Sam stumbled, held up by her steadying hand. The last thing Sam remembered was Mary fumbling with a key and opening a door. A streetlight lit up the small room, and Sam saw a bed. He took five slow steps forward and crashed onto the musty bedspread. He was asleep before Mary had shut the door.

THE CROCODILE SCREAMED LIKE A BOY AS it charged Sam. The jaws parted, the screams grew louder, and then a face appeared at the back of its mouth. Sam was staring at himself in the crocodile. Suddenly, the face blurred, and the creatures rearranged themselves. Now it was Mary's face staring out at Sam. She wasn't screaming; she was saying his name.

"Sam, wake up."

He opened his eyes to find Mary hovering over him, lit from behind by a dazzling orange glow. As his eyes adjusted, Sam remembered where he was. It was daytime, and the sun was beating hard against the thick orange curtains. The glow around Mary stung Sam's eyes, and he put an arm over his face.

"Sorry for waking you. But you were having a nightmare."

Sam didn't speak. He lay there replaying the crazy events of the last twenty-four hours. Then with a rush he came back to the present. "How did you . . ."

Mary laid a hand on Sam. "I know you have a lot of questions, so just lie there and I'll give you some answers. Then you can tell me how you ended up trapped in a crocodile park."

Sam smiled. "Deal," he said.

"I was always coming to Belize with you." Mary leaned back and rolled her eyes theatrically. "As if I would let you have this adventure all to yourself."

"But what about your father and Bassem?"

"Exactly," Mary said. "It took some planning on my part. The ski trip to Switzerland was fake. I couldn't tell you that because I wasn't sure if I was being monitored or not."

"What do you mean, fake?"

"Well, let's see," Mary said. "I created a series of daily e-mail updates that will come from an e-mail server in Switzerland. I have Photoshopped a heap of images of me skiing, which I will also drip feed to my father and Bassem. And I have arranged for charges to go on my credit card, from Switzerland, which my father will see."

"That's impressive," said Sam. "When you told me you were going to be able to watch me in the parking lot, I imagined you had gotten access to a spy satellite or something. I had no idea you'd be watching me from the hill."

"I know. It was good timing," Mary said. "When I spoke to you yesterday, before you went to Xibalba, I was in Houston, on my last stopover. I was going to tell you then, but I decided to wait and surprise you. I got in late. There were no rooms at your hotel, so I came here. But then I couldn't wait till the morning, so I called. Lucky I did, eh?"

Sam nodded. "It's good to have you here. I'm not sure how I would have escaped if it hadn't been for you." The image of Elio flashed into Sam's mind. He sat up and threw the blanket off.

"What's wrong?"

"Elio, the boy who was locked up with me. I have to help him."

"That's okay, you stay there." Mary got up and retrieved the cordless phone and phone book from the table next to the bed. "I'll look up the number for the police station while you tell me what happened to you."

Sam told Mary about the show at Xibalba, the trip to the scrap yard, being arrested, and being taken to Felix. She sat there shaking her head. "I'm so sorry, Sam," she finally said. "I had no idea what I was sending you into. I feel terrible."

Sam shrugged. "It wouldn't matter so much if I had learned something useful."

"But you have."

"What? We started with a World War Two sub. Now we have hidden gold, 2012 and the end of the world, the Maya, the Olmecs, and a madman who controls crocodiles and thinks I can lead him to more gold." Sam felt his frustration growing. "I don't understand how any of this fits together, and I'm no closer to finding my parents."

"That's not true, Sam," Mary said. "You found a man who met them. We know we are on their trail, and your mother's notes on the Mayan calendar and the end of the world in 2012 is interesting. Perhaps your parents discovered the 2012 prediction was linked to the pyramid network?"

Sam shrugged. "Felix Ramos says the link between the pyramids of Egypt and Lamanai is just a story. He thinks my parents were just after his gold."

"But we know that's not true," Mary said. "If we stay on their trail, we *will* find answers."

Sam wanted to feel encouraged, but it was easy for Mary; she'd just flown in. He had been behind the eight ball since the moment he'd arrived. She was right about one thing: he was tired. He didn't know how long he'd been asleep, but it wasn't enough. As he lay there on the bed, his eyelids felt heavy again.

Mary spoke softly as she laid the blanket back over him. "Get some more rest, Sam. Don't worry about your friend. I'll make an anonymous call to the police station about him."

Mary's words floated through Sam's mind as he drifted into darkness again. Somewhere deep down inside him, something stirred, a distant voice, warning him, but he was too tired to figure it out. He fell asleep again.

WHEN HIS EYES POPPED OPEN, SAM HAD no idea how much time had passed. An hour? Longer? He sat up and Mary, who was still sitting on the end of the bed, spun around.

"What's wrong?" she asked.

"How long was I asleep?"

Mary snorted. "Only about twenty minutes." She turned to reveal the phone stuck to her ear. "I'm calling the police station about your friend."

"Hang up," Sam said, reaching for the phone.

Mary jumped off the bed, still holding the phone to her ear. "Sam, what's wrong?"

"The police. Some of them work for Ramos."

Mary laughed. "It's okay. I won't give my name or any details. The lady has just asked me to wait on the line while she gets someone more senior."

Sam thought back to the woman at reception when he had visited the station, and he went cold. "They're tracing your call. Hang up!"

The smile left Mary's face. She stared at the phone as if it were about to attack her, then pushed the call end button and tossed it onto the bed. She looked at Sam, ashen-faced. "Are you sure?"

Sam leapt out of bed. "Get your stuff. We need to go."

They were out of the room in two minutes. Sam was pleased to see that Mary traveled light, with just a small day pack. She led him down a driveway beside the motel that led to a parking lot and a shabby swimming pool. On the other side of the parking lot was the alley where Mary had left the bike. It was hidden under an old tarpaulin behind a large Dumpster.

"What shall we do?" Mary asked.

Sam looked up and down the alleyway. They had a good view of the motel and were concealed by the Dumpster. And with the motorbike, they had a good escape route if they needed it.

"Let's wait here and see what happens," Sam said.

Mary pointed the bike down the alley for a fast get-away, and they stepped behind it to watch the motel. Neither of them spoke. The midmorning sun had warmed the metal lid of the Dumpster, and Sam felt the heat radiating off it onto his face. He leaned on the fence and shut his eyes. It was a mistake—a wave of tiredness swept over him. He popped his eyes open to see Mary watching him.

"Are you okay?" she asked.

"Just tired," Sam replied. He stepped up beside her and focused on the driveway beside the motel again. He hoped he was wrong. A tired, overworked imagination. Phone tracing—they only did that in the movies, didn't they? He wondered how long they should wait before going back to the room.

"You know, Sam, even if this turns out to be a dead end, we still had to come and have a look for ourselves. It doesn't mean the search for your parents is over."

Sam looked at Mary, but she kept staring straight ahead at the motel.

"Why are you talking like that? Half an hour ago you were Miss Positivity. Now you think this is a dead end too? What happened?"

Mary wrestled with the question for a few seconds before she answered. "Before I left home, I set a snooping program into my father's computer to search for any old e-mails from your parents to him. The search is super slow; I had to make it like that to avoid detection. I checked it while you were asleep and found this."

Mary handed her phone to Sam.

From: Phillip Force p.force@eef.com
Date: Saturday, May 8, 2010
To: Francis Verulam f.verulam@mmail.com

Dear Francis,
I regret to report that Lamanai is not the location we hoped it would be. There are no answers here. The site is a dead end. We plan to conclude our work here and depart within the next twenty-four hours. We will submit a full report on our trip within the next two weeks.

Yours sincerely,
Phillip Force

"Great," Sam said sarcastically. "So Ramos was right. No wonder he thinks I'm here looking for his gold." He was about to say something else but went quiet as a van pulled into the driveway next to the motel. "He's from Xibalba," Sam said as a man in blue overalls got out. "We need to get out of here."

Mary jumped onto the bike and started the engine. Sam stared down the long, empty alley.

"Hurry up," Mary urged.

Sam didn't move. The alley was the obvious getaway route. Too obvious. "We're not going that way," he said.

Mary didn't question Sam. She turned the bike, he climbed on, and they took off across the parking lot and past the van. There was no sign of the man in blue overalls, but when Sam turned to look behind them, he saw Azeem's yellow Mustang convertible swing into the far end of the alley, racing after them.

16

MOVING HOUSE

"WHICH WAY?" MARY SHOUTED OVER HER shoulder.

Sam watched Azeem's car gaining on them, "Just go fast!"

Mary saw the big car in her side mirror but didn't ask for details. The bike sped up, forcing Sam to hold tighter. Mary had her backpack on, so he was pushed to the very back of the passenger seat. With Sam's rear end sticking out across the mudguard, every bump in the road vibrated through him like an awkward butt massage.

"Hold on," Mary yelled as they swung into another street.

A horn blast filled the air, and as Mary increased

the revs, Sam watched the yellow car skid around the corner behind them.

"You need to lose this guy," Sam said.

"Any ideas? You know the town."

He had none. He'd only been in Orange Walk a few hours longer than Mary, and most of that time he had been on the run.

But then he saw something he recognized. "See that big white place ahead?" he asked, pointing to an old building on the left. "Go in there."

"In! You serious?"

"There's a wheelchair ramp. Look." Sam pointed over her shoulder.

"Got it," Mary said.

Sam looked back and stifled a yelp as he saw the yellow car was now less than a bus length behind them and closing fast. Azeem was hunched over the wheel, screaming words Sam couldn't hear.

The bike swerved left as Mary took them onto the ramp and up into the bus depot. Azeem skidded to a stop in a cloud of white brake smoke. Sam saw him thump the steering wheel in anger, then he turned back to watch as Mary navigated her way through the crowd.

It was a human slalom course. Some people jumped out of the way, others froze on the spot and stared at the two kids on the motorbike as they sped past. Sam didn't need to give directions; the exit was easy to spot, a big arch, identical to the one they had entered under. He assumed there was a matching wheelchair ramp, but he didn't know for sure.

Just as he spotted the ramp, Mary called out over the noise of the engine and protesting people. "Which way when we get out?"

Sam had no idea. "Go left," he said. It made sense, he told himself. Their stunt had bought them some time, but not much. Azeem would have driven up the road and around the depot. He would be coming from the right.

Mary gunned the bike down the ramp, swerved left, and powered down the street. Sam's heart sank as he saw the dead end ahead. Mary didn't say a word, but she didn't slow down, either. She turned her head left and right, and Sam realized she was looking for the way out that Sam was leading her to.

"I blew it," Sam said with a growing sense of panic. Mary kept going and Sam looked back down the road past the depot to the intersection. There was no sign of the yellow car. If they were going to turn, they needed to do it fast. Sam leaned in to speak into Mary's ear, but she swung the bike viciously to the right, and he almost slipped off. The building in front of them was four stories high and covered in scaffolding. Instead of slowing, Mary sped up, as if she was going to crash into the building. Sam would have cried out if there had been time. The bike missed the corner of the building, but there was no alleyway, only a narrow builder's walkway that led up to the second floor.

That was Mary's target.

She raced up the narrow wooden walkway and down the side of the building, slowing only a fraction. Sam looked down to the ground below, amazed at how little wood was on each side of the bike. He stayed frozen to the seat, petrified that any movement would knock them off the walkway. Then the wall of the building was gone, and ahead, Sam saw planks angled into the building. Mary steered the bike off the planks and onto the concrete and skidded to a stop.

Sam didn't trust himself to speak as he climbed off.

Mary killed the engine and put the bike on its stand. She turned to Sam, her face as white as milk. "I can't believe I just did that," she said, looking down at her shaking hands. "That was crazy."

Sam laughed weakly. "Are you telling me you haven't done something like that before?"

"No way!" said Mary. "I just saw the ramp and went for it. Did we get rid of him?"

Sam went back to the walkway to watch the narrow

strip of road. It was deserted, but after a couple of minutes, the front of Azeem's yellow Mustang rolled into view. Sam pulled his head back and listened to the rumbling V8 as it continued down the road.

"Is it him?" Mary asked.

Sam didn't answer. Tires squealed as the car spun around and roared back the other way. It didn't stop. Sam listened to it disappearing up the road before he returned to Mary. "I think we're safe."

"For now," Mary said.

She waved her hand around them. Piles of bricks dotted the concrete floor. Wheelbarrows and toolboxes were lined up under the windows facing the street. "We're lucky it's a Sunday. If people had been working here, they would have called the police."

"They still could."

Mary nodded. "You're right. We can't stay here. We need to find somewhere safe."

Somewhere safe. The words triggered something in Sam's mind. He reached behind Mary, took his notebook from her bag. They were Elio's words. He'd said them in Xibalba when he'd given him the map—*a place to go if you need somewhere safe.* Sam checked the boy's hand-drawn map and noticed the scrawl at the bottom. It was an address.

"I think I have somewhere for us to go," Sam said as he

checked his Orange Walk map. "Elio told me about it."

"Good," Mary said. "Let's give it another hour; then we'll go."

Sam sat down next to a pile of cement bags, leaned back, and tried to get comfortable. His phone was digging into his hip, so he took it out of his pocket. On the screen was a message telling him he'd received another e-mail from his uncle.

From: Jasper Force j.force@eef.com

Date: Sunday, Sep 20, 2015

To: Sam Force s.force@gmail.com

My Sam,

I have been contacted by our anonymous friend TF again. He has told me the ancient code of the Templar Knights may be of assistance to you (see below).

This may seem odd to you. I was confused myself until I thought back over our discoveries in Egypt. Remember, we learned from the diary of Mary's grandfather that the Templar Knights discovered the original Ark and learned of a second one, hidden in Amarna by the Pharaoh Akhenaten. That sacred cargo was transported to Belize in 1942 on board submarine 518 and is the reason your parents went there. It makes sense that the Templar Knights knew of the importance of Belize, but exactly how they are linked to this mystery I have yet to determine. Look out for their logo; it may lead you to new clues.

TF also asked me again to remind you not to involve Mary in any of this. My boy, I do hope you are staying out of harm's way.

Please contact me and let me know you are okay.
xxx Jasper

Sam stared at the screen. He recognized the cross his uncle had drawn. He had seen it on the hilt of the dagger in Felix Ramos's office and on the necklace the man had worn during his performance at Xibalba. Did the mysterious TF know something his parents hadn't? Sam wasn't so sure it mattered now. His parents had declared Belize a dead end and left. Their trail had gone cold. The bearded man had been right: there was nothing here for Sam.

"What are you looking at?" Mary asked.

"It's an e-mail from my uncle."

"He doesn't suspect anything, does he?" Mary asked. "He could make trouble with my father."

"No," Sam said, quickly closing the e-mail. "He still thinks I'm in Boston."

"Well, that's one good piece of news, isn't it?" Mary got up and dusted off her jeans. "This place Elio told you about . . . Is it far?"

"No," Sam said. "Just out of town."

Mary walked to the window that looked down on the street. "Looks quiet down there," she said. "Why don't we get going?"

"Sure," Sam said, glad Mary had made the call. He knew he wouldn't be able to rest until they were somewhere safer.

GETTING OUT OF THE BUILDING WAS ALMOST as dangerous as the ride in. Mary didn't trust herself to ride the bike, so she pushed it. Sam followed, his heart in his mouth as he watched her steer the bike along the narrow walkway.

When she finally got to street level, Mary sent Sam ahead to make sure there were no surprises waiting for them. The way was clear. Sam took another look at the map and picked out a route that would take then through the back alleys.

The ride only took a few minutes, but it felt like every eye in Orange Walk was on them. Mary stayed just below the speed limit, while Sam kept checking behind for any sign of danger. He called out directions from memory and was relieved to see that they were heading away from the center of town. The final street they turned into ran down to the river and ended at a concrete boat ramp. Along the riverbank, a row of aging boat sheds stuck out over the river.

Sam left Mary with the bike and followed a narrow path to number 8, the last shed. Sam smiled as he pulled out his pocketknife and opened the lock-picking attachment. Elio had known he'd make short work of the old padlock.

A steep hill covered in bushes rose behind the sheds. Mary wheeled the bike down the path and hid it among the trees opposite their new hideout. Sam took one last look outside to make sure no one had seen them, then he followed her inside.

Someone had once lived there. A rusty old bed leaned up against one wall, with a bench and sink opposite. In the middle, two chairs flanked a wooden table. The most noticeable feature of the room was the fact that the front half of the floor was missing. From the edge, Sam and Mary looked down into the water. Two large doors that could open out onto the river were bolted shut, and from the spiderwebs covering them, it was obvious the place hadn't been used for a long time.

Sam eyed the old bed longingly. The saggy brown mattress looked like a giant piece of toast, and he wasn't sure if the rusted fame would support a body, but he was willing to find out.

"Nice place, Force," Mary said with a smile.

He chuckled. "Yeah, sorry. It got five stars on the website."

Mary laughed then went serious. "What are we going to do about your friend?"

"I thought we could call the police in Belize City . . . once we get to the airport."

Mary stared at him but didn't say anything, so Sam continued. "This is a dead end. You said it yourself. The e-mail to your father proves it. And with Azeem and his boss hunting us . . . I just think it's too risky."

Mary shook her head. "There could still be important clues here. Sub 518 carried the Ark here. Where is it? If your parents left, where did they go? We can't just give up because some guy in a car chased us."

"I'm not talking about giving up!" Sam snapped. "And it wasn't just being chased by a car. I've had people after me since I got here. Since *before* I got here!"

"What do you mean?" Mary asked.

"Remember the man with the beard in Egypt?"

Mary nodded. "The one who works for the people who took your parents?"

"Yes. He found me in Boston. He told me not to come here. He said it was a dead end."

"How did he know you were coming to Belize?"

"I guess he figured I would want to come here and search for my parents. He tried to help me in Egypt. Warn me away. He said the same about Belize. Don't you see? That proves there's nothing here."

"But we can't just give up!"

"I'm not giving up!" Sam's voice thundered across the small room, and Mary winced at his outburst. He immediately felt bad. "I'm sorry . . . I know we need new clues. I just don't know where to look. We thought Lamanai was linked to the pyramid network. That e-mail my parents sent to your dad proves it isn't. There's just a crazy guy protecting some gold that he found. That's why my parents left!"

"You should have told me about the bearded man," Mary said. "We should have put off this trip."

"That's why I didn't say anything," Sam said. "I wanted to come. I just didn't think it would be . . . so hard."

Mary's face softened, and she placed a hand on Sam's arm. "You must be exhausted. You've had less than an hour of sleep since you got here. Get some rest, and then we'll make a plan." She steered him toward the bed.

Sam nodded and sat down. The bedsprings screamed in protest as he lay back. On the wall next to the bed was a narrow wooden shelf. At one end, an old bottle had the dried remains of a flower poking out of it. Someone had made a halfhearted attempt to pretty up the place. Next to the bottle, a faded piece of paper had been pinned to the wood. It was so dusty and sun-damaged, it was almost the same color as the wall, and he hadn't noticed it until he lay down.

Sam lifted his hand and touched the paper. It was dry, and the pin holding it fell out. The piece of paper fell onto the mattress next to Sam. He picked it up and studied the blacks lines on it. A drawing, someone's artwork. He ran his fingers over the paper, feeling raised lines made by charcoal. There were eyes on the page, but the rest of the drawing had faded away. At the bottom was a word. It started with the letter *B*. Sam was tired, but curiosity spurred him on. He held the drawing closer to his face. *B-A* . . .

Sam sat up, and the springs shrieked again.

At the table, Mary turned with a start. "What's wrong?"

"'Bast.' The word on this drawing. It is 'Bast.'"

"The Egyptian cat god?"

"Yes!" Sam got up and crossed to Mary. "Look at this." He slapped the drawing down in front of her.

"Someone drew an image of Bast," Mary said.

"Not 'someone,'" Sam replied. "My mother."

17

SOMETHING FISHY

THE TIREDNESS HAD FADED AWAY AS IF he'd just drunk a magic potion, or the world's most powerful energy drink. Sam paced the floor of the boat shed between the bed and table.

Mary studied the drawing. "Are you sure your mother drew this?"

"Positive," Sam replied. "She drew all the time. Every moment she sat down, she'd have her old charcoal pencil and pad out. That's where I got it from."

"So what does it mean?"

"I don't know." Sam stopped pacing and began to turn slowly, seeing the old shack with new eyes. "Help me look around."

"No problem." Mary threw up her hands. "It's not like we have much ground to cover."

Sam didn't reply; he had returned to the bed. He ran his fingers along the shelf, leaving a small, wood-colored trail in the dust. A flashback to room inspections at St. Albans made him laugh.

"Glad to see you're in a better mood," Mary said.

Sam got down on the floor and crawled under the bed.

"That's your uncle's favorite hiding place, isn't it?" Mary said.

"Yeah. Not my parents' style, but worth a look."

"I've been meaning to ask you about that hole in your pants," Mary said. "I can see your undies. It's not very classy."

Sam's movement under the bed had created a mini–dust storm. He laughed, then sneezed. He had completely forgotten about his missing patch.

"Stop looking at my butt and look for clues," he said as he rolled onto his back for a better look under the mattress.

As he expected, there was nothing.

As he shuffled out, he noticed something on the floorboards. A drawing that had been covered by a layer of dust until his body had disturbed it.

Sam recognized it. His mother had drawn the same one on the note he had found in his father's trench coat.

"Mary, come and look at this," he called out as he slid out from under the bed. "This is a Templar logo, isn't it?"

Mary peered over his shoulder. The logo had been drawn a few inches under the bed. Just out of view unless you were looking for it.

"It's almost a Templar cross," Mary said. "But one of the ends has been made into a point."

There was something else about it, Sam realized: the cross had been drawn on an angle. Standing next to the bed it looked more like an X than a cross. *X marks the spot.* Sam pressed the floorboard with his foot. It didn't budge. He looked down at the logo. The part that had been drawn wrong was on the outside. By itself it would have looked like an arrow—an arrow pointing where?

Sam turned his head, following the direction it was pointing. He walked slowly across the floor. He had almost reached the corner when the floorboard under his foot creaked.

"Out of the way," Mary said. She elbowed past and dropped to her knees. The floorboard Sam had stepped on had been cut into a short length no longer than an arm. Mary pushed on one end and the other popped up. She hooked her fingernails into the edge and lifted the board out. Underneath was one of the thick wooden beams the hut had been built on, but this section had been hollowed out. Inside the small wooden cavity were some papers.

Mary looked up at Sam. "Well done, Mr. Force."

Temple of the Mask houses a stucco mask of an Olmec god, which some believe to be of Kinich Ahau, the Sun God.

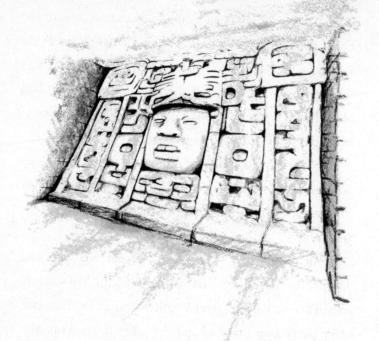

The Mayan prediction about 2012 is real, and I believe the US government knows about it!

The seeing-eye pyramid in the dollar bill has thirteen steps! The Maya and the Olmec before them believed the end of the thirteenth baktun cycle—December 21, 2012—will bring violent movement of the earth.

May 10, 2012

Dear Anne,

My trip to Lamanai paid off!

I have located the chamber!

X marks the spot.

I have found a Templar dagger. Before
the men from sub 518 found the chamber,
there were other visitors. This is proof that
this mission to save the world goes back
hundreds—no, thousands of years.

The dagger has the clues we need to lead us
to the next part of this puzzle. I will bring
it to the jetty at Lamanai so we can study
it. I have sent Elio back with this note to
fetch you. But before you come you need to

go back to our hotel. We were right to leave our possessions there, so anyone watching wouldn't suspect we were aware of them, but we need to get the copy of the map that we left in the room.

Do you remember where I hid it?

Imagine someone going through our possessions and discovering that our little family is hiding the key to the chamber at Lamanai.

Retrieve the map and Elio will bring you to me.

Before I leave the chamber, I think I should make time to conceal my other discoveries.

Remember, X always marks the spot.

Phillip

The only noise in the shed was the shuffling of paper as Sam and Mary read and reread the documents they had found.

Mary finally broke the silence.

"Do you know what this is, Sam? Proof your parents *did* find something. And it was big. It looks like they really were onto a link between the pyramids and the end of the world in 2012. Their discovery must have happened after they told my father Belize was a dead end. He always thought they had failed. But they didn't."

Sam heard Mary but didn't register what she was saying. "Elio sent us to this place, and now it turns out he knew my parents," he muttered. "Why didn't he say something to me?"

"That's just one of many questions we need answers to," Mary said. "I guess we're not leaving the country."

"I guess not," said Sam.

"We need to visit Lamanai. Your father followed the Ark there," Mary said. Taking the letter from Sam's hand, she scanned the page again. "Your father talks about someone discovering that 'our little family is hiding the key to the chamber at Lamanai.' Any idea what that means?"

"No," Sam answered, still thinking about Elio and their time in the cage room. "Hang on, what did my father say?" He grabbed the letter back. "'Our little family is hiding the key to the chamber at Lamanai.'"

"Does that mean something?" Mary asked.

"Maybe. You were right about my parents staying in my hotel. They left some stuff behind."

"What?"

"I found my dad's favorite coat, which had some research notes in it. That was in the hotel lost property.

But the police had a drawing in a frame that belonged to my mum."

"A drawing of what?"

"A drawing I did of my family. A little one."

Mary smiled. "'Our little family is hiding the key to the chamber at Lamanai.' Your father wanted your mother to go back for that drawing."

Sam nodded. "But for some reason, she didn't. And lucky for us. The map to the chamber at Lamanai is behind that drawing."

"So where is it?"

"I took it from the police, but I threw it out the window when Azeem caught me," Sam said. "I was worried they might use it to link me to my parents. I didn't know they already had."

"Doesn't matter. It was the right thing to do," Mary said. "Can you remember where?"

"Yes. We had just turned off the big bridge heading out of town. I threw the picture into a bush by the river."

Mary jumped up. "That's great. Let's go get it!"

"Hang on," said Sam. "We need to be careful. Felix Ramos still has Azeem and his goons looking for us."

Mary sat down again. "You're right," she said, then punched him in the arm.

"Hey. What was that for?"

Mary smiled. "I'm supposed to be the one who thinks things through."

Sam rubbed his arm, even though they both knew the punch hadn't hurt. "Yeah, well, maybe I've picked a few things up from you."

"That'll be it," Mary agreed. "It will be safer to wait till nightfall. And that will give you time to get some sleep."

"I'm not tired now," Sam protested, suddenly regretting his talk of caution. "I don't want to sit around all day. Maybe we can disguise ourselves?"

Mary looked at him with raised eyebrows.

"Disguises? Really? You do need some sleep. Just an hour or two."

Grudgingly, Sam got up and shuffled back to the bed. He lay back down on the mattress and looked at the spot on the shelf where his mother's drawing had been. It had been only ten minutes since he was last there, but everything had changed. Not only did he have a new lead on his parents, but Elio was suddenly in the mix. At that moment, Sam would have given anything for the chance to talk to the boy. There were still many pieces of the puzzle to find, but he finally felt they had made some real progress.

Sam decided to tell Mary that it was pointless trying to sleep. But instead of opening his mouth, he shut his eyes. Sleep came instantly.

18

ON THE LINE

Sam,

You've been asleep for two hours. I've taken the bike and gone into town to get us a change of clothes.

Don't get mad. I'll be safer alone. Azeem and his men don't know me.

It's 1 p.m. I should be back within an hour.

Sleep tight.

Mary

The first thing Sam did was check the clock on his phone. It was two thirty. He lay back on the bed and told himself not to worry. Mary knew how to look after herself.

It was no good. There was no way he could get back to sleep knowing she was out there. Sam returned to the table and laid out all the clues he had collected.

He knew that the dagger his father had written of finding in the chamber in Lamanai was the one Felix had shown him. As Sam looked at his mother's notes that he had found in the trench coat, he noticed the scribbles at the bottom of the page. He had dismissed them as doodles, but now he realized his parents had made the link between the Templars and Lamanai.

▽∨<▷◁ ⑂▽ ◁▽▷ ◁▷◁

On his phone, Sam brought up his uncle's e-mail with the Templar code from TF.

It took him less than a minute to decipher the message: *Sobek is the key.* Sobek the crocodile god. Sam thought back to his discovery in the sub. The crocodile design that had been destroyed. That had to be the key his mother was talking about.

Sam heard the motorbike and stepped outside to see Mary riding up the path to the sheds. At least, he assumed it was Mary. The rider had the same build as his friend, but this girl had long blond hair and wide red sunglasses. She skidded to a stop and laughed at the look on Sam's face.

"What? I've always wanted to go blond."

"I thought disguises were a stupid idea?"

"Changed my mind when I passed an amazing wig shop," Mary said.

"Well, I'm not wearing a wig,"

Mary laughed. "I knew you'd say that. So I got two for me."

"Two?"

"Yeah," Mary said. "I've also always wanted to try being a redhead."

Sam scowled. "This isn't a costume party we're getting ready for."

Mary got off the bike. "Come inside, grumpy. I've gotten you some clothes and the picture."

"You got it? How?" Sam said, his frustration instantly forgotten.

"You gave me a pretty good description, but I checked the GPS tracking on your phone to make sure I had the right bridge."

"You can track my phone?"

"Of course." Mary smiled slyly. "It cost a lot of money. I was worried you might lose it."

"I thought it would be a map," Mary said a few minutes later.

"It is," Sam said confidently. He had been expecting the crocodile but hoped the map hidden in it would be more obvious.

"Do you understand it?" Mary asked.

"Sure," Sam replied. "What I mean is, with a bit of time I'm sure I can work it out."

"Well, you can look at it on the way," she announced.

"On the way to what?"

"Lamanai, of course. But we need to get going."

Sam frowned. "What's the hurry?"

"Now, don't get grumpy again. I've booked us on a tour to Lamanai. By boat. So unless you want to spend an hour on the bike, we need to get a move along. And they serve food."

"Food?" Sam's stomach suddenly joined in the conversation.

"It's a dinner cruise." Mary smiled. "I thought you'd like that. And not having to ride on the back of my bike."

Sam agreed. They were both welcome bits of news, but his attention was drawn back to the crocodile drawing. Something about the design seemed familiar.

He needed time to think.

"You can study the map on the boat." Mary said. "It

takes an hour to get to Lamanai, but we need to be at the wharf in thirty minutes."

Sam took another look at the drawing, trying to soak in every detail. Then he slipped it into his notebook.

"Now," said Mary, opening her backpack, "I got you a change of clothes. Some pants."

She held up a pair of faded black jeans.

"There's a big hole in them," Sam said.

Mary looked at her friend in mock horror. "So?"

"So I already have a pair of pants with a hole and you hassled me about it."

Mary shook her head slowly. "Force, that hole is in the butt. It's embarrassing." She thrust the black jeans at Sam. "These have a hole in the knee. That's fashion."

"No way," Sam said, slapping his hands on his thighs. "These are my lucky pants, and the pocket is big enough for my notebook."

Mary muttered something under her breath as she returned to her bag. "Fine, keep them. But you have to wear the rest of the disguise. I got you a black baseball cap like mine and this." She held up a black T-shirt. "Ta daaa. I haven't heard of the band, but they look kind of freaky."

Sam stared at the T-shirt. "You didn't buy this, did you?"

"No," she admitted. "I would have bought you one, but I couldn't find a menswear store anywhere. Then I remembered the clothesline behind my motel; it had boys' clothes on it. So I . . ." She screwed up her face. "I went there and borrowed something for you."

Sam took the T-shirt and held it up. It was a size too big, but it wouldn't look too stupid. If you didn't count wearing a T-shirt with a tiger breathing fire on it as stupid.

"Have you heard of Slayers of Mayhem?" Mary asked.

Sam nodded. "Actually, I have."

19

SITE SEEING

THE FLAT-BOTTOMED SPEEDBOAT ROARED
along the river so fast that it felt like they were skidding
across glass. There were twenty-five people on the
boat. Sam had made sure he and Mary got seats in the
front, and glancing back it looked like he was riding
with a boatload of freaks. The wind in their faces gave
them a smooth, shiny look and identical hairstyles—
slicked back against the scalp. No one seemed to mind.
Everyone was pointing their phones and cameras at the
riverbank and snapping away.

Sam didn't see what the fuss was about. Dense green
vegetation grew down to the water's edge on each side,
and at the speed they were going, all anyone was getting were pictures of a blurry green wall.

A high-speed trip in an oversized dinghy wasn't what Sam had imagined when Mary said she had booked them on a dinner cruise. "Cruise" was the more misleading word, followed closely by "dinner." He poked at the stale sandwich in the cardboard box on his lap and wished he'd made Mary stop for supplies on the ride to the wharf. Her argument against that had been that the less time they spent on the streets, the better. Sam had grudgingly agreed, but now his stomach was letting him know that had been a mistake.

"I'll have that if you don't want it," Mary said, struggling to be heard over the roaring wind.

Sam wrapped an arm protectively around his meager meal. "You've got your own."

Mary held up her empty box as she eyed Sam's.

He thrust the sandwich into his mouth, and she made a show of being shocked.

"I was hoping you'd be too busy decoding that map to eat," she said.

Sam pulled the map from his pocket and began to study it.

It was the most un-map-like thing Sam had ever seen. If he hadn't read the letter from his father, he knew he wouldn't have worked out that it was a map. Maybe that was the point. He thought back over what he knew about Lamanai. A collection of pyramids and other structures by the river. He stared at the crocodile map. The squares weren't neatly added in. They had been squeezed into the design. Or had the design been drawn around them? He flicked back through the pages of his notebook to the map of Lamanai, and it hit him.

The buildings were a perfect match to the squares on the crocodile. The map was beginning to reveal itself.

Sam reread the information on Lamanai. The High Temple, the Temple of the Jaguar, the Temple of the Mask. Kinich Ahau was the Sun God, and thanks to his mum's notes, Sam knew which temple the chamber had to be inside. He also knew, thanks to Elio, that the entrance was on the riverbank. But well hidden.

To anyone without the key.

Sam blocked out the noise of the wind and the slapping of boat's hull on the rock-hard surface of the river. Since his arrival in Belize, he'd been collecting clues and information from different worlds and times. His parents had been trying to understand the common thread that linked the Maya, Olmecs, Egyptians, and Templars. Sam's only hope was that solving the mystery would lead him to them.

He thought back to the mysterious TF and the Templar code again. Sam looked at the map with new eyes. When he had found the note in the trench coat, he thought the designs weren't important, but they actually had held a message. Could this be the same? He scanned the drawing from top to bottom, seeing only random swirls and details. And then he spotted it.

A small detail that almost looked like a mistake. One of the teeth hadn't been colored in. But it was done on purpose. It formed a letter from the Templar alphabet and was one of the first phrases his uncle had mentioned. The same one he had used to find the hiding place in the fishing shed—X *marks the spot.*

The Templar code for the letter X had been hidden in the map. It was near the Temple of the Mask, and, using the buildings as reference, Sam saw the entrance was on the riverbank.

"Ladies and gentlemen, we will soon be arriving in Lamanai." The young boy standing next to the driver grinned at his group as they turned their attention to him. Sam couldn't remember his name, but the boy couldn't have been much older than him and Mary.

The secret map had distracted Sam for some time. Looking around, he saw that the river had widened considerably. The passengers scanned the right-hand riverbank, searching for their first glimpse of Lamanai.

"Is that it?" Sam scoffed. His comment immediately earned him a punch on the arm from Mary.

"Don't be rude."

Sam shrugged. No one else had heard him, and every camera and phone was aimed at the distant rocky tip poking above the forest.

"You know this is one of the largest archaeological sites in Central America, don't you?" Mary said.

"I do, actually. And less than five percent has been uncovered."

"Very impressive, Mr. Force. You do read your research," she said sarcastically.

"But you have to admit," Sam continued, "it's not nearly as impressive as the Great Pyramid at Giza."

Mary shrugged. "I'm not so sure. Imagine if the Giza pyramids were surrounded by forest."

Before Sam had a chance to consider Mary's comment, their young tour guide spoke again. "Please collect your belongings, we will be docking in a few moments."

Up ahead the forest had been cut back to reveal a semicircle of neatly cut grass. A narrow wooden jetty jutted out into the river, and the boat raced in toward it at speed. Sam held his breath as the gap between them and the jetty closed at an alarming rate. At the last second, the driver, an old man wearing large mirrored sunglasses, threw the engine into reverse and brought the boat to a dead stop with inches to spare.

Delighted at the petrified looks on the faces of his passengers, the old man laughed to himself as the tour guide leapt out and secured the boat. The tourists clambered onto the creaking wooden structure, and the boy led them off the jetty, to a hut at the edge of the forest.

An old wooden sign said LAMANAI in faded red letters, and under it was a map of the site. This map differed from the one in Sam's notebook—it had paths marked on it. He quickly sketched them onto his map, making careful note of the one that led to the Temple of the Mask.

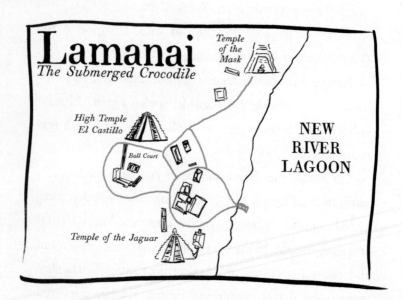

"Gather round, ladies and gentlemen," the smiling guide said. "Welcome to Lamanai. One of the oldest and largest Mayan sites in Belize."

Sam couldn't see much evidence of anything Mayan. Thick, lush forest grew almost to the edge of the river and trees obscured the tip of the pyramid they had seen from the river.

"Soon we will go to the High Temple," the guide announced. "You are welcome to climb it to watch the sun set."

Sam leaned in close to Mary's ear. "We should make a break for it now and try and find the entrance to the chamber."

"And then," the guide continued, "we will have dinner. After that, you are free to explore Lamanai."

"Dinner!" Sam exclaimed.

"It's a dinner cruise, remember?" Mary said.

"I thought that sandwich in the box was dinner."

Mary rolled her eyes. "Didn't you listen to anything Raul said on the boat?"

"Who's Raul?"

"The tour guide! Honestly, Sam Force, how do you survive without me?"

The group shuffled off, following the smiling, talkative Raul down a path that weaved between lush green ferns under a canopy formed by taller trees. The rays of the setting sun filtered down as thin yellows rays that sparkled and danced off the leaves. It was picturesque, but all forest and no ruins, Sam thought. Then he noticed the small piles of rocks that some of the group were photographing and realized they were in the middle of the ruins. The forest had claimed much of Lamanai for itself.

"This must be the ninety-five percent they haven't excavated," Sam said to Mary.

Mary's reply was interrupted by a deep-throated rumble in the trees above their heads.

"What's that?" Sam asked, staring up as leaves fell to the ground like green snow.

Mary pointed to a wide branch above them. "Look, there. A howler monkey."

A furry black monkey ran along the branch then stopped to look down at the group of trespassers under its home. Sam was about to say there was no way a little thing like that could have made such a fierce noise when it opened its mouth and let out a long, tortured growl.

"It sounds like a wild pig," Sam said.

The group snapped off another few hundred photos of the monkey, and then Raul led them off down the path.

The thick bush began to thin, and through the trees

Sam glimpsed the first large stone building. It was hard to make out the shape clearly as the forest had done a good job of camouflaging it with vines and dead leaves, but it got the attention of the other tourists.

People slowed to take photos, but Raul waved them on. "There will be time to see all this later," he said. "First we go to the High Temple."

Some of the group grumbled and moaned, but they followed the boy, and soon, more and more stone structures, in various states of disrepair, were visible among the trees. Sam wasn't impressed. He'd been expecting the kind of old temples he saw in Egypt. Lamanai had been a disappointment. But then trees parted to reveal a wide, grassy field, and Sam had a change of heart.

On the other side of the clearing, a huge stone staircase rose out of the ground and up above the trees. Murmurs of delight rippled through the group, and cameras clicked.

"Nice pyramid," Sam said.

"Its shape makes it a pyramid, but the Maya refer to them as temples, remember?" Mary said. "And they don't have anything inside, like the Egyptian ones. They performed ceremonies and made sacrifices to their gods on top. That's why it's flat up there."

"Nothing inside? What about underneath? We are looking for a chamber."

Mary shrugged. "There are no records of chambers under Mayan pyramids. But this site could predate the Maya."

Sam nodded as he thought back to his mother's notes about the Olmec. "I guess the steps make sense if the priests had to get up and down."

"And now tourists can too," Mary said.

Their tour guide motioned for the group to follow him across the clearing. "Follow me please. We must hurry to be at the top before sunset."

Sam noticed a few of the older and larger members of the group looked less than enthusiastic, and he could see why. The closer they got to the High Temple, the tougher the climb looked. The first set of stone steps were wide and angled like a steep set of stairs to a church. But they ended at a terrace, and the next steps leading off that went up at an alarmingly steep angle. Halfway up, at another terrace, a rope had been attached that ran to the top.

"Come on," Mary called out as she hurried to catch up with Raul. "The view will be amazing."

Sam didn't doubt it; he just wasn't so sure about the climb. He didn't bother trying to come up with an excuse—he knew Mary wouldn't buy it—so he hurried after her.

Less than half the group made the trip up the High Temple, and Sam outpaced most of them. It felt good to get his muscles working, and he was glad he hadn't embarrassed himself in front of Mary by making excuses to get out of it.

Mary began to tire soon after they reached the rope and Sam slowed to keep her company.

"Don't worry about me," she said cheerfully.

Sam waited anyway, taking a moment to admire the view. It was postcard perfect. A blanket of thick green forest ran to the wide blue band of the New River. The only thing spoiling the smooth green surface of the forest were the small stone tips of the other pyramids, poking up among the trees.

Using the river as a reference point Sam worked out where the Temple of the Mask was. It looked a lot farther than it did on his small map, and the golden glow in the sky reminded him that he would be making the trip in the dark.

"Hurry up, Force."

Sam turned to see Mary had passed him and was just stepping up onto the top of the pyramid. He leapt up the last few steps and joined her and the small, tired group on a flat area the size of a helicopter landing pad. There were no barriers, and Sam's first thought was that he was glad the rest of the group had stayed down below. If it had been more crowded, he had visions of camera-wielding tourists tumbling to their deaths.

At first he was happy to stay safely tucked in the middle of the group. But as the sun dropped, the spectacular golden glow drew him out for a better view, and he found himself switching his phone to camera mode.

"Now you look like a tourist," Mary said. She was sitting on the edge of the platform, looking out toward the New River. Sam took some shots and sat down beside her.

"I'm only taking a photo so I can sketch it later," he said.

Sam and Mary stared out over the forest. Behind them, tourists chatted and the high-pitched cries of howler monkeys drifted up from the forest to remind them that below their feet were thousands of living creatures who called this place home.

"If it were sand out there," Sam said, waving his arm in a slow arc, "this would be like the view from the top of the Great Pyramid at Giza."

"Have you been up there?" Mary asked.

Sam shook his head. "My mum and dad did, when I was a baby. My uncle told me about it. They bribed a guard to let them go up at night. They took some photos. That's what made me think of it."

"That's cool," Mary said. "Breaking the law like that. Your parents sound like cool people. I can't wait to meet them."

Sam was looking out toward the river. As Mary's words sank in, he turned to her. She was watching him. "I mean it, Sam. Even if it seems like I'm enjoying myself and having an adventure, I haven't forgotten why we are here. I believe we'll find your parents."

Sam turned his attention back to the view. "Thanks, Mary."

Before the sun had hit the horizon, Raul had the group moving back down the steps. He led the way with smiles and encouraging conversation about the fine BBQ feast awaiting them. Sam had begun preparing himself for his mission to find the entrance to the chamber under the Temple of the Mask, but he couldn't put the thought of a BBQ feast out of his head. *Smarter to explore on a full stomach*, he told himself. He was confident he could find the entrance now that he had located it on the map, and there would be plenty of time after dinner.

By the time they made it to the bottom of the High Temple, the sun had set and darkness had descended on Lamanai. What Sam hadn't noticed in the daylight were the light bulbs strung through the trees around the edge of the open area. Even without light, they would have known which way to go. The smell of cooking meat greeted the hungry climbers as they reached the ground.

The group followed Raul across the field to another

path. Lights in the trees showed the way, and Raul picked up the pace. He was as hungry as the rest of them. The group rounded a bend behind a thick stand of palms and entered another, smaller clearing. A large thatched roof on steel poles covered most of the ground, and under it were two long trestle tables. The rest of the tour group was already seated in front of plates of cooked meat and salad.

"Help yourselves," Raul said, waving to another table laden with food. Two men carried trays full of steaks and sausages to the table and placed them next to bowls of salad and plates of sliced bread.

Sam ran to the table and grabbed a paper plate. It was his first chance to eat properly since he had arrived in Belize, and he was ready to make the most of it.

"Wow," Mary exclaimed as Sam sat down next to her. "Is that a scale model of the High Temple?"

Sam grinned as he positioned his food mountain in front of him. "How to pack your plate is a skill you learn at boarding school," he said as he cut into a thick steak.

"Are you going to have time to look for the entrance to the chamber?" Mary asked in a quieter voice.

"Eating fast is another skill you pick up at boarding school," Sam said before he crammed a piece of the juicy meat into his mouth.

Mary watched Sam chewing happily, making no effort to stop the juice dribbling down his chin.

"They obviously don't cover table manners at St. Albans."

Sam was chewing and thinking up a suitably smart reply when Raul called for the group's attention. At the far end of the table, he picked up one of the bottles of juice that had been set in front of each guest.

"Watch this, ladies and gentlemen," he called out as he tossed a piece of bread onto a patch of grass behind Sam and Mary's table. The group watched, but nothing happened.

"Hey, Raul, the monkeys don't like your bread," one of the older tourists called out. He and his friends burst into laughter. The tour guide grinned as he moved toward the bread. Sam thought he was going to pick it up, but he stopped short, pointed the bottle of juice, and squeezed a thin stream of orange liquid.

Raul's audience looked from the soggy bread to the smiling tour guide; a woman began to speak, but her voice was drowned out by the sound of rustling leaves. All heads turned back to the patch of grass next to the table.

The noise grew, and then the piece of bread began to flicker in front of Sam's eyes. It was as if he were looking at a picture on a bad TV screen, and he couldn't work it out.

But Mary had.

"Bats," she said.

Sam stared at the bread, trying to understand what he was seeing and what Mary was saying, and then it made sense. In the dim light of the dining hut, the hundreds of black bats swirling in the air were almost invisible. Their tiny bodies only showed up as they darted in front of the bread.

"Bats!"

The word went through the group, and the excited banter grew as they understood they were witnessing a feeding frenzy. Almost as quickly, cameras came out and the moment was captured on multiple devices.

Someone threw another piece of bread and squirted their orange juice. More bread appeared, and as the amount of food grew, so did the number of bats.

"This is incredible," Mary exclaimed. "I can feel the wind from their wings."

Sam gave in and pulled out his phone to capture the moment.

The feeding frenzy went on for ten minutes, then Raul's helpers removed the bread and juice, but not before Sam grabbed a bottle and slipped it into his backpack.

Raul announced that the group had an hour to explore the Lamanai complex and handed out flashlights and maps. "Please stick to the paths. You will be quite safe. There are security people here, and other groups."

The tourists broke into small parties and began to move off. A few decided they had seen enough and were making themselves comfortable at the table. Sam knew it was time to go and he couldn't put off his talk with Mary any longer.

"Look," he said as he steered her away from the other tourists, "I think I should go by myself."

Mary opened her mouth to speak, but Sam was ready. "Hear me out. I'm pretty sure I know where to go, and I'll be faster on my own. If I find the entrance to the chamber, we can come back tomorrow and explore it properly, but I need you to stay here so you can call me if I run out of time."

Sam waited for Mary's response. In the low light, he couldn't make out her face, so he had no idea how his argument had gone down.

Finally, she said, "Good idea."

"It is? I mean, I'm glad you see it that way."

"Totally," Mary replied. "You better get going. You only have an hour."

"Plenty of time," Sam said.

He was wrong.

20
MAYHEM

FLASHLIGHT IN HAND, SAM SET OFF ON the path that led toward the Temple of the Mask. The noise of the other tourists faded, and the sounds of the forest folded in around him. From above came the now-familiar growls of howler monkeys. He moved at a fast walk, keeping the beam of the flashlight aimed down at the well-worn trail.

The track weaved between the trees and eventually came to the fork that led back to the jetty. Sam had expected to reach it sooner. He glanced nervously at the clock display on his phone. One hour didn't seem like such a long time now.

He followed the path for another fifteen minutes. He was so nervous about the time, he almost forgot he was wandering through the jungle alone. There was no sign of other tourists. The Temple of the Mask had hardly gotten a mention from Raul, and Sam realized the rest of the group must have gone to explore the closer parts of Lamanai.

The piercing screech of a howler monkey made Sam stop and look up. Leaves and branches thrashed and then fell silent, he hurried on. A few minutes later, he made out a dull glow in the distance. He increased his pace, hoping to bump into someone, but instantly canceled the wish. It would make his task even harder.

He needn't have worried.

Sam stepped out of the forest onto neatly cut grass. The beam of his flashlight wasn't strong enough to light up the temple, but he sensed the stone pyramid rising in front of him. As he approached it, he looked left and right for signs of other people. The area was empty.

Moving to the right-hand corner of the temple, Sam spotted a small track disappearing into the bush toward the river. Before he entered the forest again, Sam shone his flashlight on the large carved stone mask that gave the temple its name. The face had the wide lips of an Olmec, a fact he had learned from his mother's research. Perched on its head was the crocodile. He'd seen a photo of the face and thought it was kind of cartoonish, but now, here in the dark, it took on a very different appearance. It glared at him, the large, cold eyes warning him off.

He tried to laugh the feeling away, but the sound that came out of his mouth was weak and forced. He was glad there was no one around to hear it.

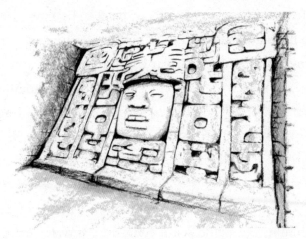

Sam shivered and immediately put it down to the drop in temperature. He swung around and found the path again. Palm fronds had blocked the way; it didn't look like it had been used for a while. Sam ducked down and slipped back into the forest.

The going was tougher now, the ground was rough, and the path quickly faded away to nothing, leaving Sam to force his way between the tree trunks and ferns. Howler monkeys screeched with indignation overhead, and every time he pushed a palm out of the way he heard the flutter of tiny bat wings.

He kept going straight, knowing he would eventually find the river. When he did, it almost killed him.

Sam pushed a large palm to one side and stepped over a root sticking out of the ground. As he looked up, he thought his flashlight had stopped working. In front of him was a wall of black. His foot came down, but instead of hitting the ground it kept going. Sam plunged forward and in that split second he realized he had found the river. The next thought, a fraction of a second later, was that he was falling. Twisting in midair, Sam reached out and grabbed the root. His fall ended abruptly as he slammed into the riverbank.

Sam's legs flailed below him. He'd let go of the flashlight, but could see it lying in the water below. As his mind cleared, Sam realized that the riverbank was higher here, but not too high. The flashlight was only a few feet down. He twisted toward the bank and lowered himself down the thick root like a rope. When he reached the end of it, he stretched his feet out and felt the ground with the tips of his boots. Letting go, he dropped the last few inches.

Sam retrieved the flashlight and shone it above him. The bank didn't look as high from the ground, and he saw exposed roots he could use to climb back up.

With his exit figured out, Sam turned his attention

to the river. He'd used up a lot of time, but he was close now.

The water ran right to the bottom of the bank, and Sam made his way slowly through the mud. It was quieter at the water's edge, as if someone had turned the volume control down on the entire jungle. All Sam could hear was the lapping of water and the squelching of his boots in the mud.

With the towering black outline of the Temple of the Mask behind him, Sam knew he was getting close to the entrance to the chamber. There was a narrow strip of sand here, and huge round boulders stuck out of the riverbank like giant brown marbles. Sam ran his hands over one of them, amazed it still held some of the warmth of the sun's rays. He could see nothing that looked like a hidden entrance, but that, he supposed, was the point.

The height of the riverbank dropped until it was only a little higher than him. The trees were growing out over the water here, and a thick wall of vines hung down over the rock. Sam looked back the way he had come, running his flashlight over the giant boulders. Then he turned back to the wall of hanging vines. These had to cover the entrance.

The vines flowed over the edge of the riverbank like a river of thick green noodles. They made it impossible to go any farther without wading out into the water. Instead, Sam got down on his knees and crawled in between the vines and the edge of the bank. It was a tight squeeze, made worse by the fact he was still wearing Mary's backpack, but there was just enough room. He needed both hands to hold the vines out of the way, so he put the flashlight away. Then, going by feel, he lifted the vines out and squeezed forward a few feet.

He stopped, turned the light on again, and inspected the riverbank. Nothing, just more rock. He put the flashlight away and repeated the procedure. He did this three more times.

All he saw was a rock wall.

Frustrated and tired, Sam turned and began the uncomfortable process all over again. He hadn't checked his phone, but he knew he'd be lucky to get back to Mary in time. To speed up his escape from the wall of vines, he didn't bother to check his progress with the flashlight—he kept pushing and squeezing along the riverbank by feel.

That decision saved him.

Sam had almost extracted himself from the vines. He could tell, even without light, because he could feel them getting thinner. But as he heard the sound of the engine, he suddenly wished he were back behind the thickest ones.

If it had been a big boat roaring up the river, Sam wouldn't have been as worried, but this was a small engine, and it was slowing down.

Sam dropped to his knees and felt the water soak through his pants, but he didn't care. He peered out through the vines trying to spot the approaching boat, but all he could see was blackness.

The rumble of the engine grew until Sam was sure it was heading right for him. Then, between the vines, he caught a glimpse of movement. Something small and dark slid past just a few feet away.

It was a Jet Ski.

Sam listened to the guttural chugging of the small craft as it passed his hiding spot. He stared at the source of the noise as if he could see it. Suddenly, a thin beam of light shot from the Jet Ski to the riverbank. Sam ducked his head and waited for the light to swing toward him, but it didn't. When he looked up, the light was still aimed directly at the riverbank, at a spot Sam had walked past. It was centered on one of the huge, round boulders. Just as quickly, there was darkness again. The Jet Ski roared to life; water churned and the craft raced off down toward the jetty.

Sam slid out from behind the vines. With his hand on the riverbank to guide him, he moved as fast as he could in the pitch dark. His heart was racing. The visitor had made him even later, but that wasn't what he was thinking about. Whoever had been on the Jet Ski had gone to one specific spot, and Sam knew it had to be the entrance to the chamber.

He stumbled on through the mud, stopping to listen to the fading sounds of the Jet Ski. Finally, he couldn't wait any longer. He pulled out his flashlight and aimed it at the rock wall. The boulder was a few feet away. Sam ran his hands over the smooth stone. Could this really be the entrance to the tomb? Hiding it behind vines made a lot more sense. But maybe not. Perhaps, Sam thought, the best way to hide the entrance was to have it in plain sight. This boulder was one of a dozen exactly like it. If the Jet Ski rider hadn't singled it out, he might have walked right past it. He *had* walked right past it.

Sam stopped and listened for the Jet Ski. The river was silent, but he turned off his flashlight anyway. On the exposed bank, he could easily be spotted from both directions. Standing in front of the boulder, he ran his hands around the edge of it. In the darkness, his sense of touch compensated for his lack of vision. He felt the seam where the boulder stuck out from the wall. It was a perfect fit. On the right-hand side, his fingers detected a circular indentation in the smooth rock face. It was so slight Sam would never have seen it, but now, in the dark, he felt the button-sized imperfection. He pushed and heard a *click*. Sliding his hand down, he felt a small rectangular hole, and inside was a keypad.

Before he had time to celebrate his discovery, Sam's phone vibrated. He didn't bother checking it. He knew it was Mary telling him to hurry. He pushed the hidden button, and the keypad disappeared again, leaving smooth rock under his hand. Now he made one quick sweep of the area with his flashlight to make sure he could find the boulder again; then he raced back along the riverbank.

Sam used his flashlight once more, to find the path back up the wall. He considered following the river all the way to the jetty to meet up with the group, but now that there was a Jet Ski out there, he didn't want to risk it.

Once he had made it to the top of the bank, Sam started using his flashlight properly again. He had no choice; the bush was so dense there was no way he could have found his way back to the Temple of the Mask. Even with light, it was tough going. He breathed a sigh of relief when he finally stumbled out onto the cut grass, but he still had a long way to go.

He sprinted across the paddock and onto the path that that led to the BBQ area. It was wide and easy to follow, and his mind drifted to the next move for

Mary and him. Maybe they didn't need to head back to Orange Walk with the tour. They could sneak off and sleep in Lamanai, and then explore the entrance to the chamber at sunrise, before anyone arrived.

Sam was still thinking this plan through when he felt his phone vibrate in his pocket again. It would be another *hurry up* from Mary. There was no time to stop, but he knew he should reply. He had passed the fork in the track and knew the BBQ area was just ahead.

He pulled out his phone and the screen lit up. Sure enough he saw a four-word text—WHERE ARE YOU? HURRY! That was the old message. The new one was longer and harder to read. Sam got halfway through and skidded to a stop. AZEEM IS HERE! GO TO THE JETTY! NOT THE BBQ!!!!

The first thing Sam did was turn off his flashlight. He stood in the dark, fighting to calm his heavy breathing. As his eyes adjusted to the darkness, he made out the glow of the lights around the BBQ area up ahead. He listened intently for sounds of people but heard only the ever-present howler monkeys. At least, he thought, their noise would have drowned out the sound of his approach.

Sam knew it had to have been Azeem on the Jet Ski. He'd been foolish to think they'd gotten rid of the man so easily.

Still watching the track ahead for signs of life, Sam began to walk backward. He'd head back to the fork in the track and follow the other path to the jetty. The boat would wait, Mary would make sure of that. There was no question of them remaining in Lamanai now.

The sharp snap of a branch made Sam spin and raise his flashlight. He was about to turn it on but stopped himself. Instead, he dropped to his knees and waited. There was another breaking branch, a loud squeal, and something scampered off through the undergrowth.

Sam got back to his feet and checked back toward the BBQ area one last time. As he did, the forest around him turned from night to day, the path and the trees on either side transformed into a vivid yellow. The source was coming from behind him, and instinctively Sam spun around. Even as he did, he knew it was a mistake. The beam of light hit him in the face, blinding him. He threw an arm up to cover his eyes, but the damage was done. Even with his eyes tightly shut, he could see the glowing yellow orb caused by the glow of the powerful flashlight.

"Stop, boy," said a familiar voice.

Sam felt the glow of the light fade away, and when he opened his eyes, he could see it had been pointed into the bush. Through squinting eyes, he made out the shape of a man stepping out from behind a tree.

"Hello, Sam," Azeem sneered. "We meet again."

Sam dropped his head, rubbed his eyes, and began to sob hysterically.

Azeem laughed. "Not so cocky now, are you, my friend? Mr. Ramos is going to be very pleased I found you. You have caused him a lot of problems."

"Please don't," Sam blurted. "Please . . . I'll tell you the location of the other two treasure sites. Just let me go."

"There are no other sites," Azeem said, but he sounded unsure.

"There are," Sam sobbed. "Here, I can show you." He slipped the backpack off his shoulders. His vision was returning now. He could see Azeem was alone and unarmed.

"What are you doing?" the man asked, taking a step onto the track.

"The map, it's in here. I can give it to you," Sam insisted. He added a few more sobs for effect as he dug through the bag. His fingers wrapped around the object he'd been looking for.

"Throw it here," Azeem insisted.

Sam pulled his hand from his backpack, but in the time Azeem took to register that it wasn't a map, Sam had pointed the juice bottle at his face and squeezed. The jet of orange liquid hit Azeem in the eyes, and it was his turn to throw an arm to his face. It was too late; the liquid was all over him. The man roared as he swung the beam of the flashlight back to Sam, but the boy had gone.

"You will pay for that," Azeem screamed as he wiped the juice from his face. "You can't hide from me. I know this place like the back of my hand."

A few feet away, Sam crouched behind the trunk of a palm. Azeem was right. He couldn't hide from him. His plan was to run, but he needed some help. He waited while the Scar-Faced Man paced up and down, calling out to Sam.

The plan had come to him the moment he had been caught. The blubbering and offer to hand over a map to the treasure were just delaying tactics. In Sam's mind, his plan was foolproof. He had witnessed the effect of the juice on the bread; surely it would work on a human.

But it wasn't. Azeem was out on the path unscathed. "I'm going to find you," he roared. "And you will be sorry."

The bush went silent, and Sam watched the high-powered beam of Azeem's flashlight swinging around toward the palm. Suddenly, he heard the fluttering of hundreds of pairs of wings as they swept through the forest. The noise grew until it was more like the roar of a wave. The beam of light suddenly tilted up, and Sam heard a cry as the first of the tiny juice-hungry mouths fell on their new meal.

There was no way of knowing how long Azeem would be held up by this new development, so Sam broke for cover. He leapt out onto the path and sprinted for the fork in the track. As he ran, he listened for signs that Azeem was coming after him, but all he heard were the screams of man under attack by a hundred sets of fangs.

The forest swallowed the cries of anguish as Sam put distance between him and Azeem. He turned on his flashlight and increased his pace. A few minutes later, he spotted the lights of the jetty ahead.

Mary was standing on the edge of the group, watching the path, and she must have spotted Sam's light bouncing through the dark. She lifted her flashlight and aimed it directly into his face, but Sam was ready for it and lowered his head as he ran up to her.

"What happened? You look terrible," she exclaimed.

Looking down at his shirt, Sam agreed. He was covered in mud from his time on the riverbank.

"Did he find you?" Mary asked.

Sam nodded. "It's okay. I gave him the slip, but we need to get out of here."

Mary glanced back up the path, which made Sam

spin and do the same. All they saw was blackness.

Mary grabbed Sam's arm. "The boat is ready to go," she said, leading him toward the jetty. "Everybody's on board. They were about to leave without us."

"Who are all these people?" Sam asked as the group of tourists stared at the mud-covered boy who had just run out of the bush.

"Another group," Mary replied. "Their boat is on . . ." She was cut off by a shout from someone in the crowd.

Sam saw a head of red hair pushing through the crowd and rolled his eyes. "That's just what we need. Come on!" he said to Mary, taking the lead and grabbing her arm.

"What's wrong?" Mary asked as they pushed through the people.

Before Sam could answer, the red-haired boy behind them did. "That guy stole my Slayers of Mayhem T-shirt," he cried out. "Stop him!"

Sam and Mary clattered onto the jetty. Their boat was easy to spot. It was the one at the far end, full of grumpy tourists. They ran toward it and were greeted by calls of "You're late" and "About time." The red-haired boy screamed out again, "Stop him!"

That's when Sam saw the security guard. The man had been talking to their tour guide but now took a keen interest in the two kids running toward him.

Sam looked back to see the Slayer of Mayhem fan already on the jetty behind them.

"Follow me," Sam said to Mary. He turned and began walking back toward the angry boy. As he did, he held up his hands. "Hey, look, I'm really sorry about this. I can explain."

The boy's face was almost as red as his hair as he huffed and puffed along the jetty.

"No way, man!" he screamed. "You took my stuff! My parents are mad. You're in big trouble!"

Sam slowed to a shuffle as the gap between them closed. His shoulders slumped in a show of total defeat. The boy began to laugh. "Yeah, that's right. Big trouble. You need to arrest this guy," he called out to the security guard. As they came together, the boy stuck out a pudgy hand to grab Sam, but Sam moved faster. He thrust his arms out and shoved the boy off the jetty.

A piercing scream erupted from the middle of the crowd on shore as the boy's mum saw her darling hit the water. Mary gaped at Sam, but he grabbed her and pulled her back toward land.

"This way," he shouted.

At the point where the jetty met the land they jumped off and ran down the narrow, sandy beach.

Angry yells, hysterical sobbing, and splashing filled the night behind them.

"Hurry," Sam urged as he turned to make sure Mary was following.

"Where are we going?"

"There!" Sam pointed at the small black blob sitting at the water's edge ahead.

"How did you know about that?" Mary asked.

The answer was, he didn't. When he hadn't seen the Jet Ski at the jetty, Sam guessed that Azeem had parked it away from prying eyes. The run down the beach had been a gamble, and it had paid off.

Sam stopped in front of the Jet Ski and pushed it out into the river. His feet dug into the sand and panic welled up as he heard an angry mob coming down the beach. Fighting the urge to look, he focused on freeing the Jet Ski.

Finally, the hull slid into the water, and the craft became weightless. Sam spun it around and leapt on. Mary was right behind him. Everything would have ended in disaster if the key hadn't been in, but it was. Sam switched the engine on. The machine roared to life, and they powered out into the river and the cover of darkness.

21

NO FRIENDS

THE SOUND OF THE ANGRY CROWD ON THE
beach drifted out to them. Sam steered the Jet Ski into
the center of the river, then swung around to the left
and began heading back to Orange Walk.

"Well, that was unexpected," Mary said over his
shoulder.

Sam could only nod. His heart was racing, and the
exertion had left him panting as if he'd run a race.
Only the sound of the engine drowned out his heavy
breathing.

"How did you know you'd be able to start it?" Mary
asked.

Sam pointed to the wristband on the end of the
rubber cord hanging off the key in the ignition. "Azeem

wasn't wearing that," he said. "So I was hoping that meant he'd left the key in the ignition."

"So he got close to you?"

Sam nodded. "Real close."

"So what now?"

"I found the entrance to the chamber," Sam said.

"That's great."

"I was hoping we could hide out at Lamanai and check it out, but we've blown that."

"We should go back to our hideout," Mary said. "Wait for things to cool down."

Sam peered ahead. The clouds had cleared and there was just enough moonlight to navigate. He kept the speed up until the river began to narrow. He could sense rather than see the jungle on each side, but as they slowed, the sounds of the wildlife drifted across the water to them. Sam drifted in toward the shore until he could make out individual trees.

"What are you doing?" Mary asked. "Our tour boat won't be far behind."

"I know," Sam said as he studied the shoreline. "That's what I'm worried about."

Minutes ticked by. As he searched, Sam kept an ear tuned for the sound of an approaching boat. He had to find the right spot fast or cut his losses and keep going. He gave himself one more minute and just as time was up, he located the perfect spot. He'd been looking for a small inlet. On the trip to Lamanai, they had passed plenty, but there were none on this section of the river. What he did find was a huge tree trunk that had fallen along the edge of the riverbank.

Sam gunned the engine and aimed the Jet Ski at it. There was just enough room between the riverbank and the trunk to slide in. It was only after he'd cut the engine he realized his mistake. He should have backed in. If they were spotted, there'd be no escape.

There was no time for regrets; the roar of outboards drowned out the sounds of the jungle. Sam and Mary peered over the trunk. A soft yellow glow grew at the bend in the river and then a powerful beam of light swung toward them as the boat rounded the corner. They ducked, and the bank behind them lit up. Sam pressed his face against the Jet Ski's vinyl seat and his mind threw up last-minute worries: Were they totally concealed? Would they be spotted as the boat passed? Should they have just kept going?

The noise of the outboard grew until it felt like the boat was on a collision course for the fallen tree. It passed so close to them, Sam could hear people talking. The wake hit the tree, and it rolled gently against the Jet Ski, then the roar of the outboard motors faded away, and the sounds of the jungle returned.

Somewhere nearby, there was a loud *splash*.

"Wonder what that was?" Mary said.

"Probably a crocodile?"

Mary's legs were dangling in the water on each side of the Jet Ski. Sam felt her pull them up onto the running boards. "Do you think?" she asked.

"This river is full of them."

Sam realized he hadn't even told Mary about his encounter with the croc in the submarine. So much had happened since then, he had almost forgotten it himself. He shivered at the memory and pulled his feet in a little farther from the edge.

When the second boat passed, Sam was sure he heard the whiny voice of the red-haired kid. He smiled as he thought of the look on the boy's face when he'd spotted his Slayers of Mayhem T-shirt.

They waited another ten minutes, then backed the Jet Ski out and resumed their trip down the river. They didn't have a light and wouldn't have risked using one anyway, so Sam kept the speed down and stuck to the middle of the river. Mary brought up the map on her phone and marked the location of the Elio's shed, but seeing how far away it was made Sam feel even worse.

He was sore and tired. He hadn't told Mary about the keypad and as their late-night river journey dragged on, the task ahead became more daunting. Familiar fears and doubts seeped into his mind. Things were even more out of control. Sam had no idea what the code was, and with Azeem still after them, how could they even get back there safely?

"Are you okay, Sam?"

"What?" Sam turned to look back at his friend.

"You haven't said anything for ages. I was just asking if everything's okay."

"I'm fine," Sam lied.

Mary laid a hand on his shoulder. "When we get back to the shed, we should get some sleep, then we can plan our trip back to the chamber."

"Cool," Sam said. He was buoyed by his friend's attitude, but he still couldn't fight the feeling that things had gone too far. They did both need some rest. Then, with a clearer mind, Sam would be able to convince Mary they should give up and leave.

It was another hour before Mary told Sam they were getting near the sheds. She held the phone up for him to see. One more bend in the river. They were lucky Elio's place was on the outskirts of town—less chance of them being spotted.

They rounded the bend and saw the lights of Orange Walk in the distance; somewhere in the darkness between them and the town was the row of boat sheds. Sam slowed the Jet Ski to a crawl and steered in toward the riverbank. He could feel a current carrying them, so he cut the engine, and they drifted in silence. Instead of the jungle sounds they had gotten so used to around Lamanai, there was nothing except the occasional honk of a car horn.

A few minutes later, the sheds appeared, their outlines lit by the lights of Orange Walk.

Sam reached out and grabbed a mooring post next to the first shed. They sat there, rocking in the water, listening for sounds that would tell them there were people around. They heard nothing and eventually Sam let go, and they drifted down to Elio's shed. Sam held the Jet Ski in place while Mary unlatched the door, and they pulled the craft inside.

Mary used the light on her phone to guide Sam up the ladder to the light switch. Neither of them spoke. Sam had closed the curtains over the one small window before they left, but he checked it to make sure no light was escaping. No point in alerting a passerby to their presence. Not that there was much chance of that. That thought made him relax. They'd made it back, and they were safe, for now at least.

"Your turn on the bed," Sam said.

Mary opened her mouth to say something, but Sam cut her off. "I wanna write in my notebook, and you haven't had any sleep since you got here."

Mary conceded his point with a nod and headed to the bed.

Sam sat down at the table and began reviewing the clues he'd collected. He couldn't tell Mary he wanted to give up if he hadn't even tried to figure out the code to the chamber. He stared at the notes from his parents, the research from his uncle. Almost immediately, the futility of it overwhelmed him, and the words and numbers swam on the pages.

Sam looked over at Mary; she was already asleep. He put his head on the table and closed his eyes. Images of crocodiles, gold, Templar codes, and Mayan pyramids floated in and out of the darkness; his mind spun, the images blurred, and darkness enveloped him.

THE BUZZING SOUND IN SAM'S SKULL WOKE him. Through half-opened eyes, he saw his glowing phone vibrating on the table just a few inches away. He reached for it and pushed himself off the table.

Glancing across the room, he noticed the empty bed. This snapped him from his sleepy state. He looked down at the screen.

There were two texts, sent ten minutes apart.

Sam read them, then grabbed the backpack and ran for the door.

WENT 2 GET SCOOTER. U WERE SLEEPING. THOUGHT IT WOULD B OK.

BUT SOMEONE WATCHING.

HIDING UNDER A CAR. CAN'T MOVE. DON'T WORRY.

Sam's anger propelled him through the streets. What had Mary been thinking? Going to get the scooter at night and by herself!

Orange Walk was quiet, and only a few people saw the running boy. Sam didn't slow until he rounded the corner of the street the boat tour building was on. It was another dead end that finished at the water's edge. The building overlooked a modern concrete pier. Lined up on each side were half a dozen boats like the one Sam and Mary had taken to Lamanai. Next to the building was a parking lot. It had been almost full that afternoon when Sam and Mary had arrived, but only a few vehicles remained.

Sam approached cautiously, keeping away from the streetlights and clinging to the shadows. He found a spot in a darkened doorway of a building that gave him a good view of the parking lot. There was no sign of life, but he knew Mary had probably thought the same thing when she arrived.

The temperature had dropped, and the breeze coming off the river chilled the sweat on Sam's body. He shivered and stretched his legs to fight off cramps.

Pain and growing concern for his friend forced Sam from his hiding spot. He ran across the road, down an alley, and behind a building, where he came to the fence that ringed the parking lot.

The longer he waited, the surer he was that the place was deserted, and the more worried he became for Mary. From his new spot, he could see the scooter, still parked where they had left it, next to the walkway down the pier. Sam had just made the decision to enter when his phone started vibrating.

"Mary, where are you?" Sam whispered anxiously.

There was a long pause, then the deep drawl of Felix Ramos oozed into Sam's ear. "Hello, Sam. Your friend is enjoying my hospitality."

"Where is she?"

"Quiet!" Felix snapped. "Listen to me. She will be quite safe as long as you do exactly what I say. Come to Xibalba immediately. And bring the map to the other two treasure locations."

"But—"

Felix cut Sam off. "Hurry, Sam. My hospitality will run out very soon. You know where I am, and you know there is no point in calling the police."

The call ended. Sam leapt to his feet and ran along the fence line. The call confirmed the area was safe— that was the conclusion his muddled mind came to. The scooter was untouched, and the key was still in its hiding place under the rear tire. The engine hummed to life and Sam spun the bike around and raced up the street.

Leaving the key had been Mary's idea—*In case we get separated*, she had said. Sam hadn't paid any attention to her statement, but now it came back to haunt him.

22

TOO EASY

SAM WAS WALKING INTO A TRAP—HE KNEW
that. Felix and Azeem were expecting him, and he had
nothing to trade. He thought back to what he'd said to
Azeem at Lamanai, his lie about the other two treasure
sites. He'd said it to buy himself time, but now he was
paying the price. No, he corrected himself, Mary was
paying the price. But as Sam rode through the streets,
he realized that instead of walking into the trap, he
could swim in.

The wet suit was the key. Sam found the spot he'd
hidden it using the GPS on his phone; then he ran to
the river.

The other critical part of the plan relied on Elio's
information about the crocodile tunnel closing at

midnight. Using the fence line of Xibalba as reference, he entered the water. It was so murky he had to use the light on his phone, but there was no time to worry about being spotted.

Sam found the tunnel with less than five minutes to spare.

A large circular door was pinned back against the riverbank. Sam kicked furiously toward it, terrified it would swing shut and lock him out.

Elio had told him the crocodiles were fed before they were released, but as Sam entered the tunnel, he couldn't stop the terrifying images of beasts racing in to attack him from behind. He channeled the fear into his legs, pumping them up and down.

The light from his phone only lit the space a few feet ahead. Beyond was a black void that seemed to go on forever. As he swam on, the blackness closed in around him; he could feel it squeezing the air from his lungs. He fought to control his breathing and stretched one arm out to run his hand along the side of the tunnel. He kicked on through the darkness. His lungs burned, and he had to work harder and harder to breathe properly. He felt himself getting light-headed, his kicking slowed, but just as he was about to pass out, his arm slipped into open water.

He had reached the pool.

With the last of his strength, Sam kicked to the surface and gulped fresh air as his eyes adjusted to the darkness. He swam to the side of the pool and eased himself up onto the concrete, listening for signs of life, but the room was deserted.

Sam aimed the light on his phone at the cage room. The familiar stench of wet beasts and rotting meat filled his nostrils as he opened the door.

"Elio, Mary," he hissed.

There was a rattle from the far end. Sam shone his phone light down the room. The cages were empty, including Elio's, but on the table he saw his backpack and his father's trench coat, exactly where he'd left them. There was another rattle and Sam moved cautiously toward it.

As he got closer, he made out legs bound with rope. He ran the last few feet. Behind the end cage, a body was tied up. It rolled to face him, and Sam was staring at Elio. The boy had a piece of black tape stuck across his mouth.

Sam dropped to his knees and removed it.

"Thank you, Sam," the boy spluttered. "I had given up hope. We must hurry."

"Why are you tied up?"

"After your escape, Azeem did not trust the locks." Elio smirked. "Please untie me."

"Where's Mary?" Sam asked as he used his pocketknife to cut the rope holding Elio's wrists. As soon as his hands were free, Elio took the knife and went to work on the rope around his legs.

"Did you see Mary?" Sam asked again.

"Yes, Sam. She was here, but Mr. Ramos took her." Elio tossed the rope aside and got up. "We must go. It is not safe here." The boy ran for the door.

Sam called out as he followed, "What do you mean she *was* here? Where are we going?"

"They left, Sam. Because of the bomb."

"Bomb! What bomb? Felix told me to come here."

"Look!" Elio stopped by the door and pointed to the cage on the ground beside him. As Sam got on his knees, Elio hit a switch that lit up the room. In the far corner of the cage, Sam saw a brown package joined by wires to a small black box. A screen on the box had a row of glowing red numbers that were counting down. They had six minutes and twelve seconds.

"You see?" Elio said. "We have to leave."

"We can swim out," Sam said. "We can share the air in my suit."

Elio shook his head. "It is after midnight. The door to the river has shut."

"It didn't look too strong. I'm sure we can force it open."

Elio shook his head again. "Your suit has run out of oxygen."

"How do you know?"

"The red light on the mouthpiece."

Sam had noticed the tiny light on the tip of the breather when he had put on the suit. But the light had been orange then, and the air had been flowing. He thought back to his last moments in the tunnel: his burning lungs, and the struggle to breathe. He'd thought it was exhaustion, but he'd run out of oxygen. He shivered at the thought of how close he'd come to drowning. "So we're trapped?"

"No," said Elio. "If we can get to Mr. Ramos's office, we can escape."

"Hang on." Sam struggled out of the wet suit. It was bulky and hard to move in, and there was no point in wearing it now. He grabbed his father's trench coat and the backpack. "What about Mary?" Sam called as he ran to catch up with Elio.

"I heard Mr. Ramos tell Azeem they are going to the chamber and then they plan to leave Belize. Azeem wanted to leave your friend here, but Mr. Ramos wants to keep her as insurance."

Elio had stopped at the door that led to Felix Ramos's office.

The boy stared at it and rubbed his head with his hand.

"What's wrong?" Sam asked.

"There should be a keypad. Right there," he said, pointing to the wall beside the handleless door. "I saw it through the glass."

Sam stepped up beside him and touched the stone wall. It was fake, but the same color as the riverbank at Lamanai. He recalled Felix telling him how he had designed every part of Xibalba.

Sam closed his eyes and ran his hand gently down the wall. His fingers felt the hidden button, and he pushed it. When he opened his eyes, a glowing number pad had appeared below.

"How did you know it was there?" Elio asked.

"Doesn't matter," Sam said. "Do you know the code?"

Elio nodded. "When they were leaving, Azeem forgot it. Mr. Ramos got mad and shouted it at him. He said, 'The code is "baktun," you fool!'"

Sam looked at the pad. "'Baktun.' Are you sure?"

"Yes, definitely."

"Are you sure?" Sam said.

Elio nodded. "Why?"

Sam pointed at the keypad. "They're numbers. Not letters."

Elio's face fell as he stared at the glowing digits. "No, no," he said, shaking his head. "'Baktun' is the code. Mr. Ramos said it, and I heard Azeem push the buttons. There were beeps, and the door clicked open."

"Hang on," Sam said, pulling his notebook out of his pants. He flicked through the pages until he found his mother's notes on the Mayan long count. "Here is it," he said, stabbing the page with a finger. "I knew I'd heard of a baktun. The fifth sun was made of thirteen baktun cycles. That has to be it."

Sam pressed one and three and was rewarded with two beeps.

Elio grabbed his arm. "No, Sam, I heard more beeps than that."

Sam entered them again. Nothing. He looked at his mother's notes. How much time did they have left? How many minutes since they had left the cage room? He shut the thoughts from his mind and concentrated.

He hit the C button, and the four sets of 13 disappeared.

"It must be the date of the end of the fifth sun." He entered 122112.

"That's it, Sam," Elio said excitedly. "That's the number of beeps I heard."

They waited. There was no sound. Elio gave the door a desperate shove. It didn't budge.

Sam went back to the notes, scanning them for another combination of six digits. There was one last chance. He entered the six numbers that made up the number of days in a baktun. After the six beeps, there was silence. The two boys looked at each other, neither able to hide the desperation on their faces. Finally, from behind the door came a muffled metallic *click*, and it swung inward a couple of inches.

"You did it," Elio said as he pushed the door open. The boy took off and Sam followed him down the corridor and up the stairs.

"Hurry, we don't have much time," Elio yelled as he ran to the door to Felix's office.

There was a bright burst of light as Elio opened it. Sam called out a warning, but it was too late. The boy had already entered.

Sam ran into the room and almost collided with Elio. The boy had stopped dead.

"What's wrong?" Sam asked, but as he said the words, he saw what had distracted Elio. Slumped over the desk was the body of a large bald man in a white suit.

"Who is it?" Sam asked.

"I have never seen him before," Elio murmured. "But he is wearing one of Mr. Ramos's expensive suits."

The man had no obvious injuries, and would have looked like he was sleeping if it hadn't been for the sickly gray color of his skin. He had been dead for some time.

As Sam approached the desk, Elio had snapped out of his shock and ran for the main door. "Sam, what are you doing? There is a fire escape this way. We can get out, but we don't have much time."

"Two minutes," Sam said, pointing behind the desk to the black timer and brown package identical to the ones in the cage room. "Go and open the fire escape. I'll be there in a minute."

As he got closer to the body, Sam could smell the stink of decay. Why had the corpse been placed there?

Holding his nose, Sam leaned over for a closer look at the papers scattered around the body. They were all from banks and had large bold letters at the top that read FORECLOSURE and FINAL NOTICE. Xibalba was in deep financial trouble, and here was the proof, under a dead man. Sam didn't understand what was going on, and he couldn't hang around to work it out. The timer told him he had less than two minutes.

An agitated Elio returned to the room. "Hurry, Sam, please!"

Sam ignored him and turned to the reason he was still there. The large panel of black fabric that had held the dagger . . . It was empty. Sam had noticed the second he entered the room, but the piece of parchment was still there. Felix had referred to it as one of the tools he used to build Xibalba. Sam didn't know what that meant either, but it was linked to Lamanai, and that was where Mary had been taken.

These orders are issued in the name of the Grand Master of the Knights Templar & the Keepers of the Light

Sir Hugh, your mission is prepare the chamber to receive the treasure. Due to the sensitive nature of this mission, it must be carried out by you alone.

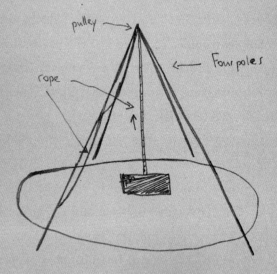

pulley

Four poles

rope

The engraving on the blade of the dagger will lead you to the chamber. This sacred location is one of three

With just a minute and a half on the timer, Sam ripped the ancient piece of paper off the wall and slipped it into his journal.

"We should go," he said as he ran toward Elio. The boy totally missed the sarcasm in Sam's voice.

"That's what I have been trying to tell you! This way!"

They went through the outer office and into the hallway. For a few sickening seconds, Sam thought the boy was going to lead them back down to the main tunnel. There was no way they'd make it in time. But he veered into a room lined with beds. At the far end was an open window. Elio leapt through it without stopping, and as Sam followed him, all he could think was that dying after jumping out a second-story window was almost worse than being blown up.

The fall didn't kill him because it was only a few feet. They were on a narrow fire escape and Elio was already sliding down the ladder fireman-style, with a foot on each side of it. Spurred on by the fact there could be only a few seconds left, Sam did the same— almost. Halfway down, one leg slipped off the side of the ladder and he only avoided falling off completely by grabbing a rung.

Shaken and sore, Sam made it to the ground.

"Hurry," Elio called as he disappeared into the darkness toward the river.

Sam sprinted after him. The timer in his mind told him time was up. As their feet beat a frantic rhythm across the staff parking lot, Sam wondered if the bombs had been fake.

Then the night became day.

The bright flash behind them lit up the way ahead. Sam could see the end of the parking lot and the river beyond. Then the concussion from the blast hit them. Sam saw Elio lifted off the ground and pushed through the air, just as the same thing happened to him. He came down in a heap and lay stunned on the concrete.

Darkness returned, but Sam was seeing stars as he lifted his head. "Elio."

The boy wasn't moving.

Sam got to his feet feeling groggy but thankful nothing was broken. He stumbled over to Elio as the boy sat up. He wobbled unsteadily and put hand to the nasty cut on his forehead.

"Now you see why we had to hurry," he said. He started to laugh at his own joke but stopped and clutched his chest.

Sam's mind felt clouded. He didn't know if it was the tumble he'd just taken or the fact he had just avoided certain death, but he knew if he stopped to dwell on it now he'd never get going. And he had a long way to go.

"Elio, listen. I have to get to Lamanai and rescue Mary. I have a Jet Ski back at the shed."

Elio shook his head, angering Sam, who thought the boy wanted to talk him out of it. "No, Sam. There are Jet Skis here."

Sam knew that. In the glare of the explosion, he had caught a glimpse of them lined up neatly at the river's edge. He shook his head. "I don't have a key. I left it in the Jet Ski at the shed."

"I can hot-wire them," Elio said as he motioned for Sam to help him up. He breathed in sharply and rubbed his chest, then waved Sam to follow him. "At night sometimes I sneak out on one and go down to the road bridge to meet my friends. We dare one another to jump off. We call it the big leap. "

"I've been over that bridge," Sam said. "It's high."

"And even scarier at night," Elio said proudly.

It was a funny conversation, Sam thought. For a moment they were two guys talking about normal stuff. There was something comforting about pretending, just for a second, that they were normal. Sam wondered if Elio felt the same way.

The feeling faded as they got to the Jet Skis. There was another timer ticking in Sam's head. Every second that passed, his chance of rescuing Mary got smaller. Felix wouldn't hang around at Lamanai for long, and Sam had no idea how he would track him down after that.

They stopped at the first Jet Ski. Sam was heartened to see Elio was already moving more freely, but the boy's face screwed up as he pulled the seat off the first Jet Ski.

"I need to tell you about your parents."

Sam stared down at him, but the boy didn't look up as he removed a panel exposing a collection of wires. In the chaos, Sam had totally forgotten about the fact that Elio knew his parents. All he had been thinking about was getting to Mary. Now, the questions he had formed in his mind came flooding back, along with a pang of guilt because he knew he couldn't head to Lamanai until he'd learned about the link between this boy and his parents.

23

FINAL COUNT

"I DON'T HAVE LONG," SAM SAID. "BUT YOU have to tell me how you know my parents."

He was thankful the boy didn't stop his work. As Elio removed wires from the circuit board, he spoke slowly and steadily.

"I was the one who first found the submarine in 2010. I was out fishing, and it was in a side stream covered in mud. Inside, I found an old notebook and a gold coin. A Templar coin. Foolishly, I went to the police."

"Felix Ramos," Sam said.

"Yes. He took the credit and kept the gold. He didn't know about the notebook. I kept that. When your parents came to Orange Walk looking for the submarine, they tracked me down. They saw through Mr. Ramos's lies. Your parents hired me to be their assistant. I helped them learn more about the submarine by giving them the notebook I found inside."

Now Elio lifted his head and looked up at Sam. "Your parents were very kind to me. I liked them. One night, I was with your father in Lamanai. He found the entrance to the chamber and sent me to get your mother. She insisted we go to their old hotel. They had left there after they suspected they were being watched. I let them stay at my family's shed."

Sam nodded but didn't mention he had found his mother's notes. He desperately wanted to hear everything Elio had to say, but he couldn't get the image of Mary out of his mind.

"Keep going," he said.

"Your mother went to get something from the hotel, but she was caught. There was nothing I could do."

Elio looked up again and Sam could see tears forming in his eyes. Sam put a hand on Elio's shoulder. "It's okay. Please, Elio, I don't have much time."

The boy sniffed and wiped his face then lowered his head. "I was scared. Mr. Ramos arrested me. He said your parents had been caught stealing and taken by the authorities."

"Which authorities? Who?"

Elio shook his head. "I don't know, Sam. Mr. Ramos told me if I ever mentioned anything, I would be put in jail. I have to support my mother; she has no one else. Mr. Ramos gave me a job."

Elio had stopped working. His hands were holding the wires. Sam could see him sobbing. "It's okay, Elio, honestly. What else?"

"That is all. I have worked for Mr. Ramos since then. But my mother is very sick. She is in the hospital. I can't afford her treatment. A week ago, I went back to Lamanai to try and find the chamber your father discovered. I hoped to find a coin. Just one would pay for my mother's treatment."

The throaty roar of the engine made both boys flinch. Elio looked up at Sam, but he wasn't smiling at his success. His face was etched with pain and guilt.

"Thank you for telling me, Elio. None of this was your fault."

"I will start another Jet Ski and come with you," he announced.

Sam watched him remove the seat and fidgeted as he felt the seconds ticking by. Suddenly, Elio stopped and lifted his head sharply. A second later, Sam heard it too—sirens.

They had run out of time.

Instead of returning to his work, Elio leapt up. Sam pushed his Jet Ski out into the river.

"It's too late," the boy called.

"What do you mean?" Sam said angrily. "We can get away."

"No." Elio pointed back to the burning ruins of Xibalba. The noise of the fire had masked the approach of the emergency vehicles. A police car was already screeching around the side of the building.

"If you leave now, they will know," Elio called as he walked up the slope to the parking lot. "Wait till I distract them and then go."

"But what about you?" Sam called.

"Go and save your friend," Elio said without looking back. And then he was running toward the approaching police car.

Sam crouched down behind the Jet Ski. The engine was ticking over contentedly, and the casing was already warming up. There was a screeching of tires and then men shouting commands. Car doors slammed, and Sam imagined the police chasing the fleeing figure. He waited for a few more seconds before sliding onto the seat of the Jet Ski.

The gears clanked as he put it into reverse, and then with his body low on the seat he reversed the craft out into the river. Once safely swallowed by the darkness,

Sam sat up and surveyed the parking lot. The police car sat in the middle of it, doors open and lights flashing. There was no sign of the officers or Elio. Conscious of the sound carrying over the water, Sam turned the Jet Ski and motored slowly up the river toward Lamanai. After a few minutes, he opened up the throttle and pushed the craft as fast as it would go.

Time was ticking.

24

LOOSE ENDS

THE WIND DIED AWAY, AND THE CLOUDS deserted the night sky. The light from the dying moon reflected off the river, and the shiny surface stood out in contrast to the dull black borders of the jungle on each side. Sam skipped across the surface, not slowing for the twists and turns of the river weaving its way to Lamanai.

He checked his phone and was surprised how far he had traveled, but he still had a way to go. His mind was plagued with thoughts of arriving to find the chamber deserted and the trail cold.

When the riverbanks suddenly veered away from sight, he knew had reached the final stretch of his run. He swung to the right, searching for the edge of the river. Soon he saw the wall of thick vines growing over the bank and dropping down into the water like the gnarly fingers of some hideous giant.

He slowed to crawling speed, then cut the engine and drifted to the point where the vines ended. In the distance, he saw a small black speedboat beached on the thin strip of sand. Sam slipped off the Jet Ski and pushed it into the vines to stop it from floating away, then he walked slowly along the riverbank, retracing the path he had taken a few hours before.

The jungle was silent; still Sam had the feeling that hundreds of sets of eyes were locked on him. But as he crept toward the speedboat, he knew his main concern should be human eyes.

He crouched down and watched the boat. When he was sure the area was deserted, he approached the boulder. There was no need for the light from his phone. The secret panel had been left open. The keypad glowed like a set of nicely arranged rubies. Unlike the keypad at Xibalba, this one didn't beep, and there was no readout screen. Sam entered the six digits and waited.

Nothing happened. His heart began to beat faster, and he checked left and right for signs of danger.

No one appeared from the shadows. The jungle stayed silent.

Sam hit the C button and entered the code again, leaning in, ears straining for the sound of the *click*. He heard nothing but pushed anyway.

The boulder moved. He put his shoulder to it and heard the faintest scrape of rock on rock as it swung inward.

The boulder was massive. Only a tiny part of it had been exposed in the rock face. As he slipped through the opening Sam saw the glint of shining metal where someone had added the lock. A modern addition to an ancient piece of engineering.

The tunnel Sam stepped into was man-made. He could feel the smooth stone beneath his feet, and the walls and roof were made of large, evenly cut stone blocks. The light began to fade, and the gentle grating sound signaled that the door was closing. Sam turned to watch the huge boulder swing gently back into place. As the strip of soft white moonlight shrank, Sam had to resist the urge to leap back through the gap.

The dull *thud* of the door slipping into place echoed around Sam as he reached for his phone, but he didn't turn on the light, he listened. Felix Ramos was somewhere ahead, and the only advantage Sam had was the man didn't know he had made it to the chamber. He had no idea what he was going to do next; he only knew that his friend was in trouble and that she would have done the same for him.

Sam stuck his hand out and felt the smooth stone of the tunnel wall. He shuffled his feet forward and began moving slowly away from the door. His fingers traced over the grooves that ran between the blocks, thin, straight lines, a reminder of the skills of the people who had constructed the tunnel.

With one hand on the wall and one hand in front of him, he shuffled forward like a blind man.

The pace was agonizingly slow. When Sam finally took out his phone, after two a.m., he also noticed there was no signal—he wouldn't be calling for help. Not that he had anyone to call. A quick flash of the light showed him the tunnel ran straight on a slight downward slope. He turned his phone off and began moving again, faster and more confidently. The next time he stopped was when he heard noises.

It sounded like tapping, slow and rhythmic. Sam listened to the repetitive noise for a while and then increased his pace. The noise got louder, and then the blackness ahead began to lighten. It happened slowly, like a sunrise; soon Sam could make out the end of the passageway, its edges lit, but the glow was coming from the space beyond.

He kept moving forward, staying to one side of

the tunnel. A few feet from the opening, Sam stopped again. The noise had continued uninterrupted, but now, without the echo caused by the tunnel's walls, Sam could identify it. Someone was digging.

Sam crept to the opening and suddenly forgot about the noise. He had been expecting a large open area, but nothing like the space he saw in front of him. A huge circular pool, twice the size of the one at Xibalba, was in the center. The same Mayan symbols were carved around the edge. The paving stones ran about fifteen feet back to walls made of huge blocks of stone. The four long poles, spaced around the pool, were also giant versions of the ones at Xibalba. They disappeared up into a cavernous space that Sam realized had to be the inside of the Temple of the Mask. This was the secret the temple had been built to hide.

The poles were painted white and glowed in the light coming from the electric lamps that had been set up around the edge of the pool. The glowing poles created the outline of a giant black pyramid. It was far more spectacular than the one Sam had seen in the show, and then he noticed another major difference. Suspended from a rope in the middle of the pyramid was a large wooden chest. It was the design on the Templar's orders Sam had taken from Felix Ramos's office.

He turned his attention back to the noise, the steady

digging sound. A small set of stairs ran from the tunnel down to the walkway around the pool. The sound was echoing off the circular wall, but Sam knew it was coming from his right. He peered around the edge of the opening and saw a pile of dirt. On the other side, he saw the big, bald head of Felix Ramos glistening in the light.

Two of the stone floor slabs had been removed and the man was standing in the bottom of a grave-sized hole that looked like it was about four feet deep. He was digging and flicking dirt over his shoulder to the pile. Then Sam spotted movement against the wall near the hole. It was Mary. Her hands were bound, and her mouth was covered with a piece of tape, but she had seen him.

He studied the chamber inch by inch, looking for any sign of danger. He had feared Azeem was with Felix, but there was no sign of him, and nowhere to hide in the huge circular room.

Sam crept down the stairs and moved slowly around the wall, using the shadows created by the electric lights. As he got closer, the pile of dirt gave him cover from the huge man. Felix continued to dig, and Sam knew he was safe as long as he could hear that sound.

The smell of the damp earth filled Sam's nostrils as he crouched behind the fresh mound. His mind was a jumble of ideas and fears. Did he charge Felix, push him over, and grab Mary? Or get Mary to run to him? He didn't have a weapon, hadn't even thought to grab a stick or a rock before he entered the tunnel. He could hear Ramos digging, but Sam knew he would have to act soon.

He edged around the pile of dirt, Mary was only a few feet away. Her eyes were wide, and she was blinking furiously. Sam motioned for her to come to him. She shook her head, and as Sam watched her, he got the feeling she was telling him to go. That was crazy, Sam thought—not when he was so close. He crawled forward and reached out for her. Maybe she just needed help getting up.

As he pulled her to her feet, Felix stopped digging. Sam froze and looked at the man in the hole. He ran a hand across his glistening dome of skin and then, without turning, he spoke.

"I must say, your ingenuity impresses me, Sam. I did not think you would be able to find this place." Now he twisted slowly and looked up at Sam with a warm smile, but he made no effort to leave the hole. He dropped the shovel and wiped his head again.

"You friend convinced me you were lying about your knowledge of the other two treasure locations," he said, nodding toward Mary. "You could have left with your life, but you came for your friend. A shame it was all for nothing." Felix laughed, and his ample stomach wobbled up and down.

Mary grunted and nodded her head frantically at Sam. He watched the man in the hole. He had made no effort to get out. Sam grabbed Mary and pulled her to him. She flinched, and he looked at her in surprise, but then he heard a noise behind him.

He let go of Mary and spun around as the mound of dirt came to life.

With a roar, a dark figure erupted out of the soil. Its arms threw back the hood of its sweatshirt and Sam saw Azeem's beaming face.

"Boo!" he shouted as he lunged forward and pushed Sam. He stumbled back against Mary and they tumbled into a heap on the ground.

Felix was still laughing as he heaved himself out of the hole. "We knew you were coming. When I added the keypad to the chamber entrance, I installed a sensor." He pulled a small remote from his pocket. "But we weren't sure if you were armed or not, so Azeem came up with the hiding place. Ingenious, yes?"

Azeem was a hideous brown mess. Only his bright toothy grin identified him as a man. The grin left his face when Felix tossed him the spade. "Keep digging."

Felix took a handkerchief from his pocket, walked

to the edge of the pool, and dipped it in the water. He wiped his face and then walked back to Sam and Mary. "You can remove the gag from your friend," he said.

Sam eased the tape off Mary's mouth. The moment it was free, a stream of words burst from her. "Sam, I'm sorry. I should never have gone to get the bike. . . . I—"

"It's okay," Sam assured her. "I would have done the same thing."

More laughter from Felix got Sam and Mary's attention. The man was staring at them with something resembling fondness in his eyes.

"Your loyalty to each other is touching," he said, wiping the damp cloth across his head.

"Why did you bring her here?" Sam asked.

"Insurance, Sam, while I tie up some loose ends. I am preparing to leave the country."

"That's why you left that body at Xibalba when you blew it up?" Sam's question was rewarded with a look of surprise on Felix's face.

"You made it up to my office? You really are quite a resourceful boy. I had assumed you would be caught up in the tragic explosion that took my life tonight."

"I don't understand," Mary said.

"Mr. Ramos's crocodile park has gone bust," Sam said. "He owes a lot of money, so he faked his death in a big explosion at Xibalba. He put a dead body in his office. And he left Elio to die."

Felix confirmed Sam's words with a smirk. "Azeem purchased the body from a morgue in Belize. I paid a dentist to swap our dental records. Young Elio was collateral damage."

"No he wasn't," Sam said. "I saved him."

Felix smiled. "I thought you might have." He turned to look at the pool. "I will be sad to leave all this. The secrets of Xibalba have been good to me."

"You didn't even find it," Sam sneered. "My father did."

Felix spun around and came at Sam with the speed of a man half his size. He clenched his fists into huge, meaty balls.

"No!" Mary shouted.

Azeem stopped and looked up, a sneer on his face. Felix glared at the man. "Keep digging," he growled. "I want to get out of here." Instead of hitting Sam, he sat down on the dirt opposite his two captives. "Your parents came to Belize, asking questions about the submarine."

"The submarine that Elio found," Sam snapped.

Felix ignored him. "They told stories about a precious

cargo on the sub and the end of the world, but I always suspected that what sub 518 carried here were men searching for Templar gold, just like your parents. So I watched them. They gave me the slip by fleeing from their hotel, but I tracked your father down at Lamanai. I saw him leave the chamber with the dagger."

Felix crossed to a bag on the ground by the hole. He opened it, and the light caught the glint of polished metal; it was the silver dagger from his office. He raised it into the air, turning it slowly and admiring the way the light made the blade sparkle. "Your father located the chamber, but I returned and found the treasure. And I paid the price," he said.

Felix tossed the dagger into the air, caught it by the handle, and drove it into his thigh.

Mary's shrill scream bounced around the walls. In the hole, Azeem spun around searching for danger. When he saw the blade sticking from his boss's leg, he laughed and resumed digging.

Felix stood there with his hands on his hips, staring down at his audience.

Sam had been as shocked as Mary, but he was closer, and the moment the blade entered the leg he knew something wasn't right. It was the sound. He hadn't seen someone stab themselves before, but he knew the dull *thud* he'd heard wasn't natural.

Mary's sobs died away as Felix wrenched the blade out as if he was pulling it from a tree trunk. Then he pulled up his trouser leg to reveal the molded blue plastic.

He let the material fall again as he turned and walked off around the edge of the pool. "Come," he called out.

Sam helped Mary to her feet, and they followed Felix to the far side of the pool. He was standing by a pile of white rocks, but as they got closer, Sam saw they were bones—huge bones bleached white by time. It was the skeleton of a massive crocodile, but as he studied the long-dead beast, he spotted another set of bones.

"There's someone under it," Mary said.

"A knight," Felix murmured respectfully. "Do you notice anything strange about the body?"

Mary spotted it before Sam. "It only has one leg," she said.

Felix nodded. "He lay there, mortally wounded, but before he died he killed his attacker. You can see where he used the dagger to kill the beast," he said, pointing to a neatly shaped slit in the crocodile's skull. "This is where your father found the dagger, Sam. But if he had searched the knight's body, he would have found the man's written orders. I did. That's how I learned the truth behind his mission. But only after I was attacked."

"I don't understand," Mary said.

"I, too, was attacked by one of the guardians of the chamber. I was pulled into the water by my leg, but I had one advantage the knight did not." Felix's empty hand disappeared behind his back and returned holding a handgun. "This," he said proudly. "I shot the beast. But the attack was my salvation. If I hadn't been pulled into the pool, I never would have seen the treasure." He pointed to the chest hanging in the middle of the pool. "It was hidden in the water. But I found it." He glared at Sam. "Not your father."

Sam stared at the old wooden box. Was this the Ark? The treasure his parents had chased around the world? His thoughts were interrupted by Azeem.

"Mr. Ramos!" the man called from the other side of the pool.

Felix scowled at the interruption, but when he saw Azeem holding up a bag, he waved Sam and Mary away from the skeletons with his gun. "Come," he said, pointing toward Azeem.

By the time they got back, Azeem had recovered three dirty canvas bags from the bottom of the hole. Felix put down the dagger and offered his hand to the Scar-Faced Man to pull him out of the hole.

"You are filthy, Azeem," Felix said. "Go and clean yourself."

Azeem looked at the pool anxiously.

Felix chuckled as he pulled a carved piece of wood from his pocket. Sam recognized the necklace with the Templar cross.

"Put the protection of Kinich Ahau to use one last time," Felix said, tossing it to Azeem.

The man hung it around his neck as he went to the edge of the pool. The moment he lowered himself into the water, ripples unsettled the glasslike surface on the far side. Something had been stirred.

Mary's horrified gasp was answered with a sneer from Azeem.

Felix was enjoying Mary's reaction too. "While you are in there, Azeem, fetch the chest. I want to show our friends what I discovered here in Lamanai."

Felix went to the nearest pole and unfastened a rope that ran up it into the darkness. Sam watched Azeem wade toward the middle of the pool, the water almost up to his neck. When he got to the center, he raised his arms. Felix fed the rope through his hands, lowering the chest down to him. Azeem took hold of it, unhooked the rope, then turned and walked confidently back.

"Your parents talked of a magical heart to this pyramid. They couldn't find it. But I did."

He pointed at the chest in Azeem's arms. "When the crocodile pulled me under the water I found what your father missed. And thanks to the knight's orders, I also discovered the truth. This chamber was nothing more than a secure place for the Templars' treasure."

Azeem slid the chest onto the stones beside the pool. He was about to climb out, but Felix stopped him. "You're still filthy, Azeem. Clean yourself."

The man slipped under the water and began rubbing the dirt off his body.

"This is how I know your parents' stories about the power of the pyramids were lies," Felix said as he opened the chest.

Sam and Mary leaned over it. Inside were a set of ancient tools made of wood and rusting metal. A hammer, a chisel, and three pottery jars with narrow necks jammed with corks.

"This is what I found. No magic. Just tools and gold. Lots of gold. I hid the last of it over there," he said, pointing to the bags by the hole. "The Templars knew their gold would be safe here in Lamanai, protected by Kinich Ahau's guardians."

Azeem had finished cleaning himself and Felix bent down and offered his hand. Azeem moved to the edge of the pool to take it, but Felix suddenly grabbed the leather cord around his neck and pulled it off him.

He stepped back, holding the wooden carving. Azeem looked down, realized what had happened, and leapt for the edge of the pool.

"Stay there," Felix said, pointing the gun at the stunned man.

Azeem's face went pale, highlighting the jagged scar on his face. "What? I don't understand." The confused look transformed to panic as he heard the noise behind him.

Sam heard it too. The sound of water churning as something broke the surface.

"Let him out," Mary said as she realized what was happening.

"Mr. Ramos, please," Azeem pleaded.

Felix kept the gun aimed down at the Scar-Faced Man as he held the wooden pendant in the air. "It is fitting I leave a tribute to the guardians."

"No, please," Azeem said, his voice becoming shrill as the panic took hold. He tried to climb out again, but Felix lashed out with his foot. The kick sent the Scar-Faced Man stumbling backward. He disappeared under the water, then popped up spluttering and pleading.

"You can't do this," Mary shouted.

"Silence!" Felix yelled. His voice boomed around the chamber but was quickly drowned out by a high-pitched scream from Azeem.

Mary screamed too as the man threw his arms in the air. For a second he seemed to be trying to keep his balance, his arms waving wildly about as if he were performing some weird water dance. Then the movement stopped, and Azeem went rigid. The water around him became red and his screaming reached a new level of loudness. He made one last effort to reach the edge of the pool, but the water behind him erupted and the man was pulled under, his scream cut off as if it were a recording that had been stopped midplay.

Mary had gone silent, shocked by the hideous spectacle, but now she rounded on Felix. "You animal," she screamed. "How could you do that?"

The water had already begun to settle and the red stain faded away. Felix turned calmly toward Mary, unaffected by her outburst. "I told you, I came here to tidy up loose ends."

Mary fought to stifle her sobs as she put a hand out for Sam, clinging to him for reassurance. Sam was silent. He had been just as shocked by what he'd witnessed, but he knew the man wouldn't have blinked an eye if it had been him in the pool. That knowledge tempered his reaction. He also knew he and Mary were in big trouble.

Felix Ramos was crazy. Sam had to keep the man calm while he tried to come up with a plan to get away, because there was no doubt he saw them as loose ends too.

25

FINAL RUN

"DID YOU FIND THE NECKLACE IN THE chest?" Sam asked as casually as he could.

Mary stared at Sam openmouthed. "Is that all you can say, Sam? He just killed a man by feeding him to a crocodile!"

Sam gripped Mary's arm and focused on Felix.

"Yes," the man replied. "If the knight had been wearing his protection, he might have lived. But the necklace was only part of it. These were the key." Felix removed one of the jars and tossed it to Sam. He hadn't been expecting to catch a piece of pottery and only just got a hand to it. His fumbling amused Felix, who laughed as he continued his story. "After I killed the crocodile,

I was close to death. I had lost a lot of blood. I should have left immediately, but I had to know what was in the chest." He crouched down next to the old wooden box. It was made of roughly cut planks, stained black and dotted with large brass nails. Felix patted it gently like it was a pet dog. He was still talking but seemed to be speaking to the box. "I couldn't believe my eyes. Bags and bags of gold coins. I was rich." He removed another of the pottery jars. Sam tensed in case it was coming his way, but Felix held it. "The tools and these things, I hardly gave them a second glance. In my haste to count the gold, I dropped one." He looked up at Sam and paused dramatically. "That act saved my life."

"How?" Sam asked, genuinely intrigued by the story.

"Who cares?" Mary shouted. But Felix looked pleased with Sam's interest.

"Another crocodile came for me. Almost as big as the one I had killed. It smelled the blood and leapt from the water. I was out of bullets. I prepared for death, but then the most remarkable thing happened. It stopped as if it had hit some invisible barrier, and then retreated to the pool. I was stunned. Then I realized the oil from the broken jar acted as a repellent."

Sam studied the jar in his hands. Engraved on the side was the same design as Felix's necklace, a Templar cross.

"There was no time to think about this miracle," Felix continued. "I had to get medical treatment. I returned the chest to the water, knowing the guardians would keep it safe just as the old knight had intended. I returned to Orange Walk, but I took the crocodile's body. While I was recovering in the hospital, the story of my fight with the beast spread. My fame grew. People came from all over the world to see the great crocodile slayer and hear my story. They wanted to know how I had survived. After my recovery, I retrieved some of the gold. Now I was rich and famous, and had a taste for more of both. Using the secret of the knight's oil, I created Xibalba and the legend of Kinich Ahau."

"So your whole crocodile power thing is built around some oil."

"Not just any oil," Felix said. He held up the pottery jar. "As my stock ran low, I spent a great deal of money getting chemists to re-create the formula. But nothing worked. Azeem's face was proof of that." Felix admired the necklace in his hand, then tossed it into the chest. "I learned that just a few drops would keep the beasts at bay and that the necklace was designed for that purpose. But now my supply is gone."

"Is that why your park went bust?" Mary sneered.

Felix glared at her then tossed the pottery jar over his shoulder, into the pool. "Come," he ordered. "You can be of use. Bring the chest."

"Stop making him angry," Sam hissed at Mary as they picked up the old wooden box.

"He's crazy, Sam," she replied.

"I know, so don't make it worse. I'm trying to get us out of here."

"Hurry," Felix called as he picked up the bags of coins. He held them in his arms as he waited for Sam and Mary. "It is fitting they should leave the way they came in."

After he'd dropped the bags in the chest, he tossed in the dagger. Slamming the lid, he strode off toward the tunnel. "Come," he ordered.

Sam looked at Mary as they lifted the box again. "Play it calm and we might just get out of here."

Felix had picked up one of the large portable electric lights and was waiting at the top of the stairs as his two prisoners struggled up with the chest. "You know the Maya believed that 2012 was not about the end of the world, but a new beginning. And they were right." Felix stared out across the pool. "This was the place of my rebirth. The beginning of my legend. At the height of my fame, I would bring my followers here to see the real Xibalba. For a fee, of course."

Sam thought back to the missing persons reports he'd seen at the police station, but he held his tongue.

Felix continued, "I followed the knight's orders and rehung the chest. But I removed the gold. I was unsure if the ropes and pulleys would hold it with so much weight."

"And the orders mention three sites," Sam said. "That's why you think there is more treasure?"

Felix nodded. "I scoured the whole of Lamanai for other chambers."

"But it wasn't just the gold. You needed the oil to keep your park alive, and your fame."

Felix shrugged. "Xibalba became a beast that had to be fed. Like the guardians in this chamber. But now it is all over." He took one last look across the cavernous space, then turned and pushed past Sam and Mary. "Come," he ordered again as he lit the tunnel ahead.

THE WALK WAS SLOW AND PAINFUL FOR Sam and Mary. They made regular stops to swap hands.

Each time he heard the chest go down, Felix would stop and swing the spotlight back at them. "Hurry," he'd snap, and then resume his march to the entrance.

By the time they got to the boulder, Felix had opened it. Sam felt the cool breeze coming off the river. The air smelled cool and fresh, almost edible. Felix stood to one side as they passed with the chest and stepped onto the sandy riverbank.

"Put it down," he ordered.

Sam had no idea how much time had passed. He hadn't had a chance to look at his phone, but it was still dark. The speedboat was rocking gently in the water. He didn't risk a look toward his Jet Ski.

"I will take it from here now," Felix said. When Sam turned, the man was holding his gun. His other hand was in his pocket, but when he removed it, Sam saw a small remote. Felix slowly raised the gun until it was pointing at Sam and Mary. He motioned to the tunnel entrance. "Inside."

"Why?" Sam asked. "We only came here to find my parents. We don't care about your gold!" he pleaded.

"I believe you, Sam," Felix said. "When you first arrived, I thought your parents had sent you for the treasure. I thought you might know of the other two locations. But now I believe you really came here to find them."

"What happened to his parents?" Mary demanded. "You can tell us now that you're going."

"Please," Sam pleaded.

Felix eyed his two prisoners coldly. "I was going to kill your parents, Sam." He paused, enjoying the look on the boy's face. "I followed your father and saw him find the entrance to the chamber. He left with the dagger and went to the jetty. He was waiting for Elio to return. That is where I planned to do it, but . . ."

"But what?" Sam blurted out.

"Men came. Foreign men in a helicopter, with guns. They took him."

"What do you mean? Who?"

Felix shrugged. "Perhaps your parents had tried to steal from other people before me. I watched your father hide the dagger just before they grabbed him. When I returned to Orange Walk, Azeem told me your mother had also been taken when she tried to return to the hotel."

"And you don't know what happened to them?"

Felix laughed. "I didn't care. They were gone, and I had the treasure to myself." He waved the gun toward the entrance to the chamber. "Now, inside."

"Why?" Mary asked.

"I told you, I came here to tidy up loose ends." He straightened his arm and pointed the gun directly at Mary's head. "I won't ask again."

Mary took a breath. Sam saw she was about to speak, and suddenly he was more afraid for her than himself. He pushed her into the tunnel.

"You should run," Felix said as the boulder began to move.

"What did he mean?" Mary asked as the boulder swung shut, plunging the tunnel into darkness.

"I'm not sure," Sam said. As he pulled his phone from his pocket, he heard a *beep* somewhere above his head.

The floor of the tunnel lit up as Sam activated his phone light. He aimed it above his head and recognized the source of the *beep* immediately. He had already seen two similar devices that night. The red numbers on the small screen told him they had only thirty seconds left.

"We need to run, don't we?" said Mary.

26

ALL IN

THEY DIDN'T MAKE IT BACK TO THE chamber. Sam could see the opening in the distance, but he'd counted the seconds in his head as they ran. When he got to twenty-seven, he grabbed Mary and pulled her to the ground. "Cover your ears."

The explosion began as a distant rumble that quickly grew to a deafening roar and a howling wind, so powerful Sam and Mary were pushed along the floor of the tunnel. As he fought to keep his face protected, Sam felt his exposed skin being stung by the tiny fragments of stone carried along in the explosion. Through the roaring winds, he heard Mary screaming.

The noise faded away, but thick, choking dust swirled around, dulling the light from Sam's phone to a weak white glow. Sharp cracks echoed down the tunnel as slabs of rock fell to the floor. Sam grabbed Mary and pulled her to her feet.

"We have to keep going," he said, ignoring her protests.

Covered in stone powder, coughing and spitting dust, Sam and Mary stumbled out of the tunnel and down the stairs. The air in the chamber was hazy with dust, obscuring the view across the pool. Sam steered Mary away from the tunnel opening in case there was another explosion. They stood close to the wall, watching gray clouds of dust swirling up into the darkness.

"I told you he was crazy," Mary said, her back to Sam.

His head was throbbing, his ears were ringing from the blast, and now Sam tensed, angered by his friend's tone. "I knew that," he snapped. "That's why we had to keep him calm."

"Fat load of good it did." Mary punctuated her statement by spitting onto the ground.

Those words, the offhand way she had delivered them, pushed Sam over the edge. His heart was still racing, he was pumped after the fright of the explosion, and his anger erupted. "It's your fault we're here!" he screamed. "You had to go for the bike in the middle of the night like this was some adventure holiday. What were you thinking? This is real, Mary. This is life and death! Our deaths!"

Sam glared at Mary as she turned. He could tell she was stunned by his outburst, and he was glad. "You dragged me into this," he said, pointing at her accusingly. "I was ready to go tonight. Give up this stupid search. I was going to tell you, but then you went and got caught, and now we're here!"

Sam's words echoed around the chamber after he'd finished. Mary sank down against the wall and pulled her knees up to her face. As she lowered her head, Sam heard her sob. "You're right," she mumbled. Then she added, "I'm sorry."

Her words sapped the last of Sam's anger from him. His shoulders slumped as he looked down at his friend crying. "No," he said, "I'm sorry."

Sam sat down next to Mary and put an arm around her. "I didn't mean it. Not like that. I'm scared. I don't know what I'm doing, and I know we are only here because of my parents. You wanted to help me, and now I've gotten you into this."

"Did you really want to leave?" Mary asked without raising her head.

"Yes," Sam said. He stared down at the layer of dust that had covered the ground. He ran a finger through it, leaving a thin, gray trail. "My parents have been gone for five years, Mary." He stopped tracing and looked up. She was watching him. "Five years. If they really are alive, then why haven't they gotten in touch with me? Haven't you wondered about that? Maybe they did believe in 2012 and the end of the world, but Felix was right, it didn't happen. So where are they?"

Sam broke Mary's gaze and resumed his finger drawing in the dust. He'd done it. He had finally shared the fear that had haunted him for months. It had been buried so deep he had never even admitted it to himself, but now he sat there hoping Mary would speak. That she would say something to convince him he was wrong. She didn't say anything for a while, and then finally she got up and brushed the dust off her clothes.

"We still have light," she said. "But we don't know how long the batteries will last. So let's use them to find a way out of here."

Sam watched her walk to the nearest portable light and pick it up. "Come on, Force, we've been in worse situations."

Sam smiled. "No we haven't."

Mary laughed as she swept the beam of light around the chamber. They were both trying to lighten the mood. "Yeah, you're probably right. Now come and help me find a way out of here."

They began a slow walk around the chamber. Mary

swept the beam of light left to right from the pool, across the floor and up the wall. There was nothing but water and stone until they got to the skeletons of the giant crocodile and the knight. Mary set the light on the ground and on their hands and knees they peered into the tangle of white bones. Sam could make out small, frayed pieces of fabric, the last traces of the knight's tunic.

"If there was anything to find here, Felix would have spotted it," Mary said, pushing her head into the tangle of bones.

Kneeling there, inches from the bodies, Sam tried to imagine what it would have been like for the man lying back against the wall as the beast lumbered out of the water and crawled toward him.

The thought drove him to his feet, and he yanked Mary with him.

"Hey," she protested.

Sam pulled her back to the wall, scanning the pool. "Sorry, I just had a thought: What if the crocodile that attacked Azeem comes back? We know they come out of the water. Felix told us."

"Blood brought them out," Mary said. "The one that attacked Felix and the one that got the knight."

Sam wasn't convinced, but as he stood staring at the water, the thought of the crocodiles triggered another thought.

"There is another way out of here," he said. "The one the crocodiles use."

"You're right!" Mary exclaimed. Sam's warnings were forgotten as she grabbed the light.

"Be careful," Sam called as she perched on the edge of the pool and dangled the light over the water to get a view of the wall below. She began shuffling sideways a few inches at a time. Sam was already approaching her when she tripped on an uneven stone. He saw her begin to fall and lunged out to grab her. Mary swung out over the water, twisting on one foot; Sam managed to haul her back, but the force of his pull shook the light from her other hand.

As Sam hauled Mary in, there was a *splash*. They turned to see the beam of light twisting and turning in the water until it hit the bottom of the pool.

The water around the unit glowed a soft blue. Mary winced and grabbed Sam's shoulder.

"I think I sprained my ankle," she said, but Sam was still staring into the pool.

"Look at that." He pointed at the light. Mary hobbled behind him as he stepped carefully to the edge. The stones on the bottom of the pool were the same gray color as the ones used for the floors and walls of the chamber, and that made the white bones on the bottom stand out.

"Those are human bones," Mary said. "And there are lots."

"We still need to find that tunnel," Sam said. He looked at Mary's foot. "You wait here. I'll get another light."

When he returned, Sam thought Mary was still staring down into the pool at the bones. But he was mistaken.

"Have a look at this," she said, pointing to the light. "See the thigh bone in front of the light?"

"Yeah."

"Go forward about a foot and there's a short, thin bone. I think it's a collarbone."

"Or a jaw," Sam said.

"But just to the right of that."

Sam could only see more bones scattered across the stones, but he kept looking and spotted something small and brown. He switched on the new unit he was holding and pointed it into the water. The extra light lit up more of the floor, and more bones, but Sam and Mary's eyes were locked on the small brown object.

"It's a mini version of those pottery jars from the chest," Sam said.

"How did it get there?"

Sam shrugged. "Maybe the knight had it on him. You know, to top up the pendant. He must have dropped it."

"We need it," Mary said, looking at Sam.

"What? You want me to jump in?"

"I can't," Mary said, pointing to her foot.

"There's a crocodile in there!"

"We haven't seen it since it took Azeem. Maybe it . . ." Her voice trailed off. "Okay, well maybe there's another way." Mary hobbled over to the skeleton mound and began pulling at the bones.

"What are you doing?" Sam asked, turning the light toward her.

"I thought we could use something from here," she said as she tugged at the tail of the crocodile. The long row of tail vertebrae held as she pulled. "It's long enough, don't you think? Give me a hand." Mary pointed to the spot where the tail joined the body. "One good kick there should do it," she said confidently.

Sam handed the light to Mary, and he positioned himself next to the crocodile. Through the ribs, he could see the body of the knight lying in his bone coffin. "Sorry," he said to the long-dead man, then brought his boot down. The cracking and splintering of bone was brief and violent. Mary gave the tail a tug.

"One more," she ordered. This time, as Sam brought his boot down, Mary pulled. He felt a satisfying *snap* under his heel, and the tail came free.

Mary picked it up by the end that had been attached to the body. The tail flopped to the ground, but, undeterred, she lifted it again, this time twisting it so the vertebrae locked together. "See," she said cheerfully. "It's perfect."

Sam wasn't so sure, but he helped Mary slide it into the water, keeping one eye on the dark area outside the range of the light. Just because they hadn't seen Azeem's attacker didn't mean it wasn't lurking out there, or one of its friends. Mary seemed to have forgotten the danger or was too preoccupied with her plan. She lay on the ground and fed the tail into the water. It flopped onto the bottom of the pool, but when she twisted her bone pointer, the vertebrae locked in place, and it straightened. Sam became more interested as she edged it closer to the small, brown flask. Just as the tip of the tail was about to touch Mary lost her grip, the bones twisted, and the whole thing flopped.

"Here, let me," Sam said, handing Mary the light. "I've got longer arms. I can get closer."

Mary stood behind Sam as he took her place at the edge of the pool. Copying her moves, he turned the tail until it was rigid, then gently swept the bottle toward the side of the pool.

"That's it," Mary said excitedly.

Sam's eyes darted from the bottle to the dark water behind, but it remained empty. With one final sweep of the tail, he edged the bottle to the bottom of the wall.

"Well done, Force. Now you can jump in and get it."

He stared down at the bottle; it was tantalizingly close. He rehearsed the move in his mind. *Drop into the water, grab the bottle, leap out.*

"Come on."

"I will," he said. "I'm just . . ."

Mary turned the light out onto the pool, moving it in a slow arc across the water. "There's nothing there. And I'll be watching."

Sam took a few breaths then realized he wouldn't be in the water long enough to need a lungful of air. He positioned himself on the edge of the pool, directly above the flask. He fixed his eyes on the small, brown object and opened his hand. Then he took one small step out and dropped.

The shock of the water took away what little breath he had as he plunged to the bottom of the pool. When his feet hit the bottom, he bent his legs, opened his hand, and reached for the flask.

It wasn't there.

He frantically patted the space around him until the tip of his little finger made contact with it. The force of his impact had moved the flask. Still crouched on the bottom of the pool, he shuffled a few inches closer and reached out. This time his hand closed on it. Now he powered himself upward, breaking the surface with a gasp. He raised his arm and carefully placed the pottery container on the stones. He turned to pull himself up, and that's when Mary screamed.

Sam twisted and saw the black shape surging across the bottom of the pool. There was no time to turn back and climb out. He worked that out in a fraction of a second. From the corner of his eye, he saw the crocodile tail sitting on the stones where he had dropped it. His arm shot out and grabbed the bone pointer. He pulled it into the water in front of him just as the living crocodile shot up from the bottom of the pool.

As it entered the beam of Mary's light, the black shape transformed into a huge pink mouth, lined with rows of jagged teeth. Sam had nowhere to go. He let out a bloodcurdling scream as the beast raced toward him. At the last second, he swung the bone tail in front him. There was a sickening *crunch* as the beast's jaws closed on the bones. Foaming white water blasted Sam in the face with so much force he had to shut his eyes. A heavy blow to his chest pushed him sideways, and he sank beneath the surface.

Sam hung there in the water, stunned and defenseless. He waited for the final attack, but it didn't come. Then he realized he was alone. Feeling for the side of the pool he reached up and pulled himself to the surface. A hand grabbed him, and he kicked as Mary pulled him onto the stones.

Sam lay there gasping for breath, but images of what had just happened flooded his mind. He scrambled to his feet and pulled Mary away from the pool. She fought him, pointing behind. Sam looked past her and saw the small pottery jar on the stones precariously close to the edge. Still breathing heavily, he pushed past Mary and scooped up the jar, searching the pool for his attacker. There was no sign of it or the tail.

Looking into the water, Sam traced the direction the crocodile had come. "I think I know why we couldn't see it. It was hiding in the tunnel."

Mary nodded, offering a weak smile. "At least we know where the tunnel is."

27

TIME ON OUR SIDE

THE FLASK WAS FULL, BUT THAT WASN'T saying much. The small pottery container fit in the palm of Sam's hand. He removed the cork stopper and sniffed the contents. The powerful stench reminded him of rotting meat. Could the contents have gone bad? There was no point in worrying about that. He would find out soon enough.

They left the oil tucked behind the skeletons and went to locate the tunnel entrance. Mary kept the light aimed at the water, searching for any sign of danger, as they walked slowly around the pool. The dust had cleared enough to reveal the far side of the chamber. They were halfway around when they spotted the dark rectangular hole in the side of the pool.

"Do you think it's still in there?" Mary asked.

"Yes," Sam answered.

"How far do you think it is to the river?"

That was the one good bit of news. Based on the map of Lamanai, Sam didn't think the tunnel to the river could be very long. Long enough to get him out on one breath? He knew with sickening clarity that he was going to find out.

"What's that?" Mary asked, bringing Sam back from his dark thoughts.

She had raised the light to the wall of the chamber above the spot where the tunnel was, and they could see a collection of marks forming a circle. Sam and Mary continued around the pool to the spot. Sam glanced anxiously into the water then joined Mary at the wall. She touched one of the marks, and her finger came away with powder on it.

"Stone dust," Sam said. "It's stuck to the marking on the wall. That's why we noticed it."

He took a step back for a better look at the whole design. Small figures forming a large circle.

"Xs, Vs, and Is," he said.

Mary nodded. "Those are Roman numerals. It's a clock."

She was right, but it didn't make sense. "The twelve should be at the top. Why is it on the side?"

"Don't know," Mary said. "And the ten is missing."

Sam stared at the lopsided clock. "The ten is an *X*."

"That's right."

"*X* marks the spot."

"What do you mean?" asked Mary, but Sam had opened his notebook.

"My father put this here," Sam announced as he looked at the note he had found in the fishing shed. "This line, 'make time'—I thought it was weird, but now it makes sense."

"How?" Mary asked

"X marks the spot. That's why the ten is missing."

"So where is it?"

Sam looked at the clock. As well as no ten, there were no hands. He traced an imaginary one from the center of the clock to where the ten was, then he kept going. He ran his finger along the wall, keeping the line straight. It angled down, and after a few feet he came to the bottom of the wall. His finger stopped on a rectangular paving stone.

It moved.

Sam waved Mary over. "I need light."

He dug his fingers into a narrow gap between the stone and the wall and pulled the carved block up. As Mary leaned over with the light, Sam saw that a space the size of a shoe box had been dug out. At the bottom was a plastic bag with a notebook, but on top Sam could see a letter.

May 10, 2012

Dear Anne,

I am about to leave the chamber and meet you at the jetty with the Templar Knight's dagger.

I believe the dagger contains the clues we need for the next stage of our hunt.

I am writing this letter in case we do not meet.

I suspect Superintendent Ramos followed me to Lamanai. I will do my best to avoid him.

If you are reading this, then I have failed. But you have not.

I trusted that my reference to "making time" would lead you to my hiding place once you found the chamber.

I have left the journal belonging to the captain of sub 518 that Elio found in the submarine. There is also a final note from the captain that he wrote here in the chamber, just before he died.

Last, there is piece of parchment belonging to the Templar Knight whose remains you will have already discovered. They are his orders-the bottom half. Very interesting.

When you read them, things will become clearer and, despite our separation, I know you will continue our work.

X always marks the spot.

Phillip

"Your father left these clues here for your mother," Mary said.

Sam nodded. "But they both got caught. Let's go back to the stairs to check this out," Sam said, glancing into the water behind Mary again.

THE JOURNAL OF CAPTAIN ROBERT SINCLAIR

June 17, 1942
And so it has begun: the grand deception planned by Jason Verdam and myself. While he remained on the Panehesy with the fake Ark, I have departed in the dead of night with the precious cargo. Our journey will take us over seven and a half thousand miles

through perilous waters. For the sake of our mission, we must avoid both German and Allied forces. We have sacrificed all but the essential equipment in favor of speed and estimate the crossing will take approximately nineteen days. I have a crew of only five, and although they are sworn Keepers of the Light, I have not shared all the details of our mission.

Our journey will be arduous, of that there is no doubt, but should I find myself weakening, I need only remind myself of what is at stake.

Day 10

I have been remiss in my commitment to keeping a record of our progress. Commanding a severely undermanned submarine is a most time-consuming endeavor. We successfully navigated our way out of the Nile without detection and are now under full power for Central America. We are making a top speed of nearly eighteen miles an hour during the day but must surface at night to recharge our batteries. This reduces our speed, but we are still making good time.

Day 15

Tempers are fraying as long shifts, due to the lack of manpower, take their toll. At night, we surface to recharge the batteries, but there is always the risk of detection. I have been studying the crocodile design engraved on the Ark. This is the key to finding the entrance to the chamber beneath the pyramid in Lamanai, the resting place for this precious chest. I have re-created the work on the hull in the control room so I may dedicate every waking moment to its study.

Day 20

We are in position off the coast of Belize near the town of Chetumal. We will remain submerged until nightfall and then plot a course for the mouth of the New River. This final stage of our journey will be the most difficult. The river is dangerously shallow and far from ideal for a craft of our type. I was assured by Jason Verulam that the charts I was supplied with will get us to our final destination, but there is no room for error. To know that the slightest miscalculation could ruin the entire mission is causing me considerable stress. The other men are sleeping, but alas, I have found rest impossible. Not until our final mission is complete will I truly be able to rest.

Day 21

We have made it. 518 has reached her final resting place. The small tributary was exactly where Jason marked it on the map, and it has been carefully excavated to fit our craft. She is hidden well. Tomorrow I will leave the others to guard our cargo and travel to the Temple of the Mask to

locate the entrance to the chamber.
The name is fitting. This temple wears a
mask to conceal its true purpose—as a
pyramid in the worldwide network.

Day 22

The journey to Lamanai from our
hidden dock is a trek through a watery
hell. Swamp and jungle so thick as to be
almost impenetrable. The going was far
harder than I anticipated, and traveling
the route with our treasure will take
all our strength. The good news is I have
found the chamber. The key to unlocking
the crocodile map was, as Jason and I
suspected, the Templar code. I found the
location on the map, but when I first
arrived, my spirits sank. There was no
sign of an entrance, even after I have
cut my way through the vines growing
over the riverbank. It took some time
for me to discover the secret: a giant
boulder, protruding from the bank. It
was so large I dismissed it immediately.

And that, I understand now, was the designer's intention. When I finally came back to the boulder, I pushed it and was amazed at how easily it swung open. So finely balanced that I could push it with one finger! Truly a marvel of ancient engineering, and proof yet again of the skills of those who came long before us.

The chamber itself was equally impressive, but the most incredible discovery was that someone else has been there before us. One of the original Keepers of the Light—a Templar Knight. It would appear he came to Lamanai on an identical mission many, many years ago. We know the Templars discovered an Ark in Solomon's Temple in Jerusalem and took it away. Perhaps the plan was to place it here in Lamanai. He was not successful. If he had been, the Keepers of the Light would have known, and our mission would have taken our Ark to another site.

This brother met with a violent end before he could complete his task. The cause of his demise was tragically obvious.

There is no sign of his Ark. This pyramid still waits for a heart, but he has prepared the way. The sarcophagus is in the bottom of the pool, and the lid has been raised on a system of ropes and pulleys. All is ready, and we will gladly make use of the brave knight's efforts.

Day 23

I am incredibly excited because today we will fulfill our sacred mission. Last night I returned to our craft and informed the men I had located the chamber. They are all fully aware of the mission now and to a man will see it through. Of that, I have no doubt. We leave after breakfast. I foresee that the transportation of the Ark will take the whole of the day and will require all of us. We will secure the sub and spend the night in the chamber. To think, after all our planning, the years of careful preparation by myself, Jason, and other Keepers of the Light, today we complete our task. I will leave my journal here for safekeeping, but I am filled with an overwhelming feeling of pride when I think that the next entry I make here will be to record our part in helping to safeguard the future of mankind and our planet.

A DAY OF TRIUMPH AND DEATH.

We have made it to the chamber with our sacred cargo. Thanks to the work of another keeper of the Light from years gone by, we secured it in its home. But then disaster. A crocodile entered the pool by way of a tunnel, and it attacked two of our men. It happened so fast, with such violence, no one was ready. We were aware of the danger. I had two men with guns keeping watch, but we became distracted, overawed by the importance of our task. The beasts seemed to wait till the moment

we lowered the stone lid of the
sarcophagus down and secured our
Ark as the new sacred heart of the
pyramid.

In the flickering light of the
torches we had lit around the
pool, dark shapes appeared. Three
men were in the water, and with
all the hallmarks of a coordinated
attack, two were hit at once.
I shall never forget the look
of horror, then pain, as unseen
monsters took hold of their legs.
Screams were stifled as the men
were pulled under. The third man
made it out, but the ugly red stain
that spread through the pool left
us in no doubt as to the fate of
our other two companions.

We are in shock. Our party has
been savagely cut from five to
three. Only the knowledge that
we have completed our mission
brings us comfort. It is too late

to leave, otherwise we would surely flee this hellhole. We are running out of oil and rags for our flaming torches. Soon we will have only our flashlights. It is the body of the long-dead knight and his attacker that fuel our fears of another visit from the guardians of this chamber. Our guns seem of little consequence when faced with beasts the size of the ones we have seen. During a closer inspection of the chamber, I found a piece of screwed-up parchment near the knight. They are his orders, or part of them. It would seem our ancient brother was aware of the guardians of Lamanai and had his own form of protection against them. Protection that I can only assume failed. Why am I writing this? I find it soothes the mind to record my thoughts like this. I will stop now. The three of us will

keep watch till morning, then leave
this place forever.

It is not to be.
   I was woken by a bloodcurdling
scream. Someone was meant to be on
watch. They had fallen asleep and let
the torch go out. In the darkness,
I fumbled for the flashlight. When
I turned it on, the beam caught
the pale white face of Tom Metson,
being dragged into the water.
   A shot rang out to my left, the
noise so loud my head felt like it
had split open. I swung the light
toward the sound and caught a
glimpse of flailing arms, and I saw
David being dragged away.
   I reached for my gun, but as I
did a blinding pain raced up my
body. Swinging the flashlight down
to my leg, I saw another crocodile,
its mouth closed around my foot.
I kicked wildly, then aimed my

gun and fired, almost at my leg.
The bullet seemed to skip off the
animal's head. In the light, its
eyes locked on to mine, and for
a moment i almost saw a look of
understanding. Then it opened its
mouth and released my foot. It
scuttled back into the darkness, and
I heard it drop into the water.

The attack lasted seconds, and
now here I lie, alone and dying. Of
that, there is no doubt.

My foot is destroyed. A messy
pulp of bone and shoe leather. The
blood pumping from it oozes down
to the pool like a red river. I
have tried to stem the bleeding by
tying a rope around my leg, but it
is pointless.

The blood will feed the hunger
of the guardians, and I know now
I will go the same way as my other
companions, and our brother the
knight before us. There is sickening

irony that we, the Keepers of the Light, should fall victim to the guardians of this chamber.

All is quiet. The water has settled. The only sound is the scratching of my pen on this paper. I can feel myself weakening. My only regret is I did not get word to Jason Verulam to let him know we have been successful.

My end is near. I can hear the water stirring. I suspect the guardians have fed and returned. I read the knight's orders again, and I am reminded that I am part of a great undertaking that has been going on for thousands of years. This brings me some comfort in my final moments.

I hope one day people will come to know of the sacrifices we made.

Capt. Robert Sinclair

pyramids that must have their sacred hearts returned to prevent the
FIFTH destruction.

The design detailed above, will enable you to raise the lid of the stone
sarcophagus. *on an island,* *from where it was*

When you have prepared the resting place, retrieve the Ark hidden by
one of your brothers. It is five days sailing from the point marked on this
map.

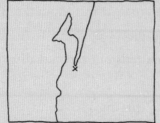

On the hilt of the dagger you will find exact directions to the ARK.

The gold is for expenses. We have sent you a great deal, rather than let
it fall into enemy hands.

The oil contained in the flasks is a powerful protection from the
guardians who dwell in the chamber. A few drops every few hours on
the wooden pendant will keep you safe.

Good luck brother Hugh. The French King is hunting down the Templers.
People think he is after our gold. You are the last Keeper of the Light
with the knowledge of what he truly seeks. Our mission was to return
this one of three. This was our sacred task. If you succeed, and the other
two Arks find their homes before 2012, the world may yet survive.

Jacques de Molay – Grand Master.

Sam looked up from Captain Sinclair's notes. "You have to read this."

"Sam, here," Mary said, holding the piece of parchment. "Ramos had it wrong. He only found the first half of the knight's orders. If he had seen this, he would have known that the talk of treasure and the other two locations wasn't about gold. It was about the Arks."

Sam looked at the pieces of paper written by different men across hundreds of years but all tied to the same incredible story.

"You know what this means, don't you, Sam?" Mary said, looking down into the water. "Your parents knew the Ark from the submarine had been installed here, but they let themselves get handed over to the people who came here to remove it. They did that to prevent 2012. They knew if they gave up the Ark they could trigger the destruction of the world."

Sam looked at the knight's orders again. "The dagger. That has some kind of map that leads to another Ark. The world didn't end in 2012. That means there must be three Arks in three pyramids."

"You're right," said Mary. "Remember, there used to be Arks in pyramids all over the world. Perhaps more than three survived. If the Knight's Ark is still hidden on the island, we could use it to bargain for your parents' freedom."

"But even if we can get out of here," Sam said, "we'll never track Felix down."

Mary smiled. "We might if he still has that chest. On one of our rest stops in the tunnel, I slipped my phone into it. We can track him using your phone."

"Wow, I'm impressed."

Mary pulled an *it was nothing* face.

"No, really," Sam insisted. "I was just thinking about giving up, but you never do."

"Okay, that's enough for my ego for now," Mary said, shuffling uncomfortably. "First we need to get out of here."

The chamber fell silent as they turned their attention to the pool, but Sam wanted to ride the new wave of enthusiasm he was feeling. "Well," he said, turning back to the knight's bones, "we better hope that crocodile repellent has a seven-hundred-year use-by date on it."

A few minutes later, the confidence had completely drained from Sam. He looked away from Mary's anxious face as he lowered himself into the water, and desperately wished he hadn't taken off the armored wet suit at Xibalba.

"Do you think it will work rubbed on your body and not on the pendant?" Mary asked.

Sam grimaced. He needed both hands to lower himself into the pool; otherwise, he would have been holding his nose. He had rubbed the stinky oil into his neck and face. He suspected that the stuff worked purely by creating such a bad smell the crocodiles were grossed out by it.

His feet touched the bottom of the pool and he felt bones around him. He knew now they were the five men of sub 518, and he silently asked for their forgiveness.

"Be careful, Sam."

"Yeah, okay," he replied, thinking that the surest way to be careful would be to get out, but he took a step away from the edge, knowing there was no alternative. He had chosen to enter the pool on the opposite side to the tunnel. His thinking was that if the oil didn't work, he might have time to make a run for it. That idea went out the window the moment he got in the water and realized he would never be able to outrace a crocodile in its own hunting ground.

"Careful, Sam," Mary said again, then checked herself. "Sorry, I just . . ."

"It's okay," Sam said as he took another step outward. "It's nice to hear your voice. Takes my mind off things."

Mary cried out. The surface of the pool looked calm to Sam, but Mary, up on the edge behind him, had a much better view.

"Get out!" she screamed.

Then Sam saw it and knew it was too late. The black shape got bigger as it swam right at him.

"Sam!" Mary called again, but as she watched, he sank beneath the water.

The crocodile was blurry and out of focus as it swam toward Sam. He sat there underwater, watching the tail sweep gracefully from side to side. Then its jaws opened as it prepared to attack.

Above him, Sam could hear Mary screaming, the noise muffled by the water, as if someone had thrown a blanket over her head. There hadn't been time to explain his plan; submerging had only occurred to him at the last second. He had rubbed the oil on his neck and face. Most of that skin was above the water. The crocodile couldn't smell it.

That was the theory.

But he was wrong.

And now there was no time to escape, no time to even move. In the last few seconds, Sam shut his eyes and stuck out his hands, like a kid fending off a school bully. He tensed and waited for the contact. Would he feel the teeth as they bit into him? What would Mary do?

He realized she had stopped screaming. He could still make out muffled noises, but it was one word over and over: *Sam*. She was calling out to him. And then he realized he was still sitting there underwater with his eyes shut. He opened them and saw nothing but the dull blue blur of the pool.

"It worked," Mary called out as he rose out of the water. "That was incredible. You were so brave, Sam, the way you let it come right at you."

It occurred to Sam there had been no other way to handle the situation, but he was too freaked out to dissuade Mary from her point of view. Besides, the crocodile might have gone, but he still had the swim through the tunnel to face.

Sam knew if he waited around he would chicken out or find a way to delay it, so he strode on across the pool without looking back.

There was no sign of the crocodile. Had it retreated into the tunnel? What would it do when it saw Sam enter? Again, they were problems he had no control over, so he pushed through the water, closing the last few feet to the tunnel entrance. Mary had run around the edge of the pool and lit the space between him and the wall with the portable light.

"Okay, I'll be back as fast as I can," he said as calmly as he could. "I'll call Jerry, the policeman. He'll help us."

There was nothing muffled about Mary's scream this time. Sam couldn't see her face behind the powerful beam from the portable light, but looking into the water he spotted what had upset her.

The crocodile came out of the tunnel like a torpedo. Sam had only just spotted it before the creature smashed into him, knocking him back off his feet. Caught totally by surprise, he went under with his mouth open. The choking sensation triggered a burst of panic that wiped the crocodile from his mind. Then its head swung around and hit him again.

As he waved his hands to find his balance, Sam made contact with the crocodile. The beast swung away, and Sam stumbled back and found his feet. His head broke the surface, and he sucked in air. Wiping the water from his face, he tried to focus on the scaly creature as it surfaced and turned toward him.

The jaws began to open.

Sam was facing the middle of the pool now, but he sensed he was near the edge. He stumbled back as the crocodile made a large, sweeping turn.

"Hurry," Mary shouted.

Sam kept backing toward the edge, keeping his eyes locked on the crocodile. Then his foot caught on a bone, and he slipped again. Losing his balance, he staggered backward, but his fall was broken when his head hit the edge of the pool with a sickening *thud*.

"Give me your hand," Mary screeched.

Sam steadied himself with one arm and reached out with the other. His head throbbed; he was seeing stars and, through the sparkly haze, the crocodile gliding toward him.

He felt Mary grab him then lose her grip.

The crocodile opened its mouth, revealing perfectly straight rows of ivory white teeth.

Mary screamed again, but Sam didn't move. He looked into the beast's mouth and spotted the big brown eyes behind the mask at the back of the throat.

Then Sam bared his teeth with a huge grin. "Hey, Mary," he called out. "I think I found us a ride out of here."

28

SUBDUED

THE UNDERWATER ROLLER-COASTER RIDE
lasted less than thirty seconds. Sam kept his eyes open,
watching for danger, but he was being pulled through
the water so fast he couldn't see a thing. The fact it was
pitch-black didn't help either.

When the blackness lightened a shade, he knew
they had made it out of the tunnel. When the ride
came to an end, Sam was relieved to discover the
water was only a few feet deep. Standing up, he saw
the riverbank in the moonlight and waded toward it.

Mary's voice greeted him in the darkness. "Were
you being chivalrous letting me go first, Force? Or was
I the guinea pig?"

"Ladies first," he answered smugly. "That's what we're taught at St. Albans."

"But you knew it was safe, right?"

"Not really," Sam confessed. "I don't think Elio's ever towed someone through an underwater tunnel in a crocmersible before."

Sam was rewarded with a playful but painful punch on the arm as the crocodile submarine cruised toward them. It stopped a few feet from the riverbank, then bubbles erupted around it as Elio emerged from the water.

"How did you find us?" Sam asked as the boy stepped onto dry land.

"After I gave the police the slip at Xibalba, I came back for a Jet Ski to come and find you. But I saw that," he said, pointing to the croc sub. "Azeem must have left it out. I knew it would be faster. When I got in, I found the GPS programmed for the tunnel at Lamanai. I followed the line all the way."

"So, that trick where you towed us out by the tail. Have you done that before?" Mary asked.

Elio shook his head. "Oh no," he said earnestly. "I have never been in this machine before. Only Azeem was allowed." He looked confused as Mary punched Sam again. "But you are glad I came?" he asked.

"Totally," Mary said. "You saved us, Elio. I'm Mary,

by the way. We were in such a hurry to get out, I never introduced myself."

"You guys can get to know each other on the ride back," Sam said. "Can you take Mary to the hideout?"

Mary cut in before Elio could answer. "Hang on. What are you going to do?"

"I have to go after Felix. I need that dagger. That's the clue my parents were following. It's my best . . . my only chance to find them."

"I want to help."

"You can't. Not with your foot the way it is." As if to prove Sam's point, Mary winced in pain as she stood up.

"So I'm supposed to ride on the tail of that thing all the way back to Orange Walk?"

"No," Sam said as he checked his phone. "Elio will take you on the Jet Ski I rode here."

"And what are you going do?"

"Go and get your phone," Sam replied.

He watched her trying to formulate an argument, but then she said, "My iPad is back at the shed. E-mail me and let me know you're okay. And be careful!"

IT WAS LIKE DRIVING A SPACESHIP. BUT it felt like he was doing it in a sleeping bag. There was only room for one inside, so Elio had given Sam a brief description of the controls, then helped him put the dive mask on and guided him under the craft.

Sam slid up through a slit in the rubber skin and crawled forward until his head and shoulders were in the cockpit, behind the mouth of the crocodile. Elio had explained that the space filled with water when the crocmersible dived, and to breathe Sam would have to use the mouthpiece attached to the roof.

He hoped it wouldn't come to that.

In front of him were two joysticks and a series of buttons arranged around a small screen. Sam hit the red one, and his dive mask glowed as the heads-up display filled the glass in front of him with numbers for speed, depth, and fuel levels. Elio had been right: the system was state-of-the-art.

Next, the screen between the joysticks lit up, showing an image from the night-vision camera on top of the machine. In the soft green glow, Sam watched Elio helping Mary along the riverbank toward the spot where he'd hidden his Jet Ski. They would be speeding back to the boat shed in Orange Walk in no time.

Sam was going the other way.

He placed his phone next to the screen and turned the craft away from the jungle. For some reason, Felix had gone up the New River. But not too far. Thanks to Mary's phone, Sam could see exactly where he was: less than a mile from Lamanai. Felix had stopped in the widest part of the river. Sam had no idea why he was there, but he knew the man wouldn't hang around. This would be his only chance to get the dagger.

Sam nudged the joysticks forward and, just as Elio had described, he felt the vibrations of the electric turbine motor. Sam couldn't hear a thing; only the picture on the screen of the craft racing across the water gave away the speed he was doing.

Sam's biggest worry was that he would find Mary's phone but not Felix. What if the man had discovered it? The small dot on his phone showed Mary's device was getting closer. When he was three hundred feet from it, he eased back on the joysticks, slowing the craft to a crawl.

Nothing showed up on the night-vision camera. With less than one hundred feet to Mary's phone, Sam pulled the joysticks back to a full stop and watched the screen. After a few moments, he saw a flash of light. He pushed the plus button under the screen and was amazed how well the camera zoomed in. The outline of the black speedboat appeared on the screen, and it was as if he was parked right next to it.

On board, he could see Felix moving about with boxes and bottles. From his vantage point, Sam saw the man lifting items, walking to the far side of the boat, and returning empty-handed.

Keeping his eyes on the screen, Sam used the right-hand joystick to move his craft around Felix's boat in a wide arc. Despite Elio's assurances that the machine was totally silent, Sam watched for signs Felix had heard him, but the man continued his work.

From his new position, Sam understood what was happening. Felix wasn't dropping things overboard. He was transferring them to another craft. This one was long and thin and incredibly low in the water. At first Sam thought it was a raft, but as he watched another box disappear, he got it.

Felix had a submarine.

It was small, only twice the length of the speedboat, but it was the perfect getaway vehicle.

There was no sign of anyone else, and Sam watched Felix struggling with something heavy. He zoomed in tighter with the camera and recognized the chest from the chamber. Instead of dropping it inside the sub, Felix lowered it onto the hull, then climbed on beside it and pushed his boat away. Next he took something from his pocket and pointed it at the boat. Another remote. The man loved his gadgets. Sam heard a dull *pop* and saw a small explosion at the waterline, then the boat began to sink.

Felix climbed inside the sub and Sam watched him pull the chest off the hull and disappear inside. At the same time, the dot on Sam's phone showing the location of Mary's device disappeared. He panicked as he saw his chance of retrieving the dagger slipping away. If Felix submerged, he would be gone forever.

Sam leaned on the joysticks and felt the nose of his crocodile craft dig into the water then pop up as it closed the gap to the glowing green outline of Felix's sub. It wasn't moving—Felix was getting himself organized before he set off—but Sam knew that it could be any moment. He stopped the crocmersible behind the sub, took off the goggles, then slid back and down through the slit in the rubber.

The freezing water outside the craft cut through Sam's clothes with a burning sensation. Ignoring the discomfort, he paddled to the sub and slid along the slender hull, feeling for a handhold. Unlike sub 518, this craft didn't have a tower, just a small dome with a hatch on top and a stumpy periscope.

Sam's hands found a row of narrow rungs and he eased himself up onto the sub, just behind the hatch. A gentle tug told him the hatch was secured, and then he felt the hull begin to vibrate.

Felix had started the engine.

From the back came the sound of churning water.

Sam crawled along the spine of the sub toward the tail. The craft lurched forward, and Sam slipped, hitting the deck painfully. Ahead he could see a propeller encased in a cage. The unit turned from left to right then stopped. Inside, Sam imagined Felix sitting in the pilot's seat, testing the steering wheel. In the next few seconds, he would speed up and then take the sub down.

Sam had run out of time.

He pulled off his shirt and began feeding it through the bars of the cage to the propeller. It sucked the fabric in like a hungry animal, but as the last of it was ripped from Sam's hands the blades locked up. Through the hull, Sam could hear the whine of the engine as it strained against the stoppage, then suddenly there was a dull *clunk*.

Sam had no time to admire the damage he'd done. Another *thump* from underneath told him Felix was coming. The water was even worse the second time. Sam bit his lip as he slid off the hull and pulled himself back toward the ladder.

The hatch swung up and fell against the side of the sub, the blow softened by two rubber stoppers. Felix grunted as he heaved himself up the stairs. His head popped out like a mutant meerkat, his bulky body blocking most of the light from inside. With his attention focused toward the rear of the craft, he didn't see Sam hanging on to the rungs, or the hatch being lifted from its resting spot.

At the last moment, Felix sensed the movement and turned, but it was too late. Sam pushed the hatch down, hitting Felix in the head. Stunned, the man let go of the side of the ladder and fell back inside. The crash of his body hitting the steel floor was followed up by the *clang* of the hatch slamming shut. Sam leapt up and heaved it open.

Five feet below, Felix was sprawled in a heap, unconscious.

It was like climbing down into a cigar tube. Sam stepped over Felix's body. The man had fallen off the ladder and hit the back of the pilot's seat. In front of it was the tiny cockpit, full of monitors and panels of colored buttons.

Felix had crammed the tube-shaped interior of the sub with his most precious possessions. Art, plastic boxes of clothes and jewels, containers of food and water. At the far end, Sam spotted his target, sitting in front of a small door. He ran to the chest and opened it. The dagger was on top. Sam grabbed one of the bags of gold coins and tipped it out. The noise of the gold pieces pouring into the chest sounded like heavy rain in the small space. Sam couldn't help running his fingers through the coins, admiring they way they glittered like a tiny yellow waterfall.

The bag was thick canvas, and Sam slipped the blade into it and tucked it into the waist of his pants. He ran back up the sub and stepped over the unconscious Felix and onto the ladder.

He knew he'd made a mistake before his foot hit the first rung. The body had moved. Felix's head had been on the ground, between the seat and the wall of the sub, but on Sam's return the man's head was directly behind the seat. He had straightened himself and waited for Sam to return.

These thoughts flashed through Sam's mind in the fraction of a second before he felt the huge, pudgy hand slap onto his ankle. Sam was straddling Felix's body, with one foot on the bottom rung, when the man reached up and pulled it off. Sam would have toppled over if he hadn't had a firm grip on the top of the ladder.

"Why won't you die?" Felix bellowed. "I should have killed you properly when I had the chance." He grabbed Sam's pants with his other hand. Sam knew if the man made it to his feet he was dead. He swung his free foot backward, catching Felix in his stomach, then released one hand from the ladder and swung his elbow back, smashing into Felix's forehead. The man grunted in pain and fell back over the seat into the cockpit.

Sam began climbing again, but suddenly the whole world twisted around him.

It felt as if the rules of gravity had been changed. One second, Sam was going up the ladder; the next, he was getting heavier and falling onto it. As loose items began sliding down the length of the sub, he realized the tail of the craft was dropping to the bottom of the river. The high-pitched hiss of air tanks emptying filled the cabin, then an alarm went off, adding to the noisy madness.

Felix roared, and Sam twisted to see him frantically pushing buttons. The panel he'd fallen onto had smashed and sparks were spitting out of the cracks. Then the sub's angle got steeper, and Felix forgot about the buttons as he scrambled for something to hold on to.

The sub was almost vertical, and Sam struggled to pull himself along the ladder. Felix screamed as he lost his grip on the instrument panel. He grabbed wildly for a handhold as he slid past. The floor of the sub had become a steep slide, and the huge man crashed into the pile of loose boxes at the tail end of the craft.

The sub lurched, and Sam almost slipped off the ladder, which had become a narrow bridge. There was a thirty-foot drop below him now. He edged forward inch by inch, but a roaring sound made him raise his head, just in time to see a wall of white foam.

Water was coming in through the hatch.

The blast pushed Sam off the ladder, at the last second he gripped the side of it and found himself hanging in a vertical chamber under a waterfall that was filling the submarine fast. The water hit Felix, and Sam stared as he watched the man come to again. He had a horrible gash on the top of his head, and the water around him turned red. The man got to his feet, dazed and disorientated, then he looked up, and his eyes locked on to Sam hanging in midair.

Felix stared at him like a predator eyeing his prey. "This time you *will* die!" he raged.

The sub was filling fast. The bloodred water was already up to Felix's waist, and then the man began to climb, using the compartments that ran the length of the craft.

Spurred on by this new threat, Sam pulled himself up onto the ladder. The water was gushing in at a steady rate now, and Sam struggled to fight against the pressure. Below, he saw Felix, clambering up the flooding space, covered in blood.

The hatch was straight ahead, but the power of the water was growing. Sam tucked his head down and edged along the narrow gangplank. It felt as if he was crawling through river rapids. Water rushed around him, filling his nose, blocking his eyes, he could take only small gulps of air through his mouth. Through the rungs of the ladder, he could see Felix was only a few feet away. Sam forced his body through the wall of water and into the hatch. He grabbed the edge of the opening, then forced his other arm through and heaved his body out of the sub. A watery cloak of chilled water enveloped his body as he slid out into the river.

Emergency lights had lit up all over the sub, casting a yellow glow into the river, so bright Sam felt like he was swimming in a well-lit pool. The sub gurgled and belched as the last of the air was expelled and the river took over. With a final blast of air and bubbles, the sub's nose sank beneath the surface.

As the glowing tube dropped, Sam saw a red stain leaking from the hatch—the bloody water from inside. Then, from out of the red clouds, a darker shape—a body.

Sam kicked frantically as he saw Felix swim up from out of the bloody haze toward him. The man broke the surface a few feet away, his face red and shiny from the bleeding wound on his head. He roared as he swam toward Sam, his clenched fists beating the water. Sam turned to swim away from the threat, but before he could build up any speed, the man had him.

Felix grabbed Sam's ankle and hauled him in. Sam wasn't ready for the sudden change in direction; the force of the pull blasted water up his nose and into his mouth. He coughed as he went under and felt the deadly embrace of Felix's thick arms. The man thrust him down; Sam felt a boot on his shoulder, and he went deeper. Off to one side, the glowing sub stood on end like a fat underwater Christmas tree lighting up the darkness. Sam could see Felix above him, kicking down with his legs. Sam tried to move, but a boot connected with his head, snapping it back viciously.

Dazed and sore, Sam knew with aching certainty that he had run out of oxygen. The silhouette of the Felix's kicking legs and swinging arms flickered above him in a red haze. Then another dark shape came gliding toward him.

The long scaly body twisted and turned in the water as it sped toward Sam. The mouth opened to reveal the pink, fleshy mouth and rows of jagged, uneven teeth. There was nothing at the back of the mouth this time, except death.

The beast came at him, and he did nothing. He had nothing to give, no way to avoid what was about to happen. He had become a spectator in his own death. There was flash of white as the crocodile suddenly veered away. It moved straight up past Sam, the white belly just inches from his face. He saw the beast rise over his head and collide with Felix. Sam saw legs and arms and tail become one dark shape. Through the water, he heard a dull crunching sound, new spurts of deep red stained the water, and then the mass of man and crocodile moved off into the darkness.

Sam reached up with one arm into the red haze above him, willing his legs to kick him to safety, but they wouldn't move. He felt himself sinking deeper; the sub, sticking vertically from the bottom of the river pointed down, like a signpost to his final resting place.

A new shadow passed over him.

This was it.

The thought dribbled lazily into his mind. He glanced up again as the limbs and body swept toward him.

But it wasn't teeth that grabbed him. They were hands, in thick rubber gloves that bit into his skin. He felt himself being shoved upward. His head broke the surface, and he opened his mouth, sucking in air and ignoring the tart taste of blood on his tongue.

The strong hands pushed him up and over the edge of an inflatable boat. He collapsed on the wooden floorboards as another figure climbed onboard. In the rising light of dawn, he saw two white eyes set in the blackest face. Words were being spoken, but they were muffled and far off. Sam tried to focus but felt a darkness coming over him that he was powerless to stop.

29

SLEEPOVER

THE MUFFLED WORDS FLOATED AROUND
Sam, but the pain in his head made it impossible to focus. He felt the sun's rays on his skin and slowly opened his eyes.

"Sam, you're awake."

The words had become recognizable, and when Sam turned his head, he knew the face, too.

"You took quite a blow to the head," Jerry said. "You've been asleep for a few hours."

Sam stared at the man as he gently prodded the bandage on his forehead. Questions began to form, but his mind felt sluggish and unwilling to do its job. He blinked again, half expecting the apparition beside him to vanish. As he studied the policeman's face, he saw streaks of black face paint around his ears and neck.

"You . . . ," he croaked, waiting for more words to come to him. ". . . you pulled me out of the river?"

Jerry nodded. "I have some questions for you, Sam."

"You have questions?" Sam looked around the small bedroom and then out the window. All he could see was forest. "Where am I? What happened?"

Instead of replying, Jerry got up and left the room. Sam propped himself up on his elbow then noticed his bare feet protruding from the sheets. Jerry returned with a newspaper and held it out to Sam, who tried to brush it away.

"I don't want to read the paper."

"Look at it," Jerry said.

He held it in front of Sam's face. It was a copy of the *Belize Times*. A large black-and-white picture dominated the front page. It was a burned-out building, and Sam recognized it. Then he read the headline: "Explosion at Xibalba kills Felix Ramos and local police officer Jerry Castillo."

Jerry folded the paper and tossed it onto a set of drawers on the other side of the room, then he sat on the bed again.

"I don't understand," Sam said.

"No. There's much you don't understand, Sam. I will tell you what I can . . . what I am allowed. Have you heard of Delta Force?"

Sam nodded. "They're special forces."

"That's right," Jerry said. "That's the cover story, anyway. The original Delta Force was created for one very specific mission: to locate the missing Arks."

"Hang on, what?" Sam pushed himself up on both arms. "The Arks?"

"That's right. Have you seen the Delta Force badge?"

Sam shook his head, and Jerry pulled his wallet from his back pocket and took out a business card. "I haven't given one of these out for over two years.

"Our logo is a pyramid with a lightning bolt inside it. It represents the secret fire and the heart of the pyramid. Anyone who knows the true story behind the Arks can see our mission there in our logo, hiding in plain sight."

"So you aren't a cop?"

"No."

"But your name really is Jerry."

"Rule number one of undercover work," Jerry said. "Tell as few lies as possible. Makes it easier."

"Why are you here?"

"I was sent to watch over the Ark."

"So you know what happened to my parents?" Sam said.

"No. I told you the truth back at the police station. We weren't aware of the Ark in the pyramid at Lamanai until after your parents . . . until after they'd gone."

"But—"

"Listen," Jerry said again, placing a hand on Sam's arm. "I'm not supposed to tell you anything, but I will, because I know what you've been through.

"Every five thousand years, the earth's crust becomes unstable, triggering a disaster that wipes out everything. After the destruction that the Maya called the end of the fourth cycle, the greatest minds of the time came up with a way to stabilize the planet."

"The network of pyramids," Sam said.

"Exactly. Pyramids, built on key energy points around the world. Powered by Arks, they create an energy field that holds the earth's crust in place. But an Ark can also produce something else. It has been known by many names over the centuries—Mfkzt, the philosopher's stone—perhaps the elixir of life is the most accurate description. But the Ark will only produce this magical substance if it is taken out of the pyramid. A small group decided to sacrifice the earth in return for their own immortality and the power that came with that. They stole one Ark for themselves from the Great Pyramid at Giza. But then, to prevent others attempting the same goal, they set out to track down and destroy every other Ark on the planet. In doing so, they knew they were condemning mankind to death in 2012."

"But they lost the Ark they stole from Giza," Sam said. "We learned that in Egypt. We also found out that more than one survived."

"That's right, Sam. And lucky for us. By 'us,' I mean mankind. A battle has gone on for thousands of years. One side is trying to find an Ark and reclaim their godlike power while the other side wants to restore the network and protect the world."

"And Delta Force is the other side?"

Jerry nodded.

"That's why the US dollar bill has the all-seeing eye on it, and the pyramid has thirteen steps," Sam said.

"That's right," Jerry said. "Members of the US government have been involved in this hunt since the country was created. Like the Delta Force logo, the signs are there, hidden in plain sight for anyone with the knowledge. Delta was created to find the Arks and install them before 2012, and make sure the other side didn't find any."

"But you only need three Arks to stabilize the planet."

"That's the minimum. But for the longest time we couldn't find any."

"Delta Force is a modern version of the Keepers of the Light?" Sam asked.

Jerry smiled. "The KOL were the first, then came the Templar Knights. You know that their logo is a pyramid?"

"I thought it was a cross?"

"Take another look with fresh eyes and you'll see it for what it really is. A bird's-eye view of the four sides of a pyramid. Again, the secret is hiding in plain sight for those who know what to look for. Over the years, other organizations have formed with the same mission as ours, but they were always infiltrated by the other side and forced to change. Did you know the Templars came to an end on Friday the thirteenth, 1307?"

"The thirteenth?"

"The date was no coincidence. Choosing the thirteenth was the other side sending a message."

"Who is the other side?" Sam asked.

"Powerful men and women. Descendants of the original destroyers of the pyramid network. Their organization has also had many names over the centuries. Today we know them simply as the Committee."

"My parents believed in a network of pyramids," Sam said. "They came to Belize to locate the Ark that was sent here in 1942."

Jerry nodded. "I know."

"Were you working with them? Do you know what happened to them?"

"No, Sam," Jerry said. "I have never met your parents. Delta Force became aware of Felix Ramos after he created Xibalba. We heard the rumors of his newfound powers and his links to the pyramid at Lamanai. I was sent in undercover, as a policeman, to see what he had found. I worked out that your parents had located the Ark in Lamanai, but also that Ramos had no idea of its existence. That suited us. We were in the countdown to 2012, and his crazy antics kept other prying eyes away. I was ordered to stay on here and make sure the true secret of the chamber at Lamanai was never discovered."

"But what about my parents?"

"Sam, your parents sacrificed themselves to protect the secret that the Ark had been installed in the Lamanai pyramid."

"You mean they're dead."

"No." Jerry shook his head, and placed a hand on Sam's arm. "I don't believe they are. They're too valuable. The Committee knows your parents are their best chance of finding an Ark."

"What do you mean?"

"2012 didn't happen. The network was restored. But the Committee hasn't given up their hunt for an Ark. If they find one in a pyramid, they will pull it out and sacrifice the world to own it. That's why I was sent here. To guard it."

"Where are the other two Arks?" Sam asked.

Jerry tensed, and he looked out the window, and then back at Sam. "We don't know."

"What do you mean?"

"The only working pyramid we have located is the one here in Lamanai. We are still searching for the other two. And trying to stop the Committee finding one of them first."

"So the Committee is holding my parents hostage until they find an Ark. But if they do find one, that will mean the end of the world?"

Jerry got up suddenly. "This is a lot to take in. Let's take a break. I'll go and make you some food."

Sam looked down at his feet sticking out from under the sheet. He shook his right leg, and the jingle of the handcuff around his ankle made Jerry stop. "I put that on for your own protection," he said. "I'll be back soon."

From: Sam Force s.force@stalbans.com

To: yarmralmevu@mmail.com

It's me. I'm okay. I'm with Jerry the policeman. He has booked us flights back home. You need to meet us at the airport at seven. Tell Elio it would be nice to see him as I am making *the big jump* home. We are leaving Orange Walk at four.

Just as he finished typing, Jerry entered the room. He crossed to the bed and took the phone. He read the e-mail then handed it back. "Sorry," he said, "I had to make sure you aren't playing any games. You've proven that you're pretty resourceful."

Sam shrugged and took the phone back. "What happened to the dagger?"

"That needs to go to headquarters. You know as well as I do that it contains information that can't fall into the wrong hands."

"Can I at least see it?"

Jerry considered the question as he watched Sam, then he turned to the drawer and came back with the canvas bag. He placed it on the bed next to the open journal.

Sam took out the dagger. It was heavier than he'd expected. He ran his fingers over the engraving of the crocodile on the blade, the details so fine they appeared

★ ★ ★

JERRY RETURNED FIFTEEN MINUTES LATER carrying a tray with an orange juice and a plate loaded with fried eggs, bacon, and toast. The questions Sam had come up with were forgotten as he devoured the food.

"You must be wondering how I found you," Jerry said as he watched Sam inhale his meal.

Sam nodded. It was one of the questions he would have asked if he hadn't been so busy eating.

"We knew Xibalba was in financial trouble and that Felix was preparing to leave. I had the chamber under surveillance to make sure he didn't accidentally stumble upon the true Ark."

"How?" Sam asked before cramming a piece of bread into his mouth.

"I installed hidden cameras inside the chamber when I first arrived."

"Hang on. So you knew we were in there?"

Jerry shifted uncomfortably and nodded. "I was watching. I would have come for you," he said, "but my first priority was to keep watch over Ramos."

"So you were there to watch Felix. Not save me."

"I followed Felix from the chamber. I didn't expect you to turn up. Or destroy the sub. You were lucky you had that crocodile repellent on, or it might have taken you instead."

"You know about the repellent, too?"

"I told you, Sam, I've been here for five years. I know all there is to know about the Lamanai pyramid and the chamber."

"So what else do you know about my parents?"

"Not much," Jerry said. "Your parents sent a message to Francis Verulam telling him Lamanai was a dead end. The Committee found out and sent a team to kidnap them. I guess they decided if there was no Ark here they would put your parents to work searching for other locations. They were flown out on a private plane, but that was untraceable. There was no flight plan filed. All I managed to find out, from an airport worker, was the name of the pilot, a Captain Sadis."

Sam had finished eating and stared at his plate.

"I shouldn't have told you that information, Sam. My bosses wouldn't be happy if they knew, but I figure it's the least I can do after what you've been through."

"So what happens now?" Sam asked.

"Now I do what I tried to do a couple of days ago. Put you on a plane home . . . don't argue," Jerry said as Sam looked up at him. "You should never have come here in the first place. I told you what I did so you can understand what's at stake and who we are up against.

I'm taking you to the airport this afternoon. What about your friend?"

"What friend?"

"Please, Sam, I saw her on the camera. The girl who is helping you. Do you want me to book her a flight out too? Can you contact her?"

"I need my phone," Sam said.

Jerry picked up the tray and put it on the chest of drawers, then he opened the top drawer and took out Sam's phone and the plastic bag containing his notebook. "I found some gold coins in your pocket. I put them in the bag," Jerry said as he placed the items on the bed.

"They're for a friend," Sam explained.

Jerry shrugged. "Felix Ramos has no more use for them. We need to be at the airport in Belize by seven. Tell the girl to meet us there, or we can pick her up if she's nearby. We'll leave here at four." Jerry picked up the tray and left the room.

The first thing Sam did was use the map on his phone to work out where he was. He was relieved to see the house was in Orange Walk. It was eleven a.m. He imagined Mary sitting in the boat shed worrying, and the thought made his fingers shake. He flicked to e-mail and entered Mary's e-mail address.

to have been made with a laser. He wrapped his hand around the hilt. The silver wire wound around it warmed under his grip, but it had been made for a larger hand and his fingers struggled to hold it.

Pointing the blade down, he admired the craftsmanship on the end. Above the grip, the hilt flattened out. Embossed on it was a large *X* with smaller symbols and lines around it. Sam thought back to his father's words—*X always marks the spot.*

Sam ran his thumb down the blade, but as he did, he lost his grip on the hilt. The dagger dropped, and its point pierced his journal. Sam looked down in shock at the long, red slice the blade had cut into his thumb. A ribbon of blood trickled across the palm of his hand. He watched it pooling in shock as Jerry reacted. He ran to the chest and grabbed the paper towel on the breakfast tray. Sam's hand was a glistening red mess as he picked up the dagger by the top of the hilt and handed it back.

Jerry shook his head. "Just as well I'm keeping this," he said, dropping it back into the canvas bag.

Jerry returned to the bed as Sam closed his blood-splattered journal and wrapped the paper towel around his wound. "That was stupid," he said sheepishly.

"You've had a rough few days, and you're exhausted,"

Jerry said. "Why don't you get a bit more rest. We're not leaving for a few hours."

Sam nodded gratefully. He lay down and shut his eyes.

He listened to the door shut and fading footsteps in the hallway. He counted another thirty seconds in his head, then opened his journal to inspect the results of his little performance.

30

THE DROP-OFF

THEY LEFT JERRY'S HOME AT FOUR.

The house turned out to be down a long driveway in the middle of a thick stand of brush. Within a few minutes, they were back in Orange Walk, and Sam spotted some familiar sites. They passed the motel Mary and he had briefly stayed at, and then the bus depot.

Staring at the old building, Sam found it hard to believe he had only been there two days. He reflected on what had happened. If he had known what was in store for him when he'd arrived, would he have gotten on the next bus to the airport?

That, he realized, was the opportunity Jerry was giving him now.

Before they left, Jerry had put on a wig, hat, and glasses. The story in the paper meant his cover was blown. His time in Orange Walk was up too.

"What will happen to the Ark?" Sam asked.

"Another operator will move in to watch over it."

"Another policeman?"

Jerry shook his head. "No, they'll create a new cover for him. I've suggested a tour guide. Someone who can spend more time up in Lamanai. The Ark in this pyramid is relatively safe. When the stone lid of the sarcophagus was lowered into place, the men from sub 518 removed the iron rings that the ropes were attached to. It is virtually impossible to shift it."

"So why the need to guard it?"

"To see if it lures members of the Committee here," Jerry said.

They stopped at the lights. Sam knew exactly where they were. The next turn would take them onto the road that led to the bridge out of town.

Jerry looked at Sam. "My bosses have leaked word that you're here in Orange Walk," he said.

"Why?" Sam asked.

The lights went green, and Jerry put the car back in gear. "To see who'll react. This is a war, remember. Our job isn't just to keep the world safe, we have to defeat the enemy."

"By using me as a pawn?"

Jerry nodded. "You understand now why I want to get you out of town. The Committee doesn't believe there is an Ark in Lamanai, but your presence could bring them here. They know you'll be looking for your parents, and that could interfere with their plans."

The traffic was bumper-to-bumper across the bridge. Horns blared as tempers frayed in the afternoon heat.

"Can I roll down the window?" Sam asked as he fumbled for the handle.

"Careful!" Jerry called out as Sam pulled the lever that opened the door instead. The warning came too late. The door swung open, and Sam toppled out onto the black tarmac. The car lurched to a stop and Jerry called out something else, but Sam didn't hear him.

The roadway had been baking in the afternoon sun; it was warm and soft. Sam felt his fingers sink into it as he sprang up. He had been going over the move since the moment he got into the car. Pretend to roll down the window, accidentally open the door, and fall onto the road. He'd been praying that the traffic would be slow on the bridge. That, like his exit move, had gone to plan.

Jerry yelled again, an angry one-word bark as Sam sprinted away from the car.

Five steps, not enough time to build up speed. In his mind, he had jumped the bridge barrier like a hurdle, but instead he climbed it and simply slipped over the edge to make the big drop.

With a rush of wind, a wide blue surface came racing up to meet him. He saw his feet hit the water, and he was under. White bubbles swirled; chaotic clouds of silver spheres engulfed him. Sam reached out with his arms and kicked to propel himself up. His head broke the surface, and the sounds of car horns and city buzz returned. Shouting drew his attention upward, and he tilted his head back. Squinting in the sun, he made out the small blobs of heads peering over the rail.

He couldn't tell if one of them was Jerry.

Sam looked away, blinded by the glare of the sun. As he kicked to keep himself above water something hit him. He thrashed out with his arm. The impact on the heavy plastic casing stung. The current gently dragged him into the shade under the bridge, and he opened his eyes to see the nose of the Jet Ski.

Sam swam to the back. Elio pulled him onto the seat and gunned the machine. They popped back out into the sun and raced up the river.

Through the curtain of white water spraying behind the Jet Ski, Sam saw Jerry watching from the rail of the bridge. They watched each other until Elio steered the craft around the bend. Just as he disappeared from sight, Jerry raised his hand. Not an angry shaking fist, but an open palm, a farewell.

The craft skipped along the surface. Elio stuck to one side, using the shadows cast from the buildings on the riverbank to avoid curious eyes. The boy didn't speak, and Sam was happy to sit back with one arm wrapped around Elio's waist and the other resting on the bulge of his journal in the thigh pocket of his cargo pants.

Around the next bend, Sam saw the ruins of an old factory on the riverbank. The rusting iron girders looked like the rib cage of a giant dead beast. Crumbling concrete pillars stuck out of the water in front, like branchless stone trees. Halfway along the pillars, a high concrete jetty jutted out into the river.

As Elio cut back the throttle and guided the Jet Ski in behind the jetty, Sam patted him on the shoulder. "I was worried Mary wouldn't get the e-mail or understand it."

Elio grinned. "She showed it to me. I knew immediately what you meant."

"So where's Mary?" Sam asked, looking up at the jetty above them.

Elio's grin faded. "She is waiting for us at the shed. We will go there soon."

"What's wrong?" Sam asked. "Is she okay?"

"Yes, yes, she is fine," the boy said, reaching inside his jacket. He took out a crumpled envelope.

"What's that?" Sam asked.

"The night your father sent me to get your mother, she wanted to go to the hotel first."

"I know, Elio, you told me."

"But before that she gave me this." He thrust the envelope at Sam; there were tears in eyes. "I was afraid, Sam. I thought if I sent it and someone came looking for your parents, then Felix would blame me. So I kept it." He lowered his head. "Please forgive me," he mumbled.

Sam looked at the envelope. His uncle's name was written on the front.

Dear Jasper,

    Phillip and I have shared our theories with you about a link to the pyramids around the world and the Ark. Well, dear brother-in-law, we have uncovered it! The implications are bigger than we ever realized. But in doing so it seems we have placed ourselves in great danger.

Jasper, I am writing this for two reasons. The first is our darling boy, Sam. Oh, how we miss him. Our desire to uncover this great secret is at odds with the heartache of being away from him. I only hope he will understand one day that we had to carry out our work. The sacrifice we are making is made easier knowing we are doing it for him. Please look after him, Jasper. For us, he is the most precious treasure in the world.

The other reason for writing this is to warn you. Remember the gentleman who has been funding our research? A kindred spirit, or so we thought.

Francis Verulam led us to believe he was part of an organization called the Keepers of the Light. A group dedicated to returning the Arks to the pyramid network. As our research has progressed,

we have begun to have doubts about his
motives.

We have been in Belize, not Jamaica as
we told you. Francis insisted we keep our
true location secret. He also revealed that
if we found the Ark he wanted it delivered
to him. This goes against the mission of
the Keepers of the Light. So eager is Mr.
Verulam to obtain the Ark that he has had
a private plane standing by at the Belize
airport. We are supposed to contact a
Captain Sadis the moment we find it.

Phillip and I have located the
resting place of the Ark from sub 518,
but now that we understand the truth
behind the pyramid network we cannot
let Francis come into possession of it. We
made the decision to lie to him and sent
a message telling him there is no Ark in
Belize. We don't know what implications

this will have. But, Jasper, if you are
reading this, then know that Francis
Verulam cannot be trusted!

Take care of yourself and please
watch over our darling Sam.

xx Anne

Elio sat quietly while Sam read the letter, and he was grateful for the silence. He had savored his mother's words and read the first few lines over and over again. His mother and father loved him and had missed him. The words filled a dark hole that had been growing in him for years. But the warm feeling faded as he read the second half of the letter.

Elio watched him fold the piece of paper, slip it back in the envelope, and slide it into the pocket with his notebook. "Is everything okay?" he asked, watching Sam anxiously.

"Yes," Sam lied.

The boy smiled with relief and turned to start the engine. "I will take you to your friend now," he said. "She will be glad to see you."

Sam didn't know anymore.

The letter had changed everything.

31

TF

"I'VE BEEN SO WORRIED ABOUT YOU," MARY
exclaimed.

Locked in her viselike embrace, Sam could manage
only an awkward nod and a muffled thanks. Eventually,
she stood back and inspected him with an overly serious frown. "That shirt is horrid. It's three sizes too big,
you know?"

Sam shrugged. "I didn't have much choice."

"Did you get the dagger?"

Sam patted the journal in his pocket. "Kind of."

"That's good. I want to know all about it. I thought
something was up with your e-mail. It's not like you
to give up. . . ."

Her voice trailed off, and Sam thought back to

his confession in the chamber about wanting to leave Belize. The awkward silence lasted only a heartbeat before she burst into more energetic chatter. "Elio went and got us some food," she said, pointing to the table, where foil packets of noodles were arrayed around an old electric kettle. "Let me fix you some dinner and you can tell me what happened. I want to know everything."

Sam watched her hobble to the table. Elio joined her, and they fussed with the kettle and noodles. He felt like he was seeing her, hearing her, for the first time. Why did she want to know about the dagger? Who was she really? He moved to the bed and sat. He felt weighed down by the burden of his new knowledge. His parents had become suspicious of Mary's father but had no proof. Now Sam did—Captain Sadis, the man Mary's father hired to fly the Ark out. He was also the pilot that Jerry had identified as the one who took his parents out of the country after they were kidnapped.

It could mean only one thing: Mary's father and the Committee were working together.

It had been a mistake to return to the shed. Sam knew that it was weakness. He didn't want to be alone. He didn't want to face the reality that he could no longer trust his best friend, his only friend.

The vibrations in his leg felt like a muscle spasm. It

took a few seconds to realize it was his phone, tucked in beside his journal in the thigh pocket of his pants.

As he took it out, Sam was careful to keep the letter out of sight. He was glad he'd managed to wrap everything in plastic before leaving Jerry's.

The message on the screen told him he had an e-mail.

From: Jasper Force j.force@eef.com
Date: Sunday, Sep 20, 2015
To: Sam Force s.force@gmail.com

Sam,

THIS IS URGENT.

My dear boy, I have been contacted by our anonymous informant, TF. He has asked for you to call him urgently. Click THIS LINK to connect to his phone. To prove his credibility I am to tell you that TF stands for Tueri Flamma—he says you will know by this that he can be trusted.

Sam, please, my boy. I know you have to contact TF. But when you can, call me to let me know you are safe.

Much love,
Jasper

"What's wrong, Sam?"

He looked up to see Mary holding a container of noodles.

"It's Uncle Jasper. He's not well. I need to call him." Sam got up. "I'll go outside; the signal isn't that good in here."

"Okay," Mary said as he walked to the door. "I'll put your noodles on the table."

The shadows were growing longer outside. Sam looked up and down the path that ran along the row of boat sheds. There was no sign of life.

Sam crossed the path into the shade of the bush on the hill opposite the shed and clicked the link in the e-mail.

The phone rang once, then a deep voice with an accent answered. "Is this Sam?"

"Yes."

"Tell me your uncle's name."

"Jasper."

"Tell me the name of his cat."

"Bast. Who is this?"

"I am sorry." The voice softened a fraction. "I had to be sure it was you."

"Who is this?" Sam said again.

"Bassem. I work for Mary's father."

Sam's mind reeled as he thought back over the past

few days. The information from TF had been invaluable. But was he part of the plot? Part of the Committee?

"I know you are suspicious. But I have been trying to help you since I found out you had gone to Belize."

"How did you know?" Sam asked.

"Please, we don't have much time. You are in danger. The Committee has discovered that you are in Belize. They will use their contacts in the police to find you."

"How do you know that?" he pleaded.

"There is no time to explain everything, Sam. What you need to know is I am a Keeper of the Light. 'Tueri Flamma,' our motto, means protect the flame. I am not loyal to Francis Verulam; I am there to protect the secret of the pyramids . . . and Mary."

"Mary!"

"Yes. She has never been part of her father's plan. She knows nothing about his links to the Committee."

"And my parents?" Sam asked.

"There is no time," Bassem said sternly. "Your parents are alive, Sam, and being held by the Committee. I think you already know that. I will tell you more when I can, but you must leave. And please take Mary. I knew she was helping you, but I had no idea she was in Belize."

"You thought she was skiing?" Sam said.

"Yes. She covered her tracks well enough to deceive her father and me. But she was not aware that the Committee has been monitoring her. They just discovered she is in Belize. Now that they know that you both know the truth, you are in great danger. Her iPad has been traced, and the police will come. You have less than an hour; you must leave now. I will contact you when I can. Please, take Mary. You can trust her."

The line went dead. Sam stared at the phone then peered through the trees to the boat shed. Could he trust Mary? Could he trust Bassem? Every time he made progress, he seemed to uncover more questions and a deeper conspiracy. It was all getting too complicated.

Sam slipped the phone back into his pocket with his journal. He had everything that was important right there in his pocket.

Turning his back on the shed, he slipped deeper into the trees and climbed the hill.

32

A BLOODY END

THE POLICE TOOK NEARLY FORTY MINUTES to arrive.

From the top of the hill, Sam could see across the river to the bush on the other side. He could also see down to the row of boat sheds. Two patrol cars stopped at the end of the road and four men crept along the path. The sun was sinking below the horizon, and the light was fading fast. In the gloom, Sam watched the men line up on each side of the door, then splintering wood shattered the evening calm. Shouts of "Police" rang out as the men ran in.

Calm returned, but only for a few seconds.

The roar of an engine echoed from the river and Sam caught a glimpse of a Jet Ski between the boat sheds. Then it was in the open and racing up the river. The driver hunched forward, his passenger holding on with her head tucked behind him, her long hair blowing in the wind.

The policemen sprinted out the door and down the path to their vehicle; tires screeched and the cars departed. As the last rays of the sun were pulled beneath the horizon, calm returned.

"I hope your friends are okay," Sam said.

"They will be fine," Elio replied. "I told Ralf and his sister they can keep the Jet Ski."

"You were going to sell that to pay for your mother's operation," Sam said.

Elio smiled and waved his hands. "It's okay. I am happy to have been able to help you."

"Here, take these," Sam said. Elio's eyes opened wide as the two gold coins dropped into his palm. "I got them off Felix. Think of it as holiday pay from Xibalba."

Elio stared at the coins, tears welling in his eyes. "Thank you, Sam." He put them in his pocket as he turned to leave. "I will signal you when everything is ready."

Sam watched Elio disappear through the trees.

"That was nice of you," said a voice behind him.

Sam turned to Mary. She was sitting against a tree,

wearing his father's trench coat and holding her bag. "Did your uncle warn you about the police? Is that what the call was about?"

He nodded.

"How did he know?"

"I'll tell you later. It's a long story."

Sam felt guilty. He had been so quick to assume Mary was in on her father's plan. Those fears had been squashed by his talk with Bassem. Mary's minder had said more in the brief call to Sam than he ever had in person, and it had changed everything. But now Sam was putting off the conversation he had to have with Mary. How did he tell her that they could never go back to their old lives? That their hunt for his parents had become part of something much bigger, much more dangerous?

Sam didn't know how to put it all into words, so he put it off.

"Did your uncle tell you they were tracking us by our phones? Is that why you made us turn everything off?"

Sam nodded.

"You know these devices can be tracked even when they are off?"

"Really?"

"Sure, but we can block them easily enough. Even wrapping them in tinfoil is enough to block the signal."

Mary opened her bag and pulled out some of the leftover packets of noodles. "These are foil," she said, ripping them open. "Give me your phone."

As Mary scattered crushed noodles around her, Sam thought back to the night outside the rowing shed in Boston. The bearded man, the foil around his leg. He had been the first of many to warn Sam away from Lamanai. How did he fit in?

It was a reminder that although his time in Belize had answered many questions, Sam still had a long way to go.

"What's wrong?" Mary asked.

"Just thinking about everything that's happened," Sam said.

"You know, you're not expected back at school for another two weeks, and my family still thinks I'm in Switzerland. We can keep going."

"I was hoping you'd say that," Sam said. "Elio is arranging a ride for us."

"To the airport?"

"No, too risky. The police and Jerry will be expecting that."

"So what's the plan?"

Sam pointed to the bend in the river; a small boat had rounded the corner, heading toward the shed. "I paid for it with one of Felix's gold coins."

"Where are we going?"

"My parents are being held by the Committee until they find an Ark," Sam said. "They won't lead them to one, because that would mean the destruction of the world, but the Templar Knight never got his Ark to Belize. He was killed by the crocodile while he prepared the chamber. His Ark is still hidden, waiting for a pyramid. If we find it before Jerry's Delta Force, I could use it as a bargaining chip for my parents."

Mary nodded. "We know from the knight's orders that the Ark he was meant to place in the pyramid at Lamanai was buried five days' sailing from Belize," she said. "We also know the exact location is on the hilt of the dagger. But Jerry has it."

Sam opened his notebook. "But I made a copy."

Mary reached for the battered book and her face wrinkled as she ran a hand over the rough red marks. "Is this blood?"

"I had a chance to make a copy, and blood was the only thing I could think of using." Sam held his hand open to show off the long red slice down his thumb.

"Gross! So what does it mean?" Mary asked.

"I'm not sure yet," Sam replied. "But *X* marks the spot." He took the notebook back and slipped it into the backpack. "What?" he said, noticing the new scowl on Mary's face.

"Before this hunt goes much further, we have to take care of one more thing, Force."

"What?"

She pointed to his pants. "You still have a big hole in your butt."

Sam began to laugh. "Okay. On the boat, we will try and unlock an ancient secret map to the last hidden Ark, and I'll fix my pants. Deal?"

"Deal," said Mary.

NOT QUITE THE END.

ACKNOWLEDGMENTS

If I had enough stone and ropes and pulleys and land and spare time, I would erect a towering monument in honor of the people that helped make this book happen. On the walls of that epic construction, with hammer and chisel, I would etch the names of Fiona Simpson and her team at Simon & Schuster, Mandy Hubbard and her gang at Emerald City, Mo—my favorite Iranian illustrator, and my awesome wife, Kirsty, and daughter, Frankie. Until I can secure a suitably large supply of stone, my heartfelt thanks to you all will be recorded here in ink on pulped wood.

xxx PV

ABOUT THE AUTHOR

Peter Vegas lives in Auckland, New Zealand, with his wife, daughter, two dogs, and a motorbike. He draws and writes at night and practices the dark arts of advertising during the day. His little corner of the Internet is petervegas.com.